Big Game: A Story

Big Game: A Story for Girls

by Mrs. George de Horne Vaizey

Copyright © 1/30/2016
Jefferson Publication

ISBN-13: 978-1523782864

Printed in the United States of America

All rights reserved. No part of this book may be reprinted or reproduced or utilized in any form or by any electronic, mechanical, or other means, now known or hereafter invented, including photocopying and recording, or in any form of storage or retrieval system, without prior permission in writing from the publisher.'

Table of Contents

Chapter One. 3
Chapter Two. 7
Chapter Three. 10
Chapter Four. 14
Chapter Five. 19
Chapter Six. 23
Chapter Seven. 28
Chapter Eight. 30
Chapter Nine. 32
Chapter Ten. 38
Chapter Eleven. 42
Chapter Twelve. 46
Chapter Thirteen. 52
Chapter Fourteen. 57
Chapter Fifteen. 60
Chapter Sixteen. 67
Chapter Seventeen. 72
Chapter Eighteen. 77
Chapter Nineteen. 82
Chapter Twenty. 88
Chapter Twenty One. 91
Chapter Twenty Two. 95
Chapter Twenty Three. 100
Chapter Twenty Four. 104
Chapter Twenty Five. 107
Chapter Twenty Six. 110

Chapter One.

Plans.

   It was the old story of woman comforting man in his affliction; the trouble in this instance appearing in the shape of a long blue envelope addressed to himself in his own handwriting. Poor young poet! He had no more appetite for eggs and bacon that morning; he pushed aside even his coffee, and buried his head in his hands.

   "Back again!" he groaned. "Always back, and back, and back, and these are my last verses: the best I have written. I felt sure that these would have been taken!"

"So they will be, some day," comforted the woman. "You have only to be patient and go on trying. I'll re-type the first and last pages, and iron out the dog's ears, and we will send it off on a fresh journey. Why don't you try the *Pinnacle Magazine*? There ought to be a chance there. They published some awful bosh last month."

The poet was roused to a passing indignation.

"As feeble as mine, I suppose! Oh, well, if even you turn against me, it is time I gave up the struggle."

"Even you" was not in this instance a wife, but "only a sister," so instead of falling on her accuser's neck with explanations and caresses, she helped herself to a second cup of coffee, and replied coolly—

"Silly thing! You know quite well that I do nothing of the sort, so don't be high-falutin. I should not encourage you to waste time if I did not know that you were going to succeed in the end. I don't think; I *know*!"

"How?" queried the poet. "How?" He had heard the reason a dozen times before, but he longed to hear it again. He lifted his face from his hands—an ideal face for a poet; clean-cut, sensitive, with deep-set eyes, curved lips, and a finely-modelled chin. "How do you know?"

"I feel!" replied the critic simply. "Of course, I am prejudiced in favour of your work; but that would not make it haunt me as if it were my own. I can see your faults; you are horribly uneven. There are lines here and there which make me cold; lines which are put in for the sake of the rhyme, and nothing more; but there are other bits,"—the girl's eyes turned towards the window, and gazed dreamily into space—"which sing in my heart! When it is fine, when it is dark, when I am glad, when I am in trouble, why do your lines come unconsciously into my mind, as if they expressed my own feelings better than I can do it myself? That's not rhyme—that's poetry! It is the real thing; not pretence."

A glad smile passed over the boy's face; he stretched out his hand towards the neglected cup, and quaffed coffee and hope in one reviving draught. "But no one seems to want poetry nowadays!"

"True! I think you may have to wait until you have made a name in the other direction. Why not try fiction? Your prose is excellent, almost as good as your verse."

"Can't think of a plot!"

"Bah! you are behind the times, my dear! You don't need a plot. Begin in the middle, meander back to the beginning, and end in the thick of the strife. Then every one wonders and raves, and the public—'mostly fools!'—think it must be clever, because they don't understand what it's about."

"Like the lady and the tiger,—which came out first?"

"Ah! if you could think of anything as baffling as that, your future would be made. Write a novel, Ron, and take me for the heroine. You might have a poet, too, and introduce some of your own love-songs. I'd coach you in the feminine parts, and you could give me a royalty on the sales."

But Ronald shook his head.

"I might try short stories, perhaps—I've thought of that—but not a novel. It's too big a venture; and we can't spare the time. There are only four months left, and unless I make some money soon, father will insist upon that hateful partnership."

The girl left her seat and strolled over to the window. She was strikingly like her brother in appearance, but a saucy imp of humour lurked in the corners of her curving lips, and danced in her big brown eyes.

Margot Vane at twenty-two made a delightful picture of youth and happiness, and radiant, unbroken health. Her slight figure was upright as a dart; her cheeks were smooth and fresh as a petal of a rose; her hair was thick and luxuriant, and she bore herself with the jaunty, self-confident gait of one whose lines have been cast in pleasant places, and who is well satisfied of her own ability to keep them pleasant to the end.

"Anything may happen in four months—and everything!" she cried cheerily. "I don't say that you will have made your name by September, but if you have drawn a reasonable amount of blood-money, father will have to be satisfied. It is in the bond! Work away, and don't worry. You are improving all the time, and spring is coming, when even ordinary people like myself feel inspired. We will stick to the ordinary methods yet awhile, but if matters get desperate, we will resort to strategy. I've several lovely plans simmering in my brain!"

The boy looked up eagerly.

"Strategy! Plans! What plans? What can we possibly do out of the ordinary course?"

But Margot only laughed mischievously, and refused to be drawn.

The cruel parent in the case of Ronald Vane was exemplified by an exceedingly worthy and kind-hearted gentleman, who followed the profession of underwriter at Lloyd's. His family had consisted of three daughters before Ronald appeared to gratify a long ambition. Now, Mr Vane was a widower, and his son engrossed a large share in his affections, being at once his pride, his hope, and his despair. The lad was a good lad; upright, honourable, and clean-living; everything, in fact, that a father could wish, if only,—but that "if" was the mischief! It was hard lines on a steady-going City man, who was famed for his level-headed sobriety, to possess a son who eschewed fact in favour of fancy, and preferred rather to roam the countryside composing rhymes and couplets, than to step into a junior partnership in an established and prosperous firm.

It is part of an Englishman's creed to appreciate the great singers of his race,— Shakespeare, Milton, Tennyson, not to mention a dozen lesser fry; but, strange to say, though he feels a due pride in the row of poets on his library shelves, he yet regards a poet by his own fireside as a humiliation and an offence. A budding painter, a sculptor, a musician, may be the boast of a proud family circle, but to give a youth the reputation of writing verses is at once to call down upon his head a storm of ridicule and patronising disdain! He is credited with being effeminate, sentimental, and feeble-minded; his failure is taken as a preordained fact; he becomes a butt and a jest.

Mr Vane profoundly hoped that none of the underwriters at Lloyd's would hear of Ronald's scribbling. It would handicap the boy in his future work, and make it harder for him to get rid of his "slips"! No one could guess from the lad's appearances that there was anything wrong,—that was one comfort! He kept his hair well cropped, and wore as high and glossy collars as any fellow in his right mind.

"You don't know when you are well off!" cried the irate father. "How many thousands would be thankful to be in your shoes, with a place kept warm to step into, and an income assured from the start! I am not asking you to sit mewed up at a desk all day. If you want to use your gift of words, you couldn't have a better chance than as a writer at Lloyd's. There's scope for imagination too,—judiciously applied! And you would have your evenings *free* for scribbling, if you haven't had enough of it in the daytime."

Ronald's reply dealt at length with the subject of environment, and his father was given to understand that the conditions in which his life was spent were mean, sordid, demoralising; fatal to all that was true and beautiful. The lad also gave it as his opinion that, so far from regarding money as a worthy object for a life's ambition, the true lover of Nature would be cumbered by the possession of more than was absolutely necessary for food and clothing. And as for neglecting a God-given gift—

"What authority have you for asking me to believe that the gift exists at all, except in your own imagination? Tell me that, if you please!" cried the father. "You spend a small income in stamps and paper, but so far as I know no human creature can be induced to publish your God-given rhymes!"

At this point matters became decidedly strained, and a serious quarrel might have developed, had it not been for the diplomatic intervention of Margot, the youngest and fairest of Mr Vane's three daughters.

Margot pinched her father's ears and kissed him on the end of his nose, a form of caress which he seemed to find extremely soothing.

"He is only twenty-one, darling," she said, referring to the turbulent heir. "You ought to be thankful that he has such good tastes, instead of drinking and gambling, like some other young men. Really and truly I believe he is a genius, but even if he is not, there is nothing to be gained by using force. Ron has a very strong will—you have yourself, you know, dear, only of course in your case it is guided by judgment and common sense— and you will never drive him into doing a thing against his will. Now just suppose you let him go his own way for a time! Six months or a year can't matter so very much out of a lifetime, and you will never regret erring on the side of kindness."

"Since when, may I ask, have you set yourself up as your father's mentor?" cried that gentleman with a growl; but he was softening obviously, and Margot knew as much, and pinched his nose for a change.

"You must try to remember how you felt yourself when you were young. If you wanted a thing, how *badly* you wanted it, and how *soon*, and how terribly cruel every one seemed who interfered! Give Ron a chance, like the dear old sportsman as you are, before you tie him down for life! It's a pity I'm not a boy—I should have loved to be at Lloyd's. Even now—if I went round with the slips, and coaxed the underwriters, don't you think it might be a striking and lucrative innovation?"

Mr Vane laughed at that, and reflected with pride that not a man in the room could boast such a taking little witch for his daughter. Then he grew grave, and returned to the subject in hand.

"In what way do you propose that I shall give the boy a chance?"

"Continue his allowance for a year, and let him give himself up to his work! If at the end of the year he has made no headway, it should be an understanding that he joins you in business without any more fuss; but if he *has* received real encouragement,—if even one or two editors have accepted his verses, and think well of them—"

"Yes? What then?"

"Then you must consider that Ron has proved his point! It is really a stiff test, for it takes mediocre people far longer than a year to make a footing on the literary ladder. You would then have to continue his allowance, and try to be thankful that you are the father of a poet, instead of a clerk!"

Mr Vane growled again, and, what was worse, sighed into the bargain, a sigh of real heartache and disappointment.

"I have looked forward for twenty years to the time when my son should be old enough to help me! I have slaved all my life to keep a place for him, and now he despises me for my pains! And you will want to be off with him, I suppose, rambling about the country while he writes his rhymes. I shall have to say good-bye to the pair of you! It doesn't matter how dull or lonely the poor old father may be."

Margot looked at him with a reproving eye.

"That's not true, and you know it isn't! I love you best of any one on earth, and I am only talking to you for your own good. I'd like to stay in the country with Ronald in summer, for he does so hate the town, but I'll strike a bargain with you, too! Last year I spent three months in visiting friends. This year I'll refuse all invitations, so that you shan't be deprived of any more of my valuable society."

"And why should you give up your pleasures, pray? Why are you so precious anxious to be with the boy? Are you going to aid and abet him in his efforts?"

"Yes, I am!" answered Margot bravely. "He has his life to live, and I want him to spend it in his own way. If he becomes a great writer, I'll be prouder of him than if he were the greatest millionaire on earth. I'll move heaven and earth to help him, and if he fails I'll move them again to make him a good underwriter! So now you know!"

Mr Vane chewed his moustache, disconsolately resigned.

"Ah well! the partnership will have to go to a stranger, I suppose. I can't get on much longer without help. I hoped it might be one of my own kith and kin, but—"

"Don't be in a hurry, dear. I may fall in love with a pauper, and then you can have a son-in-law to help you, instead of a son."

Mr Vane pushed her away with an impatient hand.

"No more son-in-laws, thank you! One is about as many as I can tackle at a time. Edith has been at me again with a sheaf of bills—"

His eldest daughter's husband had recently failed in business, in consequence of which he himself was at present supporting a second establishment. He sighed, and reflected that it was a thankless task to rear a family. The infantine troubles of teething, whooping-cough, and scarlatina were trifles as compared with the later annoyance and difficulties of dealing with striplings who had the audacity to imagine themselves grown-up, and competent to have a say in their own lives!

If things turned out well, they took the credit to themselves! If ill, then papa had to pay the bills! Mr Vane was convinced that he was an ill-used and much-to-be-pitied martyr.

Chapter Two.

The Sisters.

Mr Vane's house overlooked Regent's Park, and formed the corner house of a white terrace boasting Grecian pillars and a railed-in stretch of grass in front of the windows. The rooms were large and handsome, and of that severe, box-like outline which are the despair of the modern upholsterer. The drawing-room boasted half a dozen windows, four in front, and two at the side, and as regards furnishings was a curious graft of modern art upon an Early Victoria stock. Logically the combination was an anachronism; in effect it was charming and harmonious, for the changes had been made with the utmost caution, in consideration of the feelings of the head of the household.

Mr Vane's argument was that he preferred solid old-fashioned furniture to modern gimcracks, and had no wish to conform to artistic fads, and his daughters dutifully agreed, and—disobeyed! Their mode of procedure was to withdraw one article at a time, and to wait until the parental eye had become accustomed to the gap before venturing on a second confiscation. On the rare occasions when the abduction was discovered, it was easy to fall back upon the well-worn domestic justification, "Oh, that's been gone a *long* time!" when, in justice to one's own power of observation, the matter must be allowed to drop.

The eldest daughter of the household had married five years before the date at which this narrative opens, and during that period had enjoyed the happiness of a true and enduring devotion, and the troubles inseparable from a constant financial struggle, ending with bankruptcy, and a retreat from a tastefully furnished villa at Surbiton to a dreary lodging in Oxford Terrace. Poor Edith had lost much of her beauty and light-hearted gaiety as a result of anxiety and the constant care of two delicate children; but never in the blackest moment of her trouble had she wished herself unwed, or been willing to change places with any woman who had not the felicity of being John Martin's wife.

Trouble had drawn Jack and herself more closely together; she was in arms in a passion of indignation against that world which judged a man by the standpoint of success or failure, and lay in readiness to heave another stone at the fallen. At nightfall she watched for his coming to judge of the day's doings by the expression of his face, before it lit up with the dear welcoming smile. At sight of the weary lines, strength came to her, as though she could move mountains on his behalf. As they sat together on the horsehair sofa, his tired head resting on her shoulder, the strain and the burden fell from them both, and they knew themselves millionaires of blessings.

The second daughter of the Vane household was a very different character from her sensitive and highly-strung sister. The fairies who had attended her christening, and bequeathed upon the infant the gifts of industry, common sense, and propriety, forgot to bestow at the same time that most valuable of all qualities,—the power to awaken love! Her relatives loved Agnes—"Of course," they would have said; but when "of course" is added in this connection, it is sadly eloquent! The poor whom she visited were basely ungrateful for her doles, and when she approached empty-handed, took the occasion to pay a visit to a neighbour's back yard, leaving her to flay her knuckles on an unresponsive door.

Agnes had many acquaintances, but no friends, and none of the young men who frequented the house had exhibited even a passing inclination to pay her attention.

Edith had been a belle in her day; while as for Margot, every masculine creature gravitated towards her as needles to a magnet. Among various proposals of marriage had been one from so solid and eligible a *parti*, that even the doting father had laid aside his grudge, and turned into special pleader. He had advanced one by one the different claims to consideration possessed by the said suitor, and to every argument Margot had meekly agreed, until the moment arrived at which she was naturally expected to say "Yes" to the concluding exhortation, when she said "No" with much fervour, and stuck to it to the end of the chapter. Pressed for reasons for her obstinacy, she could advance none more satisfying than that "she did not like the shape of his ears"! but the worthy man was rejected nevertheless, and took a voyage to the Cape to blow away his disappointment.

No man crossed as much as a road for the sake of Agnes Vane! It was a tragedy, because this incapacity of her nature by no means prohibited the usual feminine desire for appreciation. Agnes could not understand why she was invariably passed over in favour of her sisters, and why even her father was more influenced by the will-o'-the-wisp Margot than by her own staid maxims. Agnes could not understand many things. In this obtuseness, perhaps, and in a deadly lack of humour lay the secret of her limitations.

On the morning after the conversation between the brother and sister recorded in the last chapter the young poet paced his attic sitting-room, wrestling with lines that halted, and others which were palpably artificial. Margot's accusations had gone home, and instead of indulging in fresh flights, he resolved to correct certain errors in the lines now on hand until the verses should be polished to a flawless whole. Any one who has any experience with the pen understands the difficulty of such a task, and the almost hopeless puzzle of changing a stone in the mosaic without disturbing the whole. The infinite capacity for taking pains is not by any means a satisfying definition of genius, but it is certainly one great secret of success.

Ronald's awkward couplet gave him employment for the rest of the morning, and lunch-time found him still dissatisfied. An adjective avoided his quest—the right adjective; the one and only word which expressed the precise shade of meaning desired. From the recesses of his brain it peeped at him, now advancing so near that it was almost within grasp, anon retreating to a shadowy distance. There was no help for it but to wait for the moment when, tired of its game of hide-and-seek, it would choose the most unexpected and inappropriate moment to peer boldly forward, and make its curtsy.

Meantime Margot had dusted the china in the drawing-room, watered the plants, put in an hour's practising, and done a *few* odds and ends of mending; in a word, had gone through the programme which comprises the duties of a well-to-do modern maiden, and by half-past eleven was stepping out of the door, arrayed in a pretty spring dress, and her third best hat. She crept quietly along the hall, treading with the cautious steps of one who wishes to escape observation; but her precautions were in vain, for just as she was passing the door of the morning-room it was thrown open from within, and Agnes appeared upon the threshold—Agnes neat and trim in her morning gown of serviceable fawn alpaca, her hands full of tradesmen's books, on her face an expression of acute disapproval.

"Going out, Margot? So early? It's not long past eleven o'clock!"

"I know?"

"Where are you going?"

"Don't know!"

"If you are passing down Edgware Road—"

"I'm not!"

The front door closed with a bang, leaving Agnes discomfited on the mat. There was no denying that at times Margot was distinctly difficult in her dealings with her elder sister. She herself was aware of the fact, and repented ardently after each fresh offence, but alas! without reformation.

"We don't fit. We never shall, if we live together a hundred years. Edgware Road, indeed, on a morning like this, when you can hear the spring a-calling, and it's a sin and a shame to live in a city at all! If I had told her I was going into the Park, she would have offered stale bread for the ducks!" Margot laughed derisively as she crossed the road in the direction of the Park, and passing in through a narrow gateway, struck boldly across a wide avenue between stretches of grass where the wind and sun had full play, and she could be as much alone as possible, within the precincts of the great city.

In spite of her light and easy manner, the problem of her brother's future weighed heavily upon the girl's mind. The eleventh hour approached, and nothing more definite had been achieved in the way of encouragement than an occasional written line at the end of the printed rejections: "Pleased to see future verses," "Unsuitable; but shall be glad to consider other poems." Even the optimism of two-and-twenty recognised that such straws as these could not weigh against the hard-headed logic of a business man!

It was in the last degree unlikely that Ronald would make any striking success in literature in the time still remaining under the terms of the agreement, unless—as she herself had hinted—desperate measures were adopted to meet desperate needs. A scheme was hatching in Margot's brain,—daring, uncertain; such a scheme as no one but a young and self-confident girl could have conceived, but holding nevertheless the possibilities of success. She wanted to think it out, and movement in the fresh air gave freedom to her thoughts.

Really it was simple enough,—requiring only a little trouble, a little engineering, a little harmless diplomacy. Ronald was a mere babe where such things were concerned, but he would be obedient and do as he was told, and for the rest, Margot was confident of her own powers.

The speculative frown gave way to a smile; she laughed, a gleeful, girlish laugh, and tossed her head, unconsciously acting a little duologue, with nods and frowns and upward languishing glance. All things seem easy to sweet and twenty, when the sun shines, and the scent of spring is in the air. The completed scheme stood out clear and distinct in Margot's mind. Only one small clue was lacking, and that she was even now on the way to discover!

Chapter Three.

A Tonic.

Margot wandered about the Park so lost in her own thoughts that she was dismayed to find that it was already one o'clock, when warned by the departing stream of nursemaids that it must be approaching luncheon hour she at last consulted her watch.

Half an hour's walk, cold cutlets and an irate Agnes, were prospects which did not smile upon her; it seemed infinitely more agreeable to turn in an opposite direction, and make as quickly as possible for Oxford Terrace, where she would be certain of a welcome from poor sad Edith, who was probably even now lunching on bread and cheese and anxiety, while her two sturdy infants tucked into nourishing beefsteak. Edith was one of those dear things who did not preach if you were late, but was content to give you what she had, without apologising.

Margot trotted briskly past Dorset Square, took a short cut behind the Great Central Hotel, and emerged into the dreary stretch of Marylebone Road.

Even in the spring sunshine it looked dull and depressing, with the gloomy hospital abutting at the corner, the flights of dull red flats on the right.

A block of flats—in appearance the most depressing—in reality the most interesting of buildings!

Inside those walls a hundred different households lived, and moved, and had their being. Every experience of life and death, of joy and grief, was acted on that stage, the innumerable curtains of which were so discreetly drawn. Margot scanned the several rows of windows with a curious interest. To-day new silk *brise-bise* appeared on the second floor, and a glimpse of a branching palm. Possibly some young bride had found her new home in this dull labyrinth, and it was still beautiful in her sight! Alas, poor bird, to be condemned to build in such a nest! Those curtains to the right were shockingly dirty, showing that some over-tired housewife had retired discomfited from the struggle against London grime. Up on the sixth floor there was a welcome splash of colour in the shape of Turkey red curtains, and a bank of scarlet geranium. Margot had decided long since that this flat must belong to an art student to whom colour was a necessity of life; who toiled up the weary length of stairs on her return from the day's work, tasting in advance the welcome of the cosy room. She herself never forgot to look up at that window, or to send a mental message of sympathy and cheer to its unknown occupant.

Oxford Terrace looked quite cheerful in comparison with the surrounding roads,—and almost countrified into the bargain, now that the beech trees were bursting into leaf. Margot passed by two or three blocks, then mounting the steps at the corner of a new terrace, walked along within the railed-in strip of lawn until she reached a house in the middle of the row. A peep between draped Nottingham lace curtains showed a luncheon table placed against the wall, after the cheerful fashion of furnished apartments, when one room does duty for three, at which sat two little sailor-suited lads and a pale mother, smiling bravely at their sallies.

Margot felt the quick contraction of the heart which she experienced afresh at every sight of Edith's changed face, but next moment she whistled softly in the familiar key, and saw the light flash back. Edith sprang to the door, and appeared flushed and smiling.

"Margot, how sweet of you! I *am* glad! Have you had lunch?"

"No. Give me anything you have. I'm awfully late. Bread and jam will do splendidly. Halloa, youngsters, how are you? We'll defer kisses, I think, till you are past the sticky stage. I've been prowling about the Park for the last two hours enjoying the spring breezes, and working out problems, and suddenly discovered it was too late to go home."

She sank down on a seat by the table, shaking her head in response to an anxious glance. "No, not my own affairs, dear; only Ron's! Can't the boys run away now, and let us have a chat? I know you have had enough of them by your face, and I've such a lot to say. Don't grumble, boys! Be good, and you shall be happy, and your aunt will take you to the Zoo. Yes, I promise! The very first afternoon that the sun shines; but first I shall ask mother if you have deserved it by doing what you are told."

"Run upstairs, dears, and wash, and put on your boots before Esther comes," said Mrs Martin fondly; and the boys obeyed, with a lingering obedience which was plainly due rather to bribery than training.

The elder of the two was a sturdy, plain-featured lad, uninteresting except to the parental eye; the younger a beauty, a bewitching, plump, curly-headed cherub of four years, with widely-opened grey eyes and a Cupid's bow of a mouth. Margot let Jim pass by with a nod, but her hand stretched out involuntarily to stroke Pat's cheek, and ruffle his curly pow.

Edith smiled in sympathetic understanding, but even as she smiled she turned her head over her shoulder to speak a parting word to the older lad.

"Good-bye, darling! We'll have a lovely game after tea!" Then the door shut, and she turned to her sister with a sigh.

"Poor Jim! everybody overlooks him to fuss over Pat, and it is hard lines. Children feel these things much more than grown-up people realise. I heard yells resounding from their bedroom one day last year, and flew upstairs to see what was wrong. There was Pat on the floor, with Jim kneeling on his chest, with his fingers twined in his hair, which he was literally dragging out by the roots. He was put to bed for being cruel to his little brother, but when I went to talk quietly to him afterwards, he sobbed so pitifully, and said, 'I only wanted some of his curls to put on, to make people love me too!' Poor wee man! You know what a silly way people have of saying, 'Will you give me one of your curls?' and poor Jim had grown tired of walking beside the pram, and having no notice taken of him. I vowed that from that day if I showed the least preference to either of the boys it should be to Jim. The world will be kind to Pat; he will never need friends."

"No, Pat is all right. He has the 'come-hither eye,' as his mother had before him!"

"And his aunt!"

Margot chuckled complacently. "Well! it's a valuable thing to possess. I find it most useful in my various plights. They are dear naughty boys, both of them, and I always love them, but rather less than usual when I see you looking so worn out. You have enough strain on you without turning nursemaid into the bargain."

Mrs Martin sighed, and knitted her delicate brows.

"I do feel such a wicked wretch, but one of the hardest bits of life at the present is being shut up with the boys in one room all day long. They are very good, poor dears, but when one is racked with anxiety, it is a strain to play wild Indians and polar bears for hours at a stretch. We do some lessons now, and that's a help—and Jack insisted that I should engage this girl to take them out in the afternoon. I must be a wretched mother, for I am thankful every day afresh to hear the door bang behind them, and to know that I am free until tea-time."

"Nonsense! Don't be artificial, Edie! You know that you are nothing of the sort, and that it's perfectly natural to be glad of a quiet hour. You are a marvel of patience. I should snap their heads off if I had them all day, packed up in this little room. What have you had for lunch? No meat? And you look so white and spent. How wicked of you!"

"Oh, Margot," sighed the other pathetically, "it's not food that I need! What good can food do when one is racked with anxiety? It's my mind that is ill, not my body. We can't pay our way even with the rent of the house coming in, unless Jack gets something to do very soon, and I am such a stupid, useless thing that I can do nothing to help."

"Except to give up your house, and your servants, and turn yourself into nurse, and seamstress, and tailor, and dressmaker, rolled into one; and live in an uproar all day long, and be a perfect angel of sympathy every night—that's all!—and try to do it on bread and cheese into the bargain! There must be something inherently mean in women, to skimp themselves as they do. You'd never find a man who would grudge tenpence for a chop, however hard up he might be, but a woman spends twopence on lunch, and a sovereign on tonics! Darling, will it comfort you most if I sympathise, or encourage? I know there are moods when it's pure aggravation to be cheerful!"

Edith sighed and smiled at one and the same moment.

"I don't know! I'd like to hear a little of both, I think, just to see what sort of a case you could make out."

"Very well, then, so you shall, but first I'll make you comfy. Which is the least lumpy chair which this beautiful room possesses? Sit down then, and put up your feet while I enjoy my lunch. I do love damson jam! I shall finish the pot before I'm satisfied... Well, to take the worst things first, I do sympathise with you about the table linen! One clean cloth a week, I suppose? It must be quite a chronicle of the boys' exploits! I should live on cold meat, so that they couldn't spill he gravy. And the spoons. They feel gritty, don't they? What is it exactly that they are made of? Poor old, dainty Edie! I know you hate it, and the idea that aliens are usurping your own treasures. Stupid people like Agnes would say that these are only pin-pricks, which we should not deign to notice, but sensible people like you and me know that constant little pricks take more out of one than the big stabs. If the wall-paper had not been so hideous, your anxieties would have seemed lighter, but it's difficult to bear things cheerfully against a background of drab roses. Here's an idea now! If all else fails, start a cheerful lodging-house. You'd make a fortune, and be a philanthropist to boot... This *is* good jam! I shall have to hide the stones, for the sake of decency.—I know you think fifty times more of Jack than of yourself. It's hard luck to feel that all his hard work ends in this, and men hate failure. They have the responsibility, poor things, and it must be tragic to feel that through their mistakes, or rashness, or incapacity, as the case may be, they have brought hard times upon their wives. I expect Jack feels the table cloth even more than you do! You smart, but you don't feel, 'This is my fault!'"

"It isn't Jack's fault," interrupted Jack's wife quickly. "He never speculated, nor shirked work, nor did anything but his best. It was that hateful war, and the upset of the market, and—"

"Call it misfortune, then; in any case the fact remains that he is the bread-winner, and has failed to provide—cake! We are not satisfied with dry bread nowadays. You are always sure of that from father, if from no one else."

"But I loathe taking it! And I would sooner live in one room than go home again, as some people do. When one marries one loses one's place in the old home, and it is never given back. Father loves me, but he would feel it a humiliation to have me back on his hands. Agnes would resent my presence, and so would you. Yes, you would! Not consciously, perhaps, but in a hundred side-issues. We should take up your spare rooms, and prevent visitors, and upset the maids. If you ran into debt, father would pay your debts as a matter of course, but he grudges paying mine, because they are partly Jack's."

"Yes, I understand. It must be hateful for you, dear. I suppose no man wishes to pay out more money than he need, especially when he has worked hard to make it, as the pater has done; but if you take him the right way he is a marvel of goodness. - This year—next year—sometime—never;—I'm going to be married next year! Just what I had decided myself... I must begin to pick up bargains at the sales."

Margot rose from her seat, flicking the crumbs off her lap with a fine disregard of the flower-wreathed carpet, and came over to a seat beside her sister.

"Now, shall I change briefs, and expatiate on the other side of the question? ... Why, Edie, every bit of this trouble depends on your attitude towards it, and on nothing else. You are all well; you are young; you adore each other; you have done nothing dishonourable; you have been able to pay your debts—what does the rest matter? Jack has had a big disappointment. Very well, but what's the use of crying over spilt milk? Get a fresh jug, and try for cream next time! The children are too young to suffer, and think it's fine fun to have no nursery, and live near Edgware Road. If you and Jack could just manage to think the same, you might turn it all into a picnic and a joke. Jack is strong and clever and industrious, and you have a rich father; humanly speaking, you will never want. Take it with a smile, dear! If you will smile, so will Jack. If you push things to the end, it rests with you, for he won't fret if he sees you happy. He *does* love you, Edie! I'm not sentimental, but I think it must be just the most beautiful thing in the world to be loved like that. I should like some one to look at me as he does at you, with his eyes lighting up with that deep, bright glow. I'd live in an attic with my Jack, and ask for nothing more!"

The elder woman smiled—a smile eloquent of a sadder, maturer wisdom. She adored her husband, and gloried in the knowledge of his love of herself, but she knew that attics are not conducive to the continuance of devotion. Love is a delicate plant, which needs care and nourishment and discreet sheltering, if it is to remain perennially in bloom. The smile lingered on her lips, however; she rested her head against the cushions of her chair and cried gratefully—

"Oh, Margot, you do comfort me! You are so nice and human. Do you really, truly think I am taking things too seriously? Do you think I am depressing Jack? Wouldn't he think me heartless if I seemed bright and happy?"

"Try it and see! You can decide according to the effect produced, but first you must have a tonic, to brace you for the effort. I've a new prescription, and we are going to Edgware Road to get it this very hour."

"Quinine, I suppose. Esther and the boys can get it at the chemist's, but really it will do roe no good."

"I'm sure it wouldn't. Mine is a hundred times more powerful."

"Iron? I can't take it. It gives me headaches."

"It isn't iron. Mine won't give you a headache, unless the pins get twisted. It's a finer specific for low spirits feminine, than any stupid drugs. A new hat!"

Edith stared, and laughed, and laughed again.

"You silly girl! What nonsense! I don't need a hat."

"That's nonsense if you like! It depresses me to see you going about in that dowdy thing, and it must be a martyrdom for you to wear it every day. Come out and buy a straw shape for something and 'eleven-three'," (it's always "eleven-three" in Edgware Road), "and I'll trim it with some of your scraps. You have such nice scraps. Then we'll have tea, and you shall walk part of the way home with me, and meet Jack, and smile at him and look pretty, and watch him perk up to match. What do you say?"

Edith lifted her eyes with a smile which brought back the youth and beauty to her face.

"I say, thank you!" she said simply. "You are a regular missionary, Margot. You spend your life making other people happy."

"Goodness!" cried Margot, aghast. "Do I? How proper it sounds! You just repeat that to Agnes, and see what she says. You'll hear a different story, I can tell you!"

Chapter Four.

Margot's Scheme.

The sisters repaired to Edgware Road, and after much searching finally ran to earth a desirable hat for at least the odd farthing less than it would have cost round the corner in Oxford Street. This saving would have existed only in imagination to the ordinary customer, who is presented with a paper of nail-like pins, a rusty bodkin, or a highly-superfluous button-hook as a substitute for lawful change; but Margot took a mischievous delight in collecting farthings and paying down the exact sum in establishments devoted to eleven-threes, to the disgust of the young ladies who supplied her demands.

The hat was carried home in true Bohemian fashion, encased in a huge paper bag, and a happy hour ensued, when the contents of the scrap-box were scattered over the bed, and a dozen different effects studied in turn. Edith sat on a chair before the glass with the skeleton frame perched on her head at the accepted fashionable angle, criticising fresh draperies and arrangement of flowers, and from time to time uttering sharp exclamations of pain as Margot's actions led to an injudicious use of the dagger-like pins. Her delicate finely-cut face and misty hair made her a delightful model, and she smiled back at the face in the mirror, reflecting that if you happened to be a pauper, it was at least satisfactory to be a pretty one, and that to possess long, curling eyelashes was a distinct compensation in life. Margot draped an old lace veil over the hard brim, caught it together at the back with a paste button, and pinned a cluster of brown roses beneath the brim, with just one pink one among the number, to give the *cachet* to the whole.

"There's Bond Street for you!" she cried triumphantly; and Edith flushed with pleasure, and wriggled round and round to admire herself from different points of view.

"It *is* a tonic!" she declared gratefully. "You are a born milliner, Margot. It will be a pleasure to go out in this hat, and I shall feel quite nice and conceited again. It's so long since I've felt conceited! I'm ever and ever so much obliged. Can you stay on a little longer, dear, or are you in a hurry to get back?"

"No! I shall get a scolding anyway, so I might as well have all the fling I can get. I'll have tea with you and the boys, and a little private chat with Jack afterwards. You won't mind leaving us alone for a few minutes? It's something about Ron, but I won't promise not to get in a little flirtation on my own account."

Jack's wife laughed happily.

"Flirt away—it will cheer him up! I'll put the boys to bed, and give you a fine opportunity. Here they come, back from their walk. I must hurry, dear, and cut bread and butter. I'll carry down the hat, and put it on when Jack comes in."

Aunt Margot's appearance at tea was hailed with a somewhat qualified approval.

"You must talk to *us*, mother," Jim said sternly; "talk properly, not only, 'Yes, dear,' 'No, dear,' like you do sometimes, and then go on speaking to her about what we can't understand. She's had you all afternoon!"

"So I have, Jim. It's your turn now. What do you want to say?"

Jim immediately lapsed into silence. Having gained his point, he had no remark to offer, but Pat lifted his curly head and asked eagerly—

"Muzzer, shall I ever grow up to be a king?"

"No, my son; little boys like you are never kings."

"Not if I'm very good, and do what I'm told?"

"No, dear, not even then. No one can be a king unless his father is a king, too, or some very, very great man. What has put that in your head, I wonder? Why do you want to be a king?"

Pat widened his clear grey eyes; the afternoon sunshine shone on his ruffled head, turning his curls to gold, until he looked like some exquisite cherub, too good and beautiful for this wicked world.

"'Cause if I was a king I could take people prisoners and cut off their heads, and stick them upon posts," he said sweetly; his mother and aunt exchanged horrified glances. Pat alternated between moods of angelic tenderness, when every tiger was a "good, *good* tiger," and naughty children "never did it any more," and a condition of frank cannibalism, when he literally wallowed in atrocities. His mother forbode to lecture, but judiciously turned the conversation.

"Kings can do much nicer things than that, Patsy boy. Our kind King Edward doesn't like cutting off heads a bit. He is always trying to prevent men from fighting with each other."

"Is he?"

"Yes, he is. People call him the Peace-maker, because he prevents so many wars."

"*Bother* him!" cried Pat fervently.

Margot giggled helplessly. Mrs Martin stared fixedly out of the window, and Jim in his turn took up the ball of conversation.

"Mummie, will you die before me?"

"I can't tell, dear; nobody knows."

"Will daddy die before me?"

"Probably he will."

"May I have his penknife when he's dead?"

"I think it's about time to cut up that lovely new cake!" cried Margot, saving the situation with admirable promptitude. "We bought it for you this afternoon, and it tastes of chocolate, and all sorts of good things."

The bait was successful, and a silence followed, eloquent of intense enjoyment; then the table was cleared and various games were played, in the midst of which Jack's whistle sounded from without, and his wife and sons rushed to meet him. They looked a typical family group as they re-entered the room, Edith happily hanging on to his arm, the boys prancing round his feet, and the onlooker felt a little pang of loneliness at the sight.

John Martin was a tall, well-made man, with a clean-shaven face and deep-set grey eyes. He was pale and lined, and a nervous twitching of the eyelids testified to the strain through which he had passed, but it was a strong face and a pleasant face, and, when he looked at his wife, a face of indescribable tenderness. At the moment he was smiling, for it was always a pleasure to see his pretty sister-in-law, and to-night Edith's anxious looks had departed, and she skipped by his side as eager and excited as the boys themselves.

"Dad, dad, has there been any more 'splosions?"

"Hasn't there been no fearful doings on in the world, daddy?"

"Jack! Jack! I've got a new tonic. It has done me such a lot of good!"

Jack turned from one to the other.

"No, boys, no,—no more accidents to-day! What is it, darling? You look radiant. What is the joke?"

"Look out of the window for a minute! Margot, you talk to him, and don't let him look round."

Edith pinned on the new hat before the mirror, carefully adjusting the angles, and pulling out her cloudy hair to fill in the necessary spaces. Her cheeks were flushed, her eyes sparkled; it was no longer the worn white wife, but a pretty, coquettish girl, who danced up to Jack's side with saucy, uplifted head.

"There! What do you think of that?"

The answer of the glowing eyes was more eloquent than words. Jack whistled softly beneath his breath, walking slowly round and round to take in the whole effect.

"I say, that *is* fetching! That's something like a hat you wore the summer we were engaged. You don't look a day older. Where did you run that to earth, darling?"

"Can't you see Bond Street in every curve? I should have thought it was self-evident. Margot said I was shabby, and that a new hat would do me good, so we went out and bought it. Do you think I am extravagant? It's better to spend on this than on medicine, and three guineas isn't expensive for real lace, is it?"

She peered in her husband's face with simulated anxiety, but his smile breathed pleasure unqualified.

"I'm delighted that you have bought something at last! You have not spent a penny on yourself for goodness knows how long."

"Goose!" cried Edith. "He has swallowed it at a gulp. Three guineas, indeed—as if I dare! Four and eleven-pence three-farthings in Edgware Road, and my old lace veil, and one of the paste buttons you gave me at Christmas, and some roses off last year's hat, and Margot's clever fingers, and my—pretty face! Do you think I am pretty still?"

"I should rather think I do!" Jack framed his wife's face in his hands, stooping to kiss the soft flushed cheeks as fondly as he had done in the time of that other lace-wreathed hat six years before. Pat and Jim returned to their dominoes, bored by such foolish proceedings on the part of their parents, while Margot covered her face with her hands, with ostentatious propriety.

"This is no place for me! Consider my feelings, Jack. I'm like a story I once read in an old volume of *Good Words*, 'Lovely yet Unloved!' When you have quite finished love-making, I want a private chat with you, while Edie puts the boys to bed. They will hate me for suggesting such a thing, but it is already past their hour, and I must have ten minutes' talk on a point of life and death!"

"Come away, boys; we are not wanted here. Daddy will come upstairs and see you again before you go to sleep."

Mother and sons departed together, and Jack Martin sat down on the corner of the sofa and leant his head on his hand. With his wife's departure the light went out of his face, but he smiled at his sister-in-law with an air of affectionate *camaraderie*.

"You are a little brick, Margot! You have done Edie a world of good. What can I do for you in return? I am at your service."

Margot pulled forward the chair that her sister had chosen as the least lumpy which the room afforded, and seated herself before him, returning his glance with an odd mixture of mischief and embarrassment.

"It's about Ron. The year of probation is nearly over."

"I know it."

"Two months more will decide whether he is to be a broker or a poet. It will mean death to Ronald to be sent into the City."

"You are wrong there. If he is a poet, no amount of brokering will alter the fact, any more than it will change the colour of his eyes or hair. It is bound to come out sooner or later. You will probably think me a brute, if I suggest that a little discipline and knowledge of the world might improve the value of his writings."

"Yes, I will! What does a poet want with a knowledge of the world, in the common, sordid sense? Let him keep his mind unsullied, and be an inspiration to others. When we were children, we used to keep birds in the nursery, in a very fine cage with golden bars, and we fed them with every bird delicacy we could find. They lived for a little time, and tried to sing, poor brave things! We threw away the cage in a fury, after finding one soft dead thing after another lying huddled up in a corner. No one shall cage Ronald, if I can prevent it! It's no use pretending to be cold-blooded and middle-aged, Jack, for I know you are with us at heart. This means every bit as much to Ron as your business troubles do to you."

Jack drew in his breath with a wince of pain.

"Well, what is it you wish me to do? I am afraid I have very little influence in the literary world, and I have always heard that introductions do more harm than good. An editor would soon ruin his paper if he accepted all the manuscripts pressed upon him by admiring relatives."

"But you see I don't ask you for an introduction. It's just a piece of information I want, which I can't get for myself. You know the *Loadstar Magazine*?"

"Certainly I do."

"Well, the *Loadstar* is—the *Loadstar*! The summit of Ron's ambition. It's the magazine of all others which he likes and admires, and the editor is known to be a man of great power and discernment. It is said that if he has the will, he can do more than any man in London to help on young writers. It is useless sending manuscripts, for he refuses to consider unsolicited poetical contributions. He shuts himself up in a fastness in Fleet Street, and the door thereof is guarded with dragons with lying tongues. I know! I have made it my business to inquire, but I feel convinced that if he once gave Ron a fair reading, he would acknowledge his gifts. There is no hope of approaching him direct, but I intend to get hold of him all the same."

Jack Martin looked up at that, his thin face twitching into a smile.

"You little baggage! and you expect me to help you. I must hear some more about this before I involve myself any further. What mischief are you up to now?"

"Dear Jack, what can I do; a little girl like me?" cried Miss Margot, mightily meek all of a sudden, as she realised that she had ventured a step too far. "I wouldn't for the whole world get you into trouble. It's just a little, simple thing that I want you to find out from some one in the office."

"I don't know any one in the office."

"But you could find out some one who did? For instance, you know that Mr Oliver who illustrates? I've seen his things in the *Loadstar*. You could ask him in a casual, off-hand manner without ever mentioning our name."

"What could I ask him?"

"Such a nice, simple little question! Just the name of the place where the editor proposes to spend this summer holiday, and the date on which he will start."

Jack stared in amazement, but the meekest, most demure of maidens confronted him from the opposite chair, with eyes so translucently candid, lips so guilelessly sweet, that it seemed incredible that any hidden mischief could lurk behind the innocent question. Nevertheless seven years' intimacy with Miss Margot made Jack Martin suspicious of mischief.

"What do you know about this editor man? Have you seen him anywhere? He is handsome, I suppose, and a bachelor?"

"You're a wretch!" retorted Miss Margot. "I don't know the man from Adam, and he may be a Methuselah for all I care; but if possible I want it to happen that Ron and I chance to be staying in the same place, in the same house, or hotel, or *pension*, whichever it may be, when he goes away for his yearly rest. We are going to the country in any case—why should we not be guided by the choice of those older and wiser than ourselves? Why should we not meet the one of all others we are most anxious to know?"

"Just so! and having done so, you will confide in the editor that Ronald is an embryo Poet Laureate, and try to enlist his kind sympathy and assistance!"

Margot smiled; a smile of lofty superiority.

"No, indeed! I know rather better than that! He will be out on a holiday, poor man, and won't want to be troubled with literary aspirants. He has enough of them all the year round. We'll never mention poetry, but we will try to get to know *him*, and to make him like us so much that he will want to see more of us when we return to town. No one can live in the same house with Ron, and have an opportunity of talking to him day by day, without feeling that he is different from other boys, and alone together in the country one can never tell what may happen. Opportunities may arise, too; opportunities for help and service. We would be on the look-out for them, and would try by every means in our power to forge the first link in the chain. Don't look so solemn, old Jack, it's all perfectly innocent! You can trust me to do nothing you would disapprove."

"I believe I can. You are a madcap, Margot, but you are a good girl. I'm not afraid of you, but I imagine that the editor will be a match for a dozen youngsters like you and Ron, and will soon see through your little scheme. However, I'll do what I can. In big offices holiday arrangements have to be made a good while ahead, so it ought not to be difficult to get the information you want. Now I must be off upstairs to see the boys before they get into bed. Shall I see you again when I come down?"

"No, indeed! I've played truant since half-past eleven, so I shall have to hang about the end of the terrace until father appears, and go in under his wing, to escape a scolding from Agnes. I had arranged to pay calls with her this afternoon. I wonder how it is that my memory is so dreadfully uncertain about things I don't want to do! Good-bye then, Jack, and a hundred thanks. Posterity will thank you for your help."

Jack Martin laughed and shrugged his shoulders. He had a man's typical disbelief in the ability of his wife's relatives.

Chapter Five.

An Explosion.

Relationships were somewhat strained in the Vane household during the next few weeks, the two elder members being banded together in an unusual partnership to bring about the confusion of the younger.

"I can't understand what you are making such a fuss about. You'll have to give in, in the end. You a poet, indeed! What next? If you would come down to breakfast in time, and give over burning the gas till one o'clock in the morning, it would be more to the point than writing silly verses. I'd be ashamed to waste my time scribbling nonsense all day long!" So cried Agnes, in Martha-like irritation, and Ronald turned his eyes upon her with that deep, dreamy gaze which only added fuel to the flame.

He was not angry with Agnes, who, as she herself truly said, "did not understand." Out of the storm of her anger an inspiration had fluttered towards him, like a crystal out of the surf. "The Worker and the Dreamer"—he would make a poem out of that idea! Already the wonderful inner vision pictured the scene—the poet sitting idle on the hillside, the man of toil labouring in the heat and glare of the fields, casting glances of scorn and impatience at the inert form. The lines began to take shape in his brain.

"...And the worker worked from the misty dawn,

Till the east was golden and red;

But the dreamer's dream which he thought to scorn,

Lived on when they both were dead..."

"I asked him three times over if he would have another cup of coffee, and he stared at me as if he were daft! I believe he *is* half daft at times, and he will grow worse and worse, if Margot encourages him like this!" Agnes announced to her father, on his weary return from City.

It was one of Agnes's exemplary habits to refuse all invitations which could prevent her being at home to welcome her father every afternoon, and assist him to tea and scones, accompanied by a minute *résumé* of the bad news of the day. What the housemaid had broken; what the cat had spilt; the parlourmaid's impertinences; the dressmaker's delinquencies; Ronald's vapourings; the new and unabashed transgressions of Margot—each in its turn was dropped into the tired man's cup with the lumps of sugar, and stirred round with the cream. There was no escaping the ordeal. On the hottest day of summer there was the boiling tea, with the hot muffins, and the rich, indigestible cake, exactly as they had appeared amidst the ice and snows of January; and the accompanied recital hardly varied more. It was a positive relief to hear that the chimney had smoked, or the parrot had had a fit.

Once a year Agnes departed on a holiday, handing over the keys to Margot, who meekly promised to follow in her footsteps; and then, heigho! for a fortnight of Bohemia, with every arrangement upside down, and appearing vastly improved by the change of position. Instead of tea in the drawing-room, two easy-chairs on the balcony overlooking the Park; cool iced drinks sipped through straws, and luscious dishes of fruit. Instead of Agnes, stiff and starched and tailor-made, a radiant vision in muslin and laces, with a ruffled golden head, and distracting little feet peeping out from beneath the frills.

"Isn't this fun?" cried the vision. "Don't you feel quite frivolous and Continental? Let's pretend we are a newly-married couple, and you adore me, and can't deny a thing I ask!

There was a blouse in Bond Street this morning... Sweetest darling, wouldn't you like me to buy it to-morrow, and show me off in it to your friends? I told them to send it home on approval. I knew you couldn't bear to see your little girl unhappy for the sake of four miserable guineas!"

This sort of treatment was very agreeable to a worn-out City man, and as a pure matter of bargaining, the blouse was a cheap price to pay for the refreshment of that cool, restful hour, and the pretty chatter which smoothed the tired lines out of his face, and made him laugh and feel young again.

Another night Mr Vane would be decoyed to a rendezvous at Earl's Court, when Margot would wear the blouse, and insist upon turning round the pearl band on her third finger, so as to imitate a wedding-ring, looking at him in languishing fashion across the table the while, to the delight of fellow-diners and his own mingled horror and amusement. Then they would wander about beneath the glimmer of the fairy-lights, listening to the band, as veritable a pair of lovers as any among the throng.

As summer approached, Mr Vane's thoughts turned to these happy occasions, and it strengthened his indignation against his son to realise that this year a cloud had arisen between himself and his dearest daughter. Margot had openly ranked herself against him, which was a bitter pill to swallow, and, so far from showing an inclination to repent as the prescribed time drew to a close, the conspirators appeared only to be the more determined. Long envelopes were continually being dispatched to the post, to appear with astonishing dispatch on the family breakfast-table. The pale, wrought look on Ronald's face as he caught sight of them against the white cloth! No parent's heart could fail to be wrung for the lad's misery; but the futility of it added to the inward exasperation. Thousands of men walking the streets of London vainly seeking for work, while this misguided youth scorned a safe and secure position!

The pent-up irritation exploded one Sunday evening, when the presence of Edith and her husband recalled the consciousness of yet another disappointment. Mr Vane had made his own way, and, after the manner of successful men, had little sympathy with failure. The presence of the two pale, dejected-looking young men filled him with impatient wrath. At the supper-table he was morose and irritable, until a chance remark set the fuse ablaze.

"Yes, yes! You all imagine yourselves so clever nowadays that you can afford to despise the experience of men who knew the world before you were born! I can see you look at each other as I speak! I'm not blind! I'm an out-of-date old fogey who doesn't know what he is talking about, and hasn't even the culture to appreciate his own children. Because one has composed a bundle of rhymes that no one will publish, he must needs assume an attitude of forbearance with the man who supplies the bread and butter! I've never been accustomed to regard failure as an instance of superiority, but no doubt I am wrong—no doubt I am behind the times—no doubt you are all condemning me in your minds as a blundering old ignoramus! A father is nothing but a nuisance who must be tolerated for the sake of what can be got out of him."

He looked round the table with his tired, angry eyes. Jack Martin sat with bent head and lips pressed tightly together, repressing himself for his wife's sake. Edith struggled against tears. Agnes served the salad dressing and grunted approval. Margot, usually so pert and ready of retort, stared at the cloth with a frown of strained distress. Only Ronald faced him with steady eyes.

"That is not true, father, and you know it yourself!"

"I know nothing, it appears! That's just what I say. Why don't you undertake my education? You never show me your work; you take the advice of a child like Margot, and leave me out in the cold, and then expect me to have faith enough to believe you a genius without a word of proof. You want to become known to the public? Very well, bring down some of that precious poetry and read it aloud to us now! You can't say then that I haven't given you a chance!"

It was a frightful prospect! The criticism of the family is always an ordeal to the budding author, and the moment was painfully unpropitious. It would have been as easy for a bird to sing in the presence of the fowler. Ronald turned white to the lips, but his reply came as unwavering as the last.

"Do you think you would care to hear even the finest poetry in the world read aloud to-night? Mine is very far from the best. I will read it to you if you wish, but you must give me a happier opportunity."

Agnes laughed shortly.

"Shilly-shally! I can't understand what opportunity you want. If it's good, it can't be spoilt by being read one day instead of another; if it's bad, it won't be improved by waiting. This is cherry-pie, and there is some tipsy cake. Edith, which will you have?"

Edith would have neither. She was still trembling with wounded indignation against her father for that cruel hit at her husband. She sat pale and silent, vowing never to enter the house again until Jack's fortunes were restored; never to accept another penny from her father's hands. She was comparatively little interested in the discussion about poetry. Ron was a dear boy; she would be sorry if he were disappointed, but Jack was her life, and Jack was working for bread!

If she had followed the moment's impulse, she would have risen and left the room, and though better counsel prevailed, she could not control the spice of temper which made the cherry-pie abhorrent.

Jack, as a man, saw no reason why he should deny himself the mitigations of the situation; he helped himself to cream and sifted sugar with leisurely satisfaction, and sensibly softened in spirit. After all, there was a measure of truth in what the old man said, and his bark was worse than his bite. If his own boy, Pat, took it into his head to go off on some scatter-brain prank when he came of age, it would be a big trouble, or if later on he came a cropper in business— Jack waited for a convenient pause, and then deftly turned the conversation to politics, and by the time that cheese was on the table, he and his father-in-law were discussing the mysteries of the last Education Bill with the satisfaction of men who hold similar views on the inanities of the opposite party. Later on they bade each other a friendly good-night; but Edith went straight from the bedroom to the street, and clung tightly to her husband's arm as they walked along the pavement opposite the Park, enjoying the quiet before entering the busy streets.

"We'll never come again!" she cried tremulously. "We'll stay at home, and have a supper of bread and cheese and love with it! You shan't be taunted and sneered at by any man on earth, if he were twenty times my father! What an angel you were, Jack, to keep quiet, and then talk as if nothing had happened! I was choking with rage!"

"Poor darling!" said Jack Martin tenderly. "You take
things too much to heart. It's rough on you, but you must remember that it's rough on the old man too. You are his eldest child, and the beauty of the family. He hoped great things for you, and it is wormwood and gall to his proud spirit to see you struggling along in cheap lodgings. We can't wonder if he explodes occasionally. It's wonderful that he is as civil to me as he is; he has put me down as a hopeless blunderer!"

'DON'T MIND WHAT HE SAYS!'

There was a touch of bitterness in the speaker's voice, for all his brave assumption of composure, and his wife winced at the sound. She clung more tightly to his arm, and raised her face to his with eager comfort.

"Don't mind what he says! Don't mind what any one says. I believe in you. I trust you! The good times will come back again, dear, and we will be happier than ever, because we shall know how to appreciate them. Even if we were always poor, I'd rather have you for my husband than the greatest millionaire in the world!"

"Thank God for my wife!" said Jack Martin solemnly.

Chapter Six.

A Managing Woman.

Meanwhile Ronald and Margot were holding a conclave on the third floor. "I must get away from home at once!" cried the lad feverishly. "I can't write in this atmosphere of antagonism. I breathe it in the air. It poisons everything I do. If I am to have only three more months of liberty, I must spend them in my own way, in the country with you, Margot, away from all this fret and turmoil. It's my last chance. I might as well throw up the sponge at once, if we are to stay here."

"Yes, we must go away; for father's sake as well as our own," replied Margot slowly. She leant her head against the back of her chair, and pushed the hair from her brow. Without the smile and the sparkle she was astonishingly like her brother,—both had oval faces, well-marked eyebrows, flexible scarlet lips, and hazel eyes, but the girl's chin was made in a firmer mould, and the expression of dreamy abstraction which characterised the boy's face was on hers replaced by animation and alertness.

"Father will be miserable to-night because he flared out at supper; but he'll flare again unless we put him out of temptation. He likes his own way as much as we like ours, and it's so difficult for parents to realise that their children are grown-up. We seem silly babies in his eyes, and he longs to be able to shut us up in the nursery until we are sorry, as he used to do in the old days. As for our own plans, Ron, they are all settled. I was just waiting for a quiet opportunity to tell you. I have been busy planning and scheming for some time back, but it was only to-night that my clue arrived. Jack, my emissary, slipped it into my hand after supper. Read that!"

She held out a half sheet of paper with an air of triumph, on which were scribbled the following lines:—

"Name, Elgood. Great walker, climber, etcetera. Goes every June with brother to small lonely inn (Nag's Head)—Glenaire—six miles' drive from S—, Perthshire. Scenery fine, but wild; accommodation limited; landlady refuses lady visitors, which fact is supposed to be one of the chief attractions; Elgood reported to be tough nut to crack; chief object of holiday, quiet and seclusion; probably dates two or three weeks from June 15."

Ronald read, and lifted a bewildered face.

"What does it all mean? How do this man's plans affect ours? I don't understand what you are driving at, Margot, but I should love to go to Scotland! The mountains in the dawning, and the shadows at night, and the dark green of the firs against the blue of the heather—oh, wouldn't it be life to see it all again, after this terrible brick city! How clever of you to think of Scotland!"

"My dear boy, if it had been Southend it would have been all the same. We are going where Mr Elgood goes, for Mr Elgood, you must know, is the editor of *The Loadstar*—

the man of all others who could give you a helping hand. Now, Ron, I am quite prepared for you to be shocked, but I know that you will agree in the end, so please give in as quickly as possible, and don't make a fuss. You have been sending unknown poems to unknown editors for the last two years, with practically no result. It's not the fault of your poems—of that I am convinced. In ten years' time every one will rave about them, but you can't afford to wait ten years, or even ten months. Our only hope is to interest some big literary light, whose verdict can't be ignored, and persuade him to plead your cause, or at least to give you such encouragement as will satisfy father that you are not deluded by your own conceit. I've thought and thought, and lain awake thinking, till I feel quite tired out, and then at last I hit on this plan,—to find out where Mr Elgood is going for his holidays, and go to the same place, so that he can't help getting to know us, whatever he may wish. Ordinary methods are useless at this stage of affairs. We must try a desperate remedy for a desperate situation!"

"I'm sure I am willing. I would try any crazy plan that had a possibility of success for the next three months. But yours isn't possible. The landlady won't take ladies. That's an unsurmountable objection at the start."

But Margot only preened her head with a smile of undaunted self-confidence.

"She'll take *me*!" she declared complacently. "She can't refuse me shelter for a night at least, after such a long, tiring journey, and I'll be such a perfect dear, that after twenty-four hours she wouldn't be bribed to do without me! You can leave Mrs McNab to me, Ron. I'll manage her. Very well then, there we shall be, away from the madding crowd, shut up in that lonely Highland glen, in the quaint little inn; two nice, amiable, attractive young people with nothing to do but make ourselves amiable and useful to our companions. Mr Elgood can't be young; he is certainly middle-aged, perhaps quite old; he will be very tired after his year's work, and perhaps even ill. Very well then, we will wait upon him and save him trouble! You shall bicycle to the village for his tobacco and papers, and I'll read aloud and bring him cups of tea. We won't worry him, but we'll be there all the time, waiting and watching for an opportunity. One never knows what may happen in the country. He might slip into the river some day, and you could drag him out. Ronald, wouldn't it be perfectly lovely if you could save his life!"

The two youthful faces confronted each other breathlessly for a moment, and then simultaneously boy and girl burst into a peal of laughter. They laughed and laughed again, till the tear-drops shone on Margot's lashes, and Ronald's pale face was flushed with colour.

"You silly girl! What nonsense you talk! I'm afraid Mr Elgood won't give me a chance of rescuing him. He won't want to be bothered with literary aspirants on his summer holiday, and he will guess that I want his help—"

"He mustn't guess anything of the kind until the end of the time. You must even never mention the word poetry. It would neither be fair to him, nor wise for ourselves. What we have to do is to make ourselves so charming and interesting that at the end of the three weeks he will want to help us as much as we want to be helped. I understand how to manage old gentlemen I've had experience, you see, in rather a difficult school. Poor father! I must run down to comfort him before I go to bed. I feel sure he is sitting in the library, puffing away at his pipe, and feeling absolutely retched. He always does after he has been cross."

Ronald's face hardened with youthful disapproval. "Why should you pity him? It's his own fault."

"That makes it all the harder, for he has remorse to trouble him, as well as disappointment. You must not be hard on the pater, Ron. Remember he has looked forward to having you with him in business ever since you were born, and it is awfully hard on him to be disappointed just when he is beginning to feel old and tired, and would be glad of a son's help. It is not easy to give up the dream of twenty years!"

Ronald felt conscience-stricken. He knew in his own heart that he would find it next to impossible to relinquish his own dawning ambitions, and the thought silenced his complaints. He looked at his sister and smiled his peculiarly sweet smile.

"You have a wide heart, Margot. It can sympathise with both plaintiff and defendant at the same time."

"Why, of course!" asserted Margot easily. "I love them both, you see, and that makes things easy. Go to bed, dear boy, and dream of Glenaire! Your chance is coming at the eleventh hour."

The light flashed in the lad's eyes as he bent his head for the good-night kiss—a light of hope and expectation, which was his sister's best reward.

Ron had worked, fretted, and worried of late, and his health itself might break down under the strain, for his constitution was not strong. During one long, anxious year there had been fear of lung trouble, and mental agitation of any kind told quickly upon him. Margot's thoughts flew longingly to the northern glen where the wind blew fresh and cool over the heather, with never a taint of smoke and grime to mar its God-given purity. All that would be medicine indeed, after the year's confinement in the murky city! Ron would lift up his head again, like a plant refreshed with dew; body and mind alike would then expand in jubilant freedom.

Margot crept down the darkened staircase, treading with precaution as she passed her sister's room. The hall beneath was in utter darkness, for it was against Agnes's economical instincts to leave a light burning after eleven o'clock, even for the convenience of the master of the house. When Mr Vane demurred, she pointed out that it was the easiest thing in the world for him to put a match to the candle which was left waiting for his use, and that each electric light cost—she had worked it all out, and mentioned a definite and substantial sum which would be wasted by the end of the year if the light were allowed to burn in hall or staircase while he enjoyed his nightly read and smoke.

"Would you wish this money to be wasted?" she asked calmly; and thus questioned, there was no alternative but to reply in the negative. It would never do for the head of the house to pose as an advocate of extravagance; but all the same he was irritated by the necessity, and with Agnes for enforcing it.

Margot turned the handle of the door and stood upon the threshold looking across the room.

It was as she had imagined. On the big leather chair beside the tireless grate sat Mr Vane, one hand supporting the pipe at which he was drearily puffing from time to time, the other hanging limp and idle by his side. Close at hand stood his writing-table, the nearer corner piled high with books, papers, and reviews, but to-night they had remained undisturbed. The inner tragedy of the man's own life had precluded interest in outside happenings. He wanted his wife! That was the incessant cry of his heart, which, diminished somewhat by the passage of the years, awoke to fresh intensity at each new crisis of life! The one love of his youth and his manhood; the dearest, wisest, truest friend that was ever sent by God to be the helpmeet of man—why had she been taken from him just when he needed her most, when the children were growing up, and her son, the longed-for Benjamin, was at his most susceptible age? It was a mystery which could never be solved this side of the grave. As a Christian Mr Vane hung fast to the belief that love and wisdom were behind the cloud; but, though his friends commented on his bravery and composure, no one but himself knew at what a cost his courage was sustained. Every now and then, when the longing was like an ache in his soul, and when he felt weary and dispirited, and irritated by the self-will of the children who were children no longer, then, alas! he was apt to forget himself, and to utter bitter, hasty words which would have grieved *her* ears, if she had been near to listen. After each of these outbreaks he suffered tortures of remorse and loneliness, realising that by his own deed he had alienated his children; grieving because they did not, could not understand!

Except, perhaps, Margot! Margot, the third little daughter, whose coming in the place of the much-desired boy had been a keen disappointment to both parents. The mother had been doubly tender to the child, as if to compensate for that passing pang; but Mr Vane recalled with contrition that he himself had remained indifferent and neglectful until two or three years later, when at last Ronald had made his tardy appearance. Then ensued constant visits to the nursery, to examine the progress of the son and heir; and after the daily questioning and inspection it was impossible to resist bestowing some little attention on the bewitching curly-headed, chubby-cheeked little damsel who clung to his trouser leg, and raised entreating eyes from the altitude of his knee. Mr Vane felt guiltily conscious of having neglected this child, and now in the content of gratified ambition he proceeded to make good that neglect by petting her to her heart's desire, until as time went on it became an open question whether his daily visits were not paid even more to the girl than to the boy. Ronald remained his father's pride, but Margot was his joy, his pet,—in years to come his comfort and companion.

There was more of the dead mother in this last daughter than in either of the elder sisters; she had her mother's gift of insight and understanding.

This was not the first time of many that she had crept downstairs after the household was in bed, to play David to his Saul, and to-night, as he turned his eyes to the doorway and recognised her slight figure, it was not surprise which he felt, but rather a shamed and uneasy embarrassment. "Margot! It's very late! Why are you not in bed?"

She shut the door and crossed the room to his side.

"I wanted to talk to you!"

"To remonstrate, I suppose, for what I said at supper! You and Ron are angry, no doubt, and feel yourselves badly used. You have come to fight his battles, as usual."

"No. I don't want to fight at all. Just to talk to you a little while, and say I'm sorry."

She seated herself on the arm of his chair as she spoke, and leant her shoulder carelessly against his; but he edged away, still sore and suspicious.

"Sorry for what?"

"For you! Because *you're* sorry. Because I knew you'd be sitting alone, doing nothing else but being sorry. So I came down to put my arms round your dear old neck, and kiss your dear old head, and tell you that I love you. Badly!"

Yes! Margot understood. In just such pretty simple words would his own Margaret have chased away the black spirit years ago. Mr Vane puffed at his pipe, staring fixedly across the room, to conceal the sudden moistening of his eyes, but his figure sank back into its old place, no longer repulsing the caress.

"It's a hard task for a lonely man to manage a family of children. He gets all the kicks, and none of the thanks!"

"That's exaggeration, dear—which you are always protesting against in others. We are tiresome and self-willed, but we know very well how much we owe to you, and your care for us. It hurts us as much as it hurts you when we disagree; but we've got to live our own lives, father!"

"And you imagine that you know better how to set about it than a man who has lived more than twice as long, and has had ten times the experience?"

Margot hesitated.

"In a way—no; in a way—*yes*! We know ourselves, daddy, as even you cannot do, and it is impossible for one person, however kind and wise he may be, to lay down the law as to what is to be the object of other lives. We all have our own ambitions; what could satisfy one, would leave another empty and aching. Agnes, for instance, and me! How different we are! Her idea of happiness would be a house worked by machinery, where every hour the same things happened at precisely the same moment, and there were never any cataracts and breaks, and nobody ever came down late to breakfast. *I* should like to have breakfast in bed, and a new excitement every single day! We are not all cut out of one pattern, and we are not children any longer, dear. Sometimes you forget that. When *you* were twenty-three, you were married, and had a home of your own."

"Ron is not twenty-one."

"When you were twenty-one, did you want your own way, or were you willing for other people to decide for you?"

Mr Vane sighed, and moved his head impatiently.

"Here we are back again at the same old argument! It's waste of time, Margot. I can't alter my ideas, but I'll try to keep a tighter rein over myself for the next few months. We mustn't have any more scenes like to-night."

"No." Margot spoke as gravely as himself. "We mustn't, daddy, for your sake as well as ours, and therefore I think it wise to remove the cause of your irritation. You said we might go away to the country together, Ron and I, and we have decided on Scotland—on a glen in Perthshire, six miles from the nearest station, where the landlady of a quaint little inn takes in a few boarders. It will be very primitive, I expect, and we shall live on cream and porridge and mountain air, and grow brown and bonnie, and study Nature as we have never had a chance of doing before. Six miles from a station, daddy! There's seclusion, if you like!"

Mr Vane knitted his brow, uncertain whether to approve or object.

"How did you come to hear of this place, if it is so out of the world?"

"Jack heard of some people who like it so much that they have gone back again and again." Margot paused for a moment, and then added resolutely, "They go to fish. Probably they will be there again this summer. They are two brothers—one of them is quite old. I don't know anything about the other. Of course, wherever we stay we shall meet other people—but you don't mind that, do you, dear? You can trust us not to associate with any one who is not what you would approve?"

"Oh yes. I am not afraid of you in that way, and Ron is sensible enough where you are concerned. He'll take care of you. I wouldn't allow you to stay at a big hotel without Agnes or some older woman, but you are welcome to your little inn, if it takes your fancy. If it rains all day, in Highland fashion, Ronald may discover that there are compensations even in Regent's Park. How soon are you off?"

"The middle of June, if all's well, and we'll stay on as long as we are happy and enjoying ourselves. Then there will be your holiday to consider, dear. I thought it would be such a good idea if you took Jack with you, while I went to the seaside with Edith and the boys. Jack and you agree so well, and have so many tastes in common. You would make splendid *compagnons de voyage*!"

Mr Vane drew back in his chair to stare at her beneath frowning brows.

"If there is one thing in this world more objectionable than another, it's a managing woman!" he cried emphatically. "Don't you develop into one, Margot, if you wish to keep any influence over me. I've seen danger signals once or twice lately, and I tell you plainly—I won't stand it! Be satisfied with what you have gained, and carry Ron away to your Highland glen, but leave my holiday alone, if you please. I'm quite capable of choosing a companion for myself if I need one."

"Yes, dear," said Margot meekly; but her smile showed no sign of contrition. She had heard this terrible indictment times without number, but as yet there had come no waning of her influence. As she felt her way carefully up the dark staircase a few minutes later, she smiled to herself with complacent satisfaction; for not only had the Scotch trip received the parental sanction, but the first step was taken towards securing a holiday for poor tired Jack. Mr Vane might protest, but the idea once suggested would take root in his mind, and by the time that it developed into action he would imagine that it was entirely his own inspiration. What did it matter? For Jack's sake even more than his own it was better that he should be so deluded; and Margot was happily above the littleness of desiring to monopolise the credit for her ideas. So long as a point was gained, she was more than content to remain inconspicuously in the background.

Chapter Seven.

Preparations.

Every one said that it would rain. It was most depressing. You had only to mention that you intended to spend your summer holiday in a Highland glen, to set the torrent of warning in full flow. "It will rain all the time.—It always rains in Scotland... You will be soaked... You will be starved... You will feel as if you have gone back to winter. You will miss all the summer in the South... You will get rheumatism... You will be bored to death." On and on it went, each newcomer adding volume to the chorus, until it became quite difficult to remember that one was starting on a pleasure trip, and not on a perilous Arctic exploration.

"Take plenty of wraps!" urged the wise ones. "Don't imagine that you will be able to wear pretty white things, as you do at home. Take old things that don't matter, for no one will see you, and you will never want to wear them again. You will shiver round the fire in the evenings. Be sure to take rugs. You won't have half enough blankets on the bed. I was in the Highlands for a month two years ago, and we had one fine day!"

"Well!" queried Margot of this last Job's comforter, "and what was *that* like? Were you glad that you were there for that one day at least?"

The speaker paused, and over her face there passed a wave of illuminating recollection. She was a prosaic, middle-aged woman, but for the moment she looked young,—young and ardent.

"Ah!" she sighed. "That day! It was wonderful; I shall never forget it. We went to bed cold and tired, looking forward to another dark, depressing morning, and woke in a dazzle of sunlight, to see the mountains outlined against a blue sky. We ran out into the road, and held out our hands to the sun, and the wind blew towards us, the soft, wet, heathery wind, and it tasted like—*nectar*! We could not go indoors. We walked about all day, and laughed, and sang. We walked miles. It seemed as if we could not tire. I—I think we were 'fey.'" She paused again, and the light flickered out, leaving her cold and prosaic once more. "The rest of the time was most unfortunate. I contracted a severe chill, and my sister-in-law had rheumatism in her ankles. Now, my dear, be sure to take good strong boots—"

Margot and Ronald listened politely to all the good advice which was lavished upon them, but, after the manner of youth, felt convinced that in their case precautions were needless. It was going to be fine. If it had been wet in previous years, all the more reason why this coming summer should be warm and dry. The sun was going to shine; the clouds were going to roll away; Mr Elgood was going to fall in love with Ron at first sight, and prove himself all that was wise, and kind, and helpful. Delightful optimism of youth, which is worth more than all the wisdom of maturer years!

Margot set about her preparations unhampered by the financial troubles which befall less fortunate girls. Her father was lavishly generous to his favourite daughter, supplementing her dress allowance by constant gifts. It was one of his greatest pleasures in life to see his pretty Margot prettily attired, a pleasure in which the young lady herself fully concurred. She had too much good taste to transport all the frills and fripperies of London to a Highland glen; but, on the other hand, she set her face firmly against the mustard-coloured tweeds affected by so many women for country wear, choosing instead a soft dull blue, a hundred times more becoming. For headgear there was a little cap of the same material, with a quill feather stuck jauntily through a fold at the side, while neat, strong little boots and a pair of doeskin gloves gave a delightfully business-like air to the costume. In the rug-strap was a capacious golf cloak, displaying a bright plaid lining. This was waiting in readiness for the six-mile drive at the end of the journey, and inside the large dress-box was a selection of well-chosen garments—a white serge coat and skirt for bright weather; cottons and lawns for the warm days that must surely come; a velveteen dress for chilly evenings, blouses galore, and even a fur-lined cloak. Margot felt a thrill of wondering satisfaction in her own prudence, as she packed this latter garment, on a hot June day, with the scent of roses filling the room from the vase on the toilet table.

She packed sketching materials also, plenty of fancy-work destined to provide presents for the coming Christmas, a selection of sixpenny novels, and one or two pet classics from her own library, which travelled about with her wherever she went.

Ronald's preparations were more easy, for surely no stock-in-trade is so simple as that of an author! His favourite stylographic pen, his favourite note-book, and that was an end of it so far as work was concerned. He took his half-plate camera with him, however; and the two handsome free-wheel bicycles were carefully swathed for the journey.

"I can't understand why you couldn't be content to go to some nice south-country place, instead of travelling to the other end of the country in this dusty weather," Agnes opined, as she assiduously fixed the label to every separate piece of the luggage which was piled together in the hall. "It's so foolish to waste time and money when there are nice places at hand. Now, there's Cromer—"

"You don't get heather-clad mountains at Cromer, Agnes, and we shan't have promenades at Glenaire, nor bands, nor crowds of fashionable people quizzing each other all day long. We prefer the real, true, genuine country."

"Oh, well, you'll be tired of it soon enough! Margot will hate it. We shall have you hurrying back at the end of a fortnight, bored to death. I don't think that lock of yours is quite safe, Margot. I shouldn't wonder if you found some things missing when you arrive. The guards have a splendid chance on these all-night journeys," prophesied Agnes cheerfully. She stared in surprise when Margot burst into a peal of laughter, and repeated, "Poor old Agnes!" as if she, secure and comfortable at home, were the one to be pitied, instead of the careless travellers into the unknown!

The sisters kissed each other in perfunctory manner, Ron shook hands, and nodded vaguely in response to half a dozen injunctions and reminders; then the travellers took their places in the cab, bending forward to wave their adieux, looking extraordinarily alike the while—young and eager and handsome, with the light of the summer sun reflected in their happy eyes.

Agnes felt a little chill as she shut the door and walked back into the quiet house. All the morning she had looked forward to the hours of peace and quietness which would follow the departure of the two children of the household; but now that the time had arrived she was conscious of an unwonted feeling of depression. The sound of that last pitying, "Poor old Agnes!" rang in her ears. Why "poor"? Why should Margot speak of her as some one to be pitied? As her father's eldest unmarried daughter and the mistress of the house, she was surely a person to be approved and envied. And yet, recalling those two vivid, radiant faces, Agnes dimly felt that there was something in life which Margot and Ron had found, and she herself had missed.

"I don't understand!" she repeated to herself with wrinkled brows. A vague depression hung over her spirits; she thought uneasily of her years, and wondered if she were growing old, unconscious of the fact that she had never yet succeeded in being young.

Chapter Eight.

Glenaire.

Margot and Ronald slept through their long journey with the fortitude of youth, enjoyed a delicious breakfast at Perth, took train again for a couple of hours, and finally set out on the last and most enjoyable stage of their journey—the six-mile drive to the head of Glenaire.

The first portion of the road gave little promise of beauty, but with every mile that was traversed the scenery began to assume a wilder and a sterner aspect. The mountains were high and bare, with few trees upon their banks, except here and there a patch of dark green firs. When the sun retired behind a cloud they looked somewhat grim and forbidding, but as it emerged from the shelter they became in a moment a soft, blooming purple; a wonder of beauty against the high, blue sky. In the valley were rolling plains of meadowland, of richest, most verdant green, with here and there a blaze of golden gorse or of thickly-growing rushes, to mark the presence of hidden water.

At long intervals was seen a little white cottage, set back from the road, where some lonely shepherd tended his sheep; and, at the sound of wheels, little linty-headed children would rush out to the gate, and stand gazing at the strangers with big round eyes, which looked light against the tan of their faces.

What a life for young and old to live all the year round, looking out on the grim bare hills; alone with God and Nature, and the dumb, patient animals! Day after day alone, in a little niche between grey rocks; alone in the summer-time, when the winds blew soft, and the buttercups made splashes of gold across the green; alone in the winter, when the mountains seemed to shut out the light, and the snow lay deep on the ground.

Margot looked with a shudder at the tall poles set here and there along the road. She had inquired as to their purpose, and had been informed that they were so placed to act as landmarks; for when the drifts lay deep, the ends of the poles served to point out the direction of the road, whereas without their aid the traveller would of a certainty be lost on the moors. Poor little linty-locked ones, imprisoned in the tiny cot in those bitter days!

Margot's thoughts flew homeward, to the well-kept roads near her own home; to the grumbling and indignation of the family, if perchance a recent fall of snow had not been swept away as speedily as might be: "The road was thick with mud. Impossible to cross without splashing one's shoes. The snow was left to melt on the pavement—disgraceful!" The Southerner railed at the discomfort of a greasy roadway; the Northerner was thankful to escape death by the aid of a warning pole!

Suddenly and unexpectedly the road took a quick swerve to the right, and lo, a narrow glen leading apparently into the very heart of the mountains.

Glenaire village at last! A little group of cottages, two whitewashed kirks, a schoolhouse, a post office, a crowded emporium where everything was to be purchased, from a bale of wincey to a red herring or a coil of rope; a baker's shop, sending forth a warm and appetising odour; a smithy, through the open door of which came out a glare of heat, astonishingly welcome after the long, chill drive; bare-footed children playing at tares by the wayside; an old man in a plaid, smoking a pipe and turning on the new arrivals a kindly, weather-beaten face,—these were the impressions left on Margot's mind as the horses put on an extra spurt, knowing full well that rest and food were near at hand.

After the little group of houses there came another stretch of road for perhaps three-quarters of a mile; a road which wound along between moorland on the right, and on the left a straggling tarn, thickly surrounded by rushes. The cone-shaped mountain at the head of the glen towered ever nearer and nearer, until it seemed as if it must be impossible to drive a hundred yards farther. Seen in the broad light of a summer afternoon it was wonderfully beautiful; but it was a wild and lonesome spot, and, given cloud or rain, its very grandeur and isolation would increase the sense of gloom.

Margot had time to shiver at an imaginary picture before an exclamation from Ron attracted her attention. There it stood! the little white inn, nestled beneath the shelter of a rock, so near to the head of the glen that the road came to an abrupt ending but a few yards farther on. A door in the middle; two small-paned windows on either side; a row of five windows overhead; to the right a garden stocked with vegetables and a tangle of bright-coloured flowers; to the left the stable-yard. This was the Nag's Head, and in the doorway stood the redoubtable Mrs McNab herself, staring with steely eyes at the daring feminine intruder.

The one overpowering impression made by Mrs McNab was cleanliness! She was so obtrusively, aggressively, immaculately clean, that the like of her had never before dazzled the eyes of the benighted Southern visitors. Her lilac print gown was glossy from the press of the iron; the hands folded across the snowy apron were puffed and lined from recent parboiling; her face shone like a mirror from a generous use of good yellow soap. White stockings showed above her black felt slippers; her hair—red streaked with grey—was plastered down on each side of her head, and, for greater security, tied with a broad black ribbon. A stiff white collar was fastened by a slab of pebble rimmed in silver, which proudly imagined itself to be an ornamental brooch. There was not a single feminine curve in her body; stiff and square she stood, like a sentinel on guard, her lips pressed into a thin line; in her eyes a smouldering flame.

Margot took her in, with one swift comprehensive glance, as the driver reined up his tired horses before the door. A temper; a quick temper, a temper easily provoked, but a kindly woman nevertheless. No country bumpkin, but a shrewd, capable business woman, with two light blue eyes fixed stolidly on the main chance; a woman, moreover, blessed with a sense of humour; else why those deep lines stretching from nose to chin; that radiating nest of wrinkles round the eyes?

Margot's courage revived at the sight. She sprang down lightly from her perch and advanced towards the house, smiling in her most fascinating manner.

"How do you do, Mrs McNab? We have arrived, you see. So glad to be here at last!"

The mistress of the inn stared into her face, stolidly unmoved.

"It was two brithers I was expecting. I'm no caring for leddies!"

"You like gentlemen better? Oh, so do I—*Much*!" cried Margot with a gush. "But they need us to look after them, don't they? My brother is not at all strong. The drive has been delightful, but rather cold, all the same. I am afraid he may be chilled." She stretched out a little ungloved hand, and laid it lightly on the hard red fist. "Feel! We *should* love some tea!"

Mrs McNab looked down at the delicate little hand, up into the pleading eyes, and over her set square face there passed a contortion,—there is really no other word to describe it,—a contortion of unwilling amusement. The chin dropped, the lips twitched, the red lines which did duty for eyebrows wrinkled towards the nose. Similarly affected, an Irishwoman would have invoked all the saints in her calendar, and rained welcomes and blessings in a breath; an Englishwoman would have smiled a gracious welcome; but Mrs McNab drew away from the beguiling touch, turned a broad back on her guests, and with a curt "Come yer ways!" led the way into the house.

Behind her back Margot beamed and grimaced triumphantly to her confederate. Victory was in the air! Mrs McNab could not refuse to grant a night's shelter to a tired and chilly traveller, and by to-morrow—Margot smiled to herself, recalling the contortion of the dour Scotch face,—by to-morrow she was complacently satisfied that Mrs McNab would no longer wish to be rid of her unexpected guest!

Chapter Nine.

The Brothers Elgood.

Inside the inn a mingling of odours greeted the nostrils. Furniture polish, soft soap, various whiffs from the bar, which by good fortune opened into the stable-yard, and was distinct from the house itself; a sweet, heavy odour of milk from the dairy; a smell of musk from the plants ranged along the window-sills. In the dining-room the tablecloth was laid, with a large home-cured ham in the place of honour. The floor was covered with oilcloth; the furniture was covered with horsehair. On the mantelpiece stood two large specimens of granite, and a last year's almanac. Red rep curtains were draped across the window, so as to conceal all the view except a glimpse of the road. The walls were hung with a fearsome paper, in which bouquets of deep blue flowers were grouped on a background of lozenges of an orange hue. Over the mantelpiece hung a coloured print of Queen Victoria; over the sideboard a print entitled "Deerstalking," representing two Highlanders in plaids and bonnets standing over the prostrate form of a "monarch of the waste." In the corner by the window were massed together quite an imposing collection of "burial cards," memorialising McNab connections dead and gone, all framed to match in black bands with silver beadings.

Anything less homelike and inviting can hardly be imagined to welcome tired travellers at the end of a long and chilly journey. Margot shivered as she crossed the portals, and rubbed her hands together in disconsolate fashion, even her cheery optimism failing at the sight.

"It's so—*slippery*!" was the mental comment. "What an appalling room to sit in! What must it be like in bad weather! And no fire! We'd die of cold if we sat here all the evening. If the worst comes to the worst, I'll hug my hot bottle. What a mercy I remembered to bring it!"

Mrs McNab was speaking in hard, aloof accents, after the manner of one who, having been interrupted in her work by unwelcome intruders, is still determined to perform her duty toward them, as a matter of distasteful necessity. Shades of the obsequious landladies of the South! The tired guests quailed before the severity of this Northern welcome.

"If it's tea you're wanting, the kettle's on the hob. It will be waiting for you before ye're ready for it. Ye'll be wanting a wash, I'm thinking."

It was a statement, not a question, and, in response to it, brother and sister meekly ascended the staircase to the rooms allotted to their use in the front of the house—two whitewashed cribs, provided with nothing which was not absolutely necessary; a small, white-covered bed; a wooden chest of drawers, made to do duty for a dressing-table also, by the presence of a small mirror set fair and square in the middle of a coarse-grained mat; a few pegs on the wall, a deal washstand, and a couple of chairs—that was all; but everything was exquisitely clean and orderly, and what did one want with luxurious upholstery when a peep through the open windows revealed a view which sent the blood racing through the veins in very ecstasy of delight? Purple mountains and a blue sky; golden yellow of gorse—a silver sheet of water, reflecting the dark fringe of the pines—it was wonderfully, incredibly beautiful in the clear afternoon light.

Margot thrust her head out of the window, forgetful of cold and fatigue. What joy to think of waking up every morning for a month to a scene like this! Thirty mornings, and on every one of them the sun would shine, and the air blow clear and sweet. She would put on her thick, nailed boots, and clamber up the glen, to see what lay at the other side of the pass; she would take her sketching materials, and sit on that sunny knoll, trying to make some sort of a picture to send home to the poor father in his smoky prison-house. On hot days she would wade in the cool grey tarn...

The little maid was knocking at the door, and announcing that tea was ready, while Margot was still weaving her rose-coloured dreams. It was a cold douche in more ways than one, to return to the depressing atmosphere of the dining-room, but the meal itself was tempting and plentiful. Scones and toast, eggs and strawberry-jam, besides the solid flank of ham, and, better than all, plenty of delicious cream and fresh butter.

Margot poured out tea for herself and Ron, and, taking the hot-water-jug on her knee, warmed her numbed hands on it as she ate. For the first five or ten minutes no time was wasted in talking; then, the first pangs of hunger being appeased, the two young people began to compare impressions.

"Do you suppose this is the only sitting-room? Do you suppose we shall have to sit here in the evenings and when it rains? Fancy a long wet day, Ron, shining on horsehair chairs, with your feet on an oil-clothed floor, gazing at funeral cards! I should go to bed!"

"It wouldn't be a bad idea. Rest cure, you know! If we are very energetic in fine weather, we may be glad of a rest; but there *is* another room. I caught sight of a sanctuary filled with woollen mats and wax flowers, with a real live piano in the corner. 'The best parlour,' I should say, and the pride of Mrs McNab's heart. I don't know if she will allow you to enter."

"She will; but she won't have a fire. It has been spring-cleaned, and has a waterfall of green paper in the grate—I can see it all!" Margot declared, with a shudder. She hugged the hot-water-jug still closer, and shivered expressively. "I shall be obliged to raid the kitchen—there's nothing else for it!"

"You daren't!"

Margot laughed derisively, but her answer was checked by the sudden appearance of a man's figure pacing slowly past the window. Brother and sister sprang from their chairs, with a simultaneous impulse, rushed across the room, and crouched behind the moreen curtains. "Is it?" they queried breathlessly of each other—"Mr Elgood? Can it be?"

If it were Mr Elgood, he was certainly not imposing, so far as looks were concerned. A dumpy little man, of forty years or more, dressed in a baggy suit of grey tweed, with carpet slippers on his dumpy little feet. He had evidently started out of the inn to enjoy a smoke in the open air, sublimely unconscious of the scrutiny that was levelled upon him the while. His uncovered head showed a large bald patch, his face was round and of a cherubic serenity.

"I could twist him round like a teetotum!" whispered Margot, holding up a pert first finger and peering complacently.

"He looks terribly commonplace!" sighed Ronald disconsolately. "Not in the least the sort of man I expected."

Together they peered and peeped, ducking behind the curtains as the stranger approached, and gazing out again the moment his back was turned. Every now and then he halted in his promenade, stuck his hands inside his baggy pockets, and tilted slowly to and fro on the points of his carpeted toes. Anon he took his pipe from his mouth, and blew out big whiffs of smoke, glancing around the while with an expression of beatific contentment. The whole appearance of the man was an embodiment of the holiday spirit, the unrestrained enjoyment of one who has escaped from work, and sees before him a pageant of golden idle hours. Margot and Ronald smiled in sympathy even as they looked. He was a plain little man, a fat little man, a middle-aged little man, but they recognised in him the spirit of abiding youth, and recognising, felt their hearts warm towards him.

"He is nice, Ron, after all! I like him!"

"So do I. A capital chap. But he can't possibly be Elgood of the *Loadstar*."

Even as he spoke the last word the door was thrown suddenly open, and Mrs McNab entered, carrying a plate of hot scones. She stopped short to stare in surprise, while the two new arrivals hurried back to the table, obviously discomposed at being discovered playing the part of Peeping Tom.

Seated once more before the tea-tray, Margot made an effort at composure; decided that honesty was the best policy, and said in her most charming manner—

"We were looking at the gentleman who is walking up and down! Another of your guests, I suppose? It is interesting to see people who are staying in the same house."

Mrs McNab planted the scones in the centre of the table, and gathered together the soiled plates with a wooden stolidity. To all appearances she might not have heard a word that had been said. Margot seized the hot-water-jug, and shivered ostentatiously, trusting to pity to prevail where guile had failed; and sure enough the pale blue eye turned on her like a flash of steel.

"What's ailing ye with the water-jug?"

"I'm ailing myself!" returned Margot meekly. "So cold! I can't get warm. Tired out after the long journey."

She tried her best to look delicate and fragile, but the healthy bloom on her cheeks contradicted her words, and the landlady's reply showed no softening of heart.

"Cramped, more like! Better go ye're ways for a guid sharp trot, to bring the blood back to your veins. Ye'll be in time for the afternoon's post; but unless ye're expecting news of your own, ye needna fash for the rest. Mr Elgood's gane to fetch them."

"Mr Elgood?" Information had come at last, and in the most unexpected fashion. "The gentleman we have been watching?"

The thin lips lifted with a suspicion of scorn.

"Oh, him! That's just the brither. The real Mr Elgood's away till the village. You passed it on the road."

She disappeared into the "lobby," and brother and sister nodded at each other solemnly, the while they munched the hot buttered scones.

"We'll go! As soon as we have finished. I long to see what he is like. I'm glad it is not—" Margot nodded towards the window, and Ron assented with a lofty superiority—

"Yes—he is not the type! A good sort, no doubt, but hardly an intellectual leader. One could not imagine him writing those grand articles."

"He may be useful, though, for he looks a friendly little soul, and if we get intimate with him we must know his brother, too... These scones are the most delectable things! Do you think She will be shocked if we eat them all? I feel a conviction that I shall get into the way of calling her 'She'—with a capital S. 'She who must be obeyed!' I thought She would be softened by the sight of me hugging the jug, and offer to light a fire at once; but not a bit of it! Her cure was much more drastic. I'll accept it this time, as it suits my purpose, but when to-morrow comes,—we'll see!"

Margot nodded her head meaningly, pushed her chair back from the table, and picked up the golf cape which lay over the back of a chair. "After all, I believe 'She' is right! It will do us good to have a scamper, and the unpacking can wait until the light goes." She peered discreetly through the window, and held up a detaining hand. "Wait a moment until the 'Brither' has turned back towards the village. Then we'll sally out of the door and meet him face to face."

Ron picked up his grey cap,—a coat he disdained, though he also was far from warm,—and followed his sister into the bare entrance-hall, with its pungent mingling of odours. From the back of the house could be heard the jangling of milk-pails, and a feminine voice raised in shrill invective; but no one was in sight, and the conspirators emerged unseen from the door of the inn, and turned to the left, endeavouring somewhat unsuccessfully to appear unconscious of the approaching figure.

"Good afternoon! Good afternoon!" cried the stranger, in a full genial voice.

"Good afternoon!" cried the confederates, in eager response; then they passed by, and were conscious, by the cessation of the crunching footsteps, that the "Brither" had halted to look after them as they went.

"He likes our looks! He is going to be friendly... I don't wonder!" soliloquised Margot, looking with fond eyes at the tall figure of the youth by her side; at the clean-cut, sensitive face beneath the deerstalker cap.

"He was pleased to see us. All men admire Margot," said Ron to himself, noting with an artist's appreciation the picture made by the graceful figure of the girl, with her vivid, healthful colouring, the little cap set jauntily on her chestnut locks, the breeze showing glimpses of the bright tartan lining of her cloak.

Starting under such promising auspices, brother and sister merrily continued their way along the winding road which skirted the border of the tarn. Fresh from London smoke and grime, the clear mountain air tasted almost incredibly pure and fresh. One wanted to open the mouth wide and drink it in in deep gulps; to send it down to the poor clogged lungs,—most marvellous and reviving of tonics!

"It makes me feel—*clean*!" gasped Margot, at the end of a deep respiration, and Ron's eyes lighted with the inward glow which showed that imagination was perfecting the idea.

Margot loved to watch the lad at moments like these, when he strode along, forgetful of her presence, oblivious of everything but his own thoughts; his face set, save for those glowing eyes, and now and then an involuntary twitch of the lips. In her own poor way she could grasp the trend of his mind, could toil after him as he flew.

That word "clean" had suggested wonderful thoughts. God's wind, blowing fresh over the ageless hills, untainted by the soil of the city; the wind of the moorland and the heights! Must not a man's soul perforce be clean who lived alone in the solitude with God? Dare he remain alone in that awful companionship with a taint upon his life?...

Ronald dreamt, and Margot pondered, making no excuses for the silence which is a sign of truest understanding, until the scattered village came in sight, and curiosity awakened once more.

"Why did they have two churches, I wonder? There can't be enough people to fill even one, and every one is Presbyterian in the Highlands. Why don't they all meet together?" cried Margot, in her ignorance.

At the door of the outlying cottages the fair-haired matrons stood to stare at the new arrivals. They all seemed fresh and rosy, and of an exquisite cleanliness; they each bore a linty-haired infant in their arms, or held by the hand a toddling mite of two or three summers; but they made no sign of welcome, and, when Margot smiled and nodded in her friendly fashion, either retreated hastily into the shadow, or responded in a manner painfully suggestive of Mrs McNab's contortion. Then came the scattered shops; the baker's, the draper's, (fancy being condemned to purchase your whole wardrobe in that dreary little cell!) the grocer and general emporium in the middle of the row; last of all, the post office and stationer's shop combined.

Brother and sister cast a swift glance down the road, but there was no male figure in sight which could by any possibility belong to a visitor from the South.

"You go in, and I'll mount guard at the door. Buy some postcards to send home!" suggested Ron; and, nothing loath, Margot entered the little shop, glancing round with a curious air. There was no other customer but herself; but a queer little figure of a man stood behind the counter, sorting packets of stationery. He turned his head at her approach, and displayed a face thickly powdered with freckles of extraordinary size and darkness. Margot was irresistibly reminded of an advertisement of "The Spotted Man," which she had once seen in a travelling circus, and had some ado to restrain a start of surprise. The eyes looking out between the hairless lids, looked like nothing so much as a pair of larger and more animated freckles, and the hair was of the same washed—out brown. Whether the curious-looking specimen was fourteen or forty was at first sight a problem to decide, but a closer inspection proved the latter age to be the more likely, and when Margot smiled and wished him a cheery good afternoon, he responded with unusual cordiality for an inhabitant of the glen.

"Good efternoun to ye, mem! What may ye be seeking, the day?"

Margot took refuge in the picture postcards, which afforded a good excuse for deliberation. The great object was to dally in the post office as long as possible, in the hope of meeting the real Mr Elgood; and to this end she turned over several packets of views, making the while many inquiries; and the spotted man was delighted to expatiate on the beauties of his native land, the more so, as, presumably, it was not often that so lavish a purchaser came his way.

They were in the middle of the fourth packet of views, and the selected pile of cards had reached quite a formidable height, when a familiar whistle from the doorway started Margot into vivid attention, and a minute later a tall dark man stepped hastily into the shop.

What a marvellous thing is family likeness! In height, in complexion, and feature alike this man appeared diametrically the opposite of the stout little person encountered outside the inn; yet in his thin, cadaverous face there was an intangible something which marked him out as a child of the same parents. The brother on whom Margot was now gazing was considerably the younger of the two, and might have been handsome, given a trifle more flesh and animation. As it was, he looked gaunt and livid, and his shoulders were rounded, as with much stooping over a scholar's desk.

Big Game: A Story for Girls

"A fine big bundle for ye the day, Mister Elgood! I'm thinking the whole of London is coming down upon ye," the postmaster declared affably, as he handed over a formidable packet of letters. Envelopes white and envelopes blue, long manuscript envelopes, which Margot recognised with a reminiscent pang; rolled-up bundles of papers. The stranger took them over with a thin hand, thrust them into the pockets of his coat, with a muttered word of acknowledgment, and turned back to the door.

Now for the first time Margot stood directly in his path, and waited with a thrill of curiosity and excitement to see whether he would echo his brother's welcome. In this Highland glen the ordinary forms and ceremonies of society were hopelessly out of place, and it seemed as if perforce there must be an atmosphere of *camaraderie* between the few visitors whom Fate had thrown together in the spirit of holiday-making.

Margot's prettiest smile and bow were in waiting to greet the faintest flicker of animation on the grave, dark face, but it did not come. Mr Elgood's deep-set eyes stared at her with an unseeing gaze—stared as it were straight through her, without being conscious of her presence. She might have been a chair, a table, a post of wood by the wayside, for all the notice bestowed upon her by the man whose favour she had travelled some hundreds of miles to obtain.

Another moment and he had left the shop, leaving Margot to draw out her purse and pay for her purchases in a tingling of pique and disappointment.

"That gentleman will be staying up at the Nag's Head with yourself," vouchsafed the spotted postmaster affably. "A fine gentleman—a ferry fine gentleman! They say he will be a ferry great man up in London. I suppose you will be hearing of his name?"

Margot's response was somewhat depressed in tone.

"Yes. She had heard of Mr Elgood... She would take four, not five, postcards of the Nag's Head. No; there was nothing else she was needing. The two penny packets of notepaper were certainly very cheap, the coloured tints and scalloped borders quite wonderful to behold; but she did not require any to-day, thank you. Perhaps another time. Good morning!"

Outside in the road Ronald was pacing up and down, twirling his stick, and looking bright and animated. He came hurrying back to meet Margot, hardly waiting to reach her side before breaking into speech.

"Well—well! You saw him? Did you notice the shape of his head? You can see it all in his face—the force and the insight, the imagination. The face of a scholar, and the body of a sportsman, A magnificent combination! Did you notice his walk?"

"Oh, I noticed him well enough. I noticed all there was to see. I have no complaints to make about his appearance."

"What have you to complain of then? What has gone wrong?"

"He never noticed me!"

Ron laughed; a loud boyish laugh of amusement!

"Poor old Margot! That was it, was it? An unforgivable offence. He lives up in the clouds, my dear; compared with him, you and I are miserable little earth-worms crawling about the ground. It will take some time before he is even aware of our presence. We will have to make friends with the brother, and trust by degrees to make him conscious of our existence. It's worth waiting for!"

Ronald was plainly afire with enthusiastic admiration of his hero; but for once Margot refused to be infected.

"I'm not a worm!" she murmured resentfully. "Worm, indeed! I'm every bit as good as he!"

For twenty yards she walked on in silence, tilting her chin in petulant scorn. Then—

"Do you remember the old story of Johnny-head-in-air, Ron?" she asked mischievously. "He had a fall. A fall and a dousing! If he isn't very careful, the same sad fate may await your wonderful Mr Elgood!"

Chapter Ten.

An Excellent Beginning.

Dinner was served at seven o'clock at the Nag's Head, and was a substantial meal, consisting of spiced salt beef, gooseberry pie, and cheese. Mrs McNab carved the joint at the sideboard, and directed the movements of the maid by a series of glares which appeared to be fraught with wondrous significance.

"Brither Elgood" took the head of the table, and beamed upon his companions with cherubic good-nature, while his brother sat on his left, immersed in thought and his dinner. An elderly man with a strong Glasgow accent came next, accompanied by a homely, kindly-looking wife. (Margot sighed with relief to find that after all she was not the only lady of the company). Across from them sat a bowed old man, wearing a clerical collar with his tweed coat, and a thin, weedy-looking youth, evidently his son. An eminently staid and respectable company, but hardly of thrilling interest!

Ronald's handsome, clear-cut face stood out like a cameo among them, while Margot's fluffy net blouse looked a garment of superfine smartness. There was no opportunity of talking to either of the brothers Elgood, separated as they were by the length of the table. The clergyman, Mr Moffat, remarked that it had been a fine day, an ex–ceptionally fine day! Mrs Macalister, the Glasgow lady, handed the mustard with the suggestion that it was always an improvement to a boiled round; but with these thrilling exceptions the newcomers were left to their own devices. Conversation even among the older residents was spasmodic and intermittent, and in no sense could the meal be termed sociable or cheerful.

As soon as it was over "the real Mr Elgood" darted upstairs to his own room, the remaining gentlemen strolled out of doors to smoke their pipes, and Mrs Macalister escorted Margot to the best parlour across the landing.

It was a chill, yet fusty little apartment, the shrine of the accumulated treasures of Mrs McNab's lifetime. Time was when she had been cook to a family in Edinburgh, before McNab won her reluctant consent to matrimony. Photographs of different members of "The Family" were displayed in plush frames on the mantelpiece, table, and piano-top. Mr Moncrieff in Sheriff's attire, "The Mistress" in black satin; Master Percy in cap and gown, Miss Isabel reclining in a hammock, Master Bunting and Miss Poppet in various stages of development. There was also a framed picture of "The House"; a tambourine painted with purple iris by Miss Isabel's own hands; an old bannerette in cross-stitch pendent from the mantelpiece, a collection of paper mats, shaded from orange to white, the glass-covered vase of wax flowers which had attracted Ron's notice, one or two cheap china vases, a pot of musk placed diametrically in the centre of a wicker table, a sofa, and two "occasional chairs" gorgeously upholstered in red satin and green plush.

Mrs Macalister seated herself in the larger of the chairs, Margot took possession of the smaller, and heroically stifled a yawn. Another evening she would wrap herself in her golf cape and go out into the clear cool evening air; but now at last fatigue overpowered her; fatigue and a little chill of disappointment and doubt. How would it be possible to become intimate with a man who sat at the opposite end of the table, shut himself in his own room, and was apparently oblivious of his surroundings? With characteristic recklessness Margot had put on her very prettiest blouse, hoping to make a good impression on this first evening, but for all the attention it had received it might as well have been black delaine! She sighed and yawned again, whereupon Mrs Macalister manifested a kindly concern.

"You're tired out, poor lassie! Ye've had a weary journey of it. From London, I believe? I have a daughter married in Notting Hill. Will that be anywhere near where you stay? I'm hoping she'll be up to visit us in the New Year, and bring the baby with her. I have five children. The eldest girl is settled in Glasgow. I say, that's something to be thankful for, to have a married daughter near by. There was a young lawyer paying her attention who's away to the Cape. If it had been him, I'd have broken my heart! It's bad enough to have Lizzie in London, where, if the worst comes to the worst, ye can get to her for thirty-three shillings, but I couldn't bear one of my girls to go abroad..."

"But the men have to go—it's their duty to the Empire; and somebody must marry the poor things," Margot declared, still stifling yawns, but roused to a sleepy interest in Lizzie and her sisters. She foresaw that Mrs Macalister would need but the slightest encouragement to divulge her entire family history, and wondered whether time would prove her to be more of a solace or a bore. As a rule, she herself preferred to monopolise the larger share of a conversation, but to-night she was too tired to do more than offer the necessary remarks by the way.

"Oh ay, that's right enough. I don't object to their marrying, so long as it isn't one of my girls. I sent Isabel off on a visit to a school friend when young Bailey began to grow particular. A mother can manage these things, if she's any gumption, without letting the young people suspect that there is any interference. They like their own way, young people do, and Isabel is obstinate, like her father. Mr Macalister can be led, but he'll never be driven. Ye have to ca' canny to get the better of him."

Margot murmured a few words of polite but somewhat vague import, being rather puzzled to decide in what light she was expected to view Mr Macalister's characteristics. It occurred to her that as the good lady was determined to talk, the conversation might be carefully directed into more interesting channels, and valuable information gleaned concerning the other guests of the house.

"Have you been staying here long? Are you going to make a long visit?" she inquired; whereupon her companion began again with increased vigour.

"We've been a matter of a week, and as for the future, it just depends! Mr Macalister's been failing for the past year. He's just unduly set on his business, and his nerves," (she pronounced it "nearves") "are in a terrible condition. The doctor warned him he would have a collapse if he didn't get a rest at once. 'Take him away where he can't get letters and telegrams every hour of the day,' he told me. 'Take him to the quietest place you can find, and keep him there as long as ye can!' So here we are; but how long he'll put up with it, is past my knowledge. He begins to weary already, and of course no man will ever believe that any one else will take his place. They're conceited creatures, my dear. Mr Macalister—"

"It is nice for him having so many companions. I suppose you know the other visitors quite well?" Margot felt that for one evening she had heard as much as she cared for about Mr Macalister, and headed the subject in the desired direction with unflinching determination. "The Mr Elgood who took the head of the table seems very agreeable."

"Oh ay, he's a friendly wee body!" Mrs Macalister allowed, patronisingly. "There's no harm in him, nor in his brother neither, though he keeps himself to himself, and is always busy with his fishing, or writing, or what not. My husband went fishing with him one day, but they didn't seem to hit it exactly. Mr Macalister is very genial-like when he's in health, and he can't do with any one who's stand-off. He always says—"

"But Mrs McNab seems to prefer the younger brother. He must be nice, or she would not like him so much," interrupted Margot once more; and Mrs Macalister smiled with unruffled good-humour.

"Oh ay, they're just two dour, silent bodies who understand each other and each other's ways. He goes and has a crack with her now and then, and I've even heard them laugh,"—her voice took an awed and incredulous tone—"but at the table he never raises his voice. Mr Macalister says he is very close. He couldn't get anything out of him at all, and all his friends say Mr Macalister ought to have been a lawyer, for he's just wonderful for getting to the bottom of things. Of course when a man's run down, he isna at his best. Ye can't judge him, as I say, as you can when he's in his usual—"

Margot groaned in spirit! To keep Mr Macalister out of the conversation was evidently a hopeless feat. She saw before her a long succession of interviews when she would sit caged up in this little room, listening to the expressions of his virtues and failings! To-night she felt a moral conviction that she would soon fall asleep under the strain, and making an excuse of writing home, escaped to her own room, scribbled a few words on the back of a postcard, wrapped herself in her golf cape, and went out into the road in search of Ron.

It was still broad daylight, but now the sky was grey and colourless, and the mountains had ceased to smile. Like grim watching sentinels they stood on either side, closing in the Glen in a solitude that was almost awesome to behold. It seemed impossible to believe that twenty-four hours earlier one had been in the great city, and had considered Regent's Park countrified! Margot hurried forward to meet Ron, who was strolling along by himself, the other men of the party being out of sight. He looked at her with some anxiety, as she approached, and asked an eager question—

"What's the matter? Aren't you well? I thought you were not coming out. You look quite white!"

"I'm cold and tired, and—scarey! The beauty seems to have disappeared, and it's all so grim and grey. I made an excuse and came out to you with a card to post—but we needn't take it to-night, it's too far to the village."

"Nonsense! the walk is just what you need. You are tired with sitting still, and a sharp trot will warm you up, and help you to sleep. Come along. I'll give you a start to the bend of the road, and race you to the nearest tree."

Margot was not in the least in the mood for running races, but as a means of getting warm it was not to be despised, so she started promptly, running with swift, easy steps, and gradually quickening pace, as Ron gained upon her from the rear. She had not been educated at a girls' public school and been captain of the sports committee for nothing, and, given a short handicap, could often come off best. As the following footsteps grew nearer and nearer she spurted bravely forward, the ends of her cape streaming wildly in the breeze, her uncovered hair ruffled into curling ends. The tree was but a few yards distant; she was laughing and panting, dodging from right and left, to prevent Ron from passing by from behind, when round a bend in the road a figure appeared directly in her path, the figure of Brither Elgood himself, his round eyes bulging with surprise and curiosity. He came to an abrupt standstill in the middle of the road, and the racers followed his example, looking, if the truth were told, a trifle abashed to be discovered in so childish an amusement.

"Halloa! What is the matter? Is the Inn on fire?"

Margot laughed merrily. The voice, the tone, the manner, were those of a friend of a lifetime, rather than an acquaintance of an hour. It was impossible to answer formally; moreover, the humour of the idea made its appeal.

"No, indeed! On ice, more likely! We were so cold that a race seemed the only chance of getting warm! I hope we didn't startle you too much!"

"I like being startled," returned Mr Elgood complacently. He stood still, swinging his cane, looking from brother to sister with bright, approving eyes. "I was afraid you were feeling tired after your journey, but evidently you have not yet reached the age of fatigue. That's right! Thats quite right! I am glad that you have joined us at the Nag's Head. We are a respectable and harmonious party, but we need life—young life! We may weary *you*, but you will refresh and enliven us. In the name of our little company, I welcome you to the Glen?"

"Thank you, sir," said Ron simply, while Margot, as usual, hastened to amplify his words.

"I hope we shall be friends. I hope we shall all be friends. I was dreadfully tired really, but I felt worse staying in the house, and in that little parlour after dinner I nearly fell asleep."

Mr Elgood's eyes lit up with a flash of humour.

"But when a man's out of health you canna judge him! When he's in his usual, Mr Macalister's a verra interesting character!" he said solemnly. Then, meeting Margot's start and smile, he began to laugh again, and to shake in his happy, jelly-like fashion. "Ah—ha, I know! I guessed what was in store for you, as I saw you led away. She's a good woman that; a good, kind, womanly woman. Her devotion does her credit. When you and I get a wife, sir, we shall do well if we find one half so loyal and devoted."

He looked at Ron as he spoke, bringing his eyebrows together in a quick, scrutinising glance; but Ron's face was blank and unresponsive. Enshrined in his heart was a dim figure, half goddess, half fairy, a creature of thistledown, of snow, of blossom tossed before the wind; a lovely illusive vision who in due time was to appear and complete his life. It was a violation of the shrine to suggest a Mrs Macalister! He stood still, his brows knitted, his lips pressed together in a thin, warning line. Margot was impatient at his lack of response, but all the same he looked wonderfully handsome and interesting, and she could see that Mr Elgood regarded him with awakened interest, conscious that here was a character cut out of a pattern of its own, not made in the same mould as the vast majority of his fellows.

They turned and walked together along the winding road. Evidently friendship progressed quickly in this quiet glen, and guests living beneath the same roof accepted each other in simple, natural fashion, as members of a common household. Margot felt a sense of protection in the presence of this little man, so much older than herself, so friendly, so absolutely unsentimental in manner. His head was on a level with her own, and she read a frank admiration in his eyes, but it was an admiration of which Agnes herself could not have disapproved. He was the kind of man one would have chosen for an uncle—an indulgent bachelor uncle with plenty of money, and a partiality for standing treat!

"Tell me about the people in the Inn! I am always so interested in people!" she cried eagerly. "My brother likes other things better—books and pictures and mountains—but I like the living things best. I know a good deal about Mr Macalister's health, and about Lizzie, and Isabel, and their husbands and babies, and their lovers before they were married. They come from Glasgow—and the old clergyman is Scotch too, I suppose. Is every one Scotch except ourselves and you? We come from London—"

Mr Elgood's face shadowed quickly.

"Yes! but don't mention it. Never mention it!" he cried quickly. "I live there, too, or as nearly live as is possible in the surroundings. Now for three or four weeks I've escaped, and my one endeavour is to forget that such a place exists. I ask every one as a favour never to mention as much as the name in my hearing. You'll remember, won't you, and be good enough to indulge me? For the moment Miss—Miss Vane, I am a Heelander, born and bred, a strapping young chieftain of five-and-twenty. The Elgood of Elgood, an it please you, in bonnet and kilt, and my foot is on my native heather!"

He tilted his cap on one side, and threw a swagger into his walk, cleverly remindful of the swirl of tartan skirts, then turning upon Margot, queried quickly—

"Why do you laugh? It's rude to laugh! Is it so impossible to think of me in the character?"

"I laugh because I'm pleased," Margot answered, truthfully enough. "I do love to pretend! Let's bury London and our lives there, and pretend that we are *all* Highlanders! We will be your guests up in your mountain fastness, and you will take us about, and show us the scenes of your historic feuds with neighbouring clans, and we will swear to help you, if any new trouble should arise!"

"Right oh!" cried Mr Elgood, laughing. "I shall be only too proud. I'm a sociable beggar—during holiday time—and want to do nothing but smoke and talk. To talk nonsense, of course. Nothing dull or improving." He cast a sudden, suspicious look at the girl's face. "You are not clever by any chance, are you? I can't stand cleverness in the country."

Margot laughed gaily.

"I think I am—rather!" she declared audaciously. "I couldn't confess to being stupid, even to please a Highland chief, but it's in a very feminine way. I don't know anything about politics or science, and I've forgotten almost all that I learnt at school, but I take an interest in things, and understand people pretty well. I am generally clever enough to get my own way!"

She laughed again, remembering the purpose of the moment, and its close connection with this newly-made acquaintance. Instinctively she turned towards Ron, and the two pairs of brown eyes met, and flashed a message of mischief, affection, and secret understanding—a glance which made the watcher sigh with a sudden realisation of his own lost youth, his bald head, and increasing bulk. They were only a pair of children, these newcomers; kindly, affectionate, light-hearted children, whose companionship would be a tonic to a lonely, tired man. The broad cherubic countenance showed a passing shadow of wistfulness, as he slacked his pace and said in hesitating tones—

"I am afraid I have tacked myself on to you, without waiting for an invitation. I will say good evening now, unless I can act as guide, or help you in any way. Have you any special object in your walk?"

"Only the post office in the village. Do please come with us if you will! We should be delighted to have you!" cried Margot eagerly; and Ron looked down into the little man's face with his beautiful dreamy eyes, and said simply, "Please come, sir," with a sincerity which there was no denying.

Mr Elgood beamed with satisfaction. "Come awa, then, ma bonnie men!" he cried jauntily, and waved his stick in the air.

For the very first evening Margot could not help thinking that they had made an excellent beginning!

Chapter Eleven.

An Awkward Meeting.

Being a prudent damsel, and wise in her day and generation, Margot set before herself the subjugation of Mrs McNab as her first duty in Glenaire. To this end she repaired to her bedroom after breakfast on the morning after her arrival, made her bed, carefully put away every article of clothing, and tidied the oddments on the dressing-table; went through the same performance in Ron's little crib adjoining her own, and sailed downstairs in a glow of virtuous satisfaction.

Mrs McNab had apparently only one maid to help her to attend to her eight guests and to keep the inn in its present condition of immaculate order and cleanliness, though a shaggy-headed man—presumably the master of the house—could be seen through the staircase window, meekly brushing boots, and cleaning knives in a corner of the flagged yard. He had a small, wizened face, to which the unkempt hair, tufted eyebrows, and straggling whiskers gave a strong resemblance to a Skye terrier dog. Margot watched him now and then for a minute or two as she passed up and down, and heard him speaking once or twice, but he "had the Gaelic," and the sing-song voice and mysterious words sounded weirdly in her ears. Sometimes, as he put the final polish on the boots, he would break into song,—a strange, tuneless song which quavered up and down, and ended on long-sustained notes. Once even she saw the slippered feet move in jaunty dance-step to and fro, but at the sound of a clatter of saucepans from the kitchen close at hand he retired into his corner, and polished with redoubled energy. Mrs McNab evidently kept her husband in order, even as she did her house!

Elspeth, the maid, was a girl of eighteen or twenty, with a thin figure encased in a lavender print gown, and flaxen hair pulled so tightly back from her forehead that her eyebrows seemed to be permanently elevated by the process. Her face shone from the effects of constant soaping, and was absolutely void of expression. From morn till night she rushed breathlessly from one duty to another, rated continuously by Mrs McNab's strident voice, with never so much as a bleat of protest. When waiting at table, she snored loudly from nervousness, and the big red fist trembled as she carried the dishes to and fro, but her face remained blankly expressionless as before. Margot smiled at her radiantly every time that they met, and mentally decided to bequeath to her half her own wardrobe before leaving the Glen. In comparison with such a lot of drudgery, her own life seemed inexcusably idle and self-indulgent!

It took a considerable amount of courage to beard in her own den a woman of whom the members of her own household stood in such evident awe, but there was at least no nervousness apparent in Margot's manner as she tapped at the kitchen door at eleven o'clock that first morning, and thrust her pretty face round the opening to request permission to enter. Mrs McNab had descended from her work upstairs, and surely her heart must be softened by the spectacle of those two immaculately tidy rooms!

"Mrs McNab, I'm cold! May I come in and warm myself by your fire?"

The mistress of the inn turned a stonily surprised face from the table, before which she stood chopping suet with a short-handled knife; she did not suspend her work, but simply heightened her voice to make it heard above the harsh, monotonous noise.

"Cold, are ye? Havers! It's a fine June day. There's no call for any one to feel cold, if they don't sit about idling away their time. Put on yer cloak, and go a turn down the Glen!"

Margot suppressed a thrill of indignation at that accusation of idleness. Had she not made two whole beds, and even stooped to pick stray pins off the carpet? She pushed the door open and walked boldly forward.

"I'll go out as soon as I'm warm. If I caught a chill, I should give a lot of trouble, and you have enough to do without fussing over me. I know you would be a good nurse, Mrs

McNab—good housekeepers always are. I know without being told that you have a cupboard chock full of medicines and mixtures, and plasters and liniments, and neat little rolls of lint and oilskins. Is it this one?" She laid her hand on a closed door, drawing the while nearer and nearer to the fire. "What a perfectly beautiful oak chest! That's genuine! One can see it at a glance. The lovely elbow-grease polish can never be imitated. So different from the faked-up, over-carved things glittering with varnish that one sees so often nowadays. What a shame to keep it hidden away in the kitchen!"

Mrs McNab pounded stolidly away at the suet.

"I dinna ken where the shame can be!" she responded drily. "It's my own chest, and my mither's before me, and it's a pity if I mayna keep it where it pleases meself. There's no call that I know of to turn out my things, so that ither folks can have the fun of staring at them!"

Mrs McNab's manner was certainly the reverse of gracious, but, remembering the momentary softening of the grim face which she had witnessed the night before, Margot was determined not to be easily discouraged. Having gone so far, one could not retreat without irrevocably burning one's boats. Now or never victory must be wrested from the enemy!

With a charming little air of domesticity she seated herself upon the polished fender-stool at the side of the open grate, catching up her skirt so that it should not be caught by the blaze, and smiling across the room in her most confiding fashion.

"Please let me stay, Mrs McNab! It's such a lovely cosy kitchen, and my brother is out, and I feel so lost! Couldn't I do something to help? Are those gooseberries in that basket? Do they need picking? I can't cook, but I can pick gooseberries with any man living. Do let me! You said I was idling away my time. Give me a chance to work!"

Mrs McNab grunted sourly.

"There's no call for you to do anything of the sort. I never was one to take work upon myself that I couldna perform. The girl would have picked them before now, if she didna go about making more work than she gets through. She can do them when she gets downstairs!"

Poor, struggling, machine-like Elspeth! Margot felt a pang of pity for her unappreciated efforts, and the determination to spare her one task at least brought with it renewed courage.

"Let me do them as a pleasure to myself! I should feel so proud when the pie came to table, if I had helped to prepare it, and it would be an excuse to sit by this lovely fire. Please?"

"Kitchen work is no for the likes of you. Ye wouldna like it if ye soiled yer fine new gown!"

"If I asked you very nicely, perhaps you would lend me an apron!"

Mrs McNab threw down her chopper, and turned to wipe her hands on a roller towel. Perhaps she had come to the conclusion that as a pure saving of time it would be wise to give in without further demur; perhaps the twinkling appeal of the brown eyes touched a vulnerable spot in her heart; perhaps the service itself was of some value at the moment.

Margot did not concern herself as to causes, but was content to realise that she had won the victory. She meekly allowed herself to be tied into a coarse white apron, and set to work on the big basket of berries with nimble fingers. Picking gooseberries is not a task which requires much skill or experience; perhaps quickness is the criterion by which it can best be tested, and Mrs McNab's sharp glances soon discovered that her new apprentice was no laggard at the work. The little green balls fell from Margot's fingers into the basin with quite extraordinary quickness. She kept her eyes on her work, but her tongue wagged.

Margot talked, and Mrs McNab grunted, but the grunts grew ever softer and less repellent. The first attempt at a joke was met with a sniff of disdain, but a second effort produced a dry cackle, and that was a triumph indeed! When the suet had been reduced to shreds, there was bread to sift, and eggs to beat; and then Mrs McNab washed her hands and dropped her working apron preparatory to going upstairs to see after "the girl." She made no demur at leaving Margot alone in the kitchen, for, having undertaken a task, she was plainly expected to carry it through.

It was astonishing how much fruit one basket could hold! One wide-lipped basin had already been filled, and another pressed into the service, yet even a vigorous tilt to the side failed to show any signs of the bottom of the basket. Margot had achieved her double purpose of warming herself and breaking the ice of her hostess's reserve, and now was in a fidget to be off to join Ron on the hillside; but the fear of Mrs McNab was strong upon her, and she dare not move until her task was complete.

There she sat upon the low fender-stool, the big white apron concealing the blue tweed dress, her pretty, flushed face bent over her work, to all appearances the most industrious of Cinderellas, while the pendulum of the old oak clock clicked noisily to and fro, and through the open door came a whiff of clean cool air, laden with the scent of flowers and sweet-briar, with the pungent aromatic odour of growing herbs, with the heavy sweetness of the dairy.

Margot thought with a shudder of the gloomy underground regions in Regent's Park, where the servants of the house spent the greater part of their lives. In her own future spells of authority she determined to be very, very indulgent to pleas for "outings"; nay, even to make it a matter of duty to plan days of sunshine and liberty for the patient, uncomplaining workers.

The sun was beginning to peep forth from behind the clouds, and its rays dancing across the kitchen floor were an almost irresistible temptation to one newly escaped from town. Margot gave the basket an impatient shake, and, as another means to the desired end, popped a couple of berries into her mouth. So sweet did they taste, so fresh and ripe, that another two soon followed suit, and henceforth she ate as steadily as she worked. There could be no hesitation in so doing, for in fruit-picking it is an unwritten law that the worker is free to take his toll.

It was while Margot's hand was raised to her mouth for the eighth or ninth time that a footstep sounded on the flagged floor of the scullery behind her back, and a man's voice and laugh startled her into vivid attention. In both was a note which immediately recalled her companion of the night before,—the cheery, warm-hearted pseudo-chieftain of the Glen—yet in both rang a difference which told that the newcomer was not he, but probably one closely connected by birth and association.

The Mr Elgood; the Editor; the all-powerful dispenser of Ronald's fortunes! Margot felt convinced that it could be no one else, and experienced a moment of keen anticipation, followed by a shock of disgust, as she grasped the meaning of his words.

"Ah-ha! So I've caught you pilfering again. What will Mrs McNab say when she finds all her good fruit disappearing like this? You'll have to bribe me not to carry tales. Better turn me into a confederate—eh? Are they ripe?"

A long thin hand descended over Margot's shoulder, the fingers deliberately feeling after the plumpest and yellowest of the berries. *He had mistaken her for Elspeth*! Stupefaction mingled with wrath,—*Elspeth*! A vision of the square-built, flat-headed, hopelessly graceless figure rose before Margot's outraged vision, and resentment lighted into a blaze. Could any apron in the world be large enough to cause a resemblance between two such diametrically different figures! Margot appreciated her own beauty in an honest, unaffected fashion, as one of the good gifts which had been showered upon her, and for the moment the sense of injury eclipsed that of embarrassment.

With an impetuous movement she turned her face over her shoulder—that vivid pink and white face which made such a startling contrast to Elspeth's stolidity—and stared with widely-opened hazel eyes into that other pair of eyes so near her own.

It was the younger Mr Elgood sure enough,—but seen close at hand, with that mischievous smile curling his lips, he had an extraordinary youthful and boyish appearance. Margot received an instantaneous impression of kindliness and strength, of a glinting sense of humour, before the change came. Such a change! If she had been a wild animal prepared to spring, horror and dismay could not have been more eloquently depicted upon his face. The eyes widened, the features stiffened into a mask, the outstretched hand fell limply to his side. He opened his lips to say something, several things, but the words were unintelligible; a mere broken stammer of apology, as he wheeled round and walked hastily from the room.

The door slammed behind him; she heard his footsteps over the flagged hall. Poor Margot! Never before in her life had she so keenly desired to make a good impression; never had she so signally failed. It was indeed an unpromising beginning to the campaign!

Chapter Twelve.

A Moorland Walk.

A second time that day Margot came into close contact with Mr George Elgood. She was strolling slowly up and down the road with "the Chieftain," waiting for Ron to make his appearance before starting for a ramble over the countryside, when through the doorway of the inn out dashed the "Editor," making in the same direction, in the headlong, unseeing fashion which was plainly a characteristic. When about twenty yards distant, he lifted his eyes from the ground, became suddenly conscious of the two figures slowly strolling towards him, stopped short in the middle of the path, and, wheeling round, darted quickly in the opposite direction.

The cut was too glaring to be ignored. Margot's cheeks flamed with annoyance, which the sound of a low chuckle by her side did not help to subdue. She reared her little head to its haughtiest angle, and spoke in frosty accents.

"I am afraid I am in the way. Pray don't let me interfere with your plans. Won't you join your brother before he goes too far? He is walking very fast—"

There was a note of satire in the last words which made the Chieftain chuckle once more.

"Not I," he replied easily. "I can have his society any time I like. Yours is infinitely more refreshing. Keeps up a pretty good pace, don't he? Scared, you know. Scared to death! Running to cover like a frightened hare!"

"Scared of what?"

"Of you?"

Margot had known the answer to the question before she had put it, but, woman-like, was none the less affronted. Accustomed to be sought after and admired by mankind in general, it was a disagreeable experience to find herself repelled by the man of all others whom she was most anxious to ingratiate. Her face stiffened, and her rounded little chin projected itself proudly, the while her companion looked on with twinkling amusement.

"That makes you feel pretty mad, don't it?" he inquired genially. "You are not accustomed to that sort of treatment. Most of 'em run the other way, don't they? I should, in their place! But you mustn't be hard on old George. When I said 'you,' I used the word as a plural, not as applying with any special significance to your charming self. It is womankind as a whole which he finds terrifying. Run a mile any day rather than meet a woman face to face! You must not imagine that there is anything unusual in his avoidance of yourself. It's always the same tale."

Margot paused a moment, to reflect dismally that in this case there was small hope for the fulfilment of her scheme, then ventured the natural feminine question—

"Has he been crossed in love?"

"Who? George?" George's brother appeared to find something mysteriously ludicrous in the suggestion, for he shook with delighted laughter. "Rather not! Never had enough to do with a woman to give himself a chance. He's an old hermit of a bachelor, Miss Vane, absorbed in his work, and becoming more of a slave to it every year of his life. Even on a holiday he can't take it easy like other folks. He has some writing on hand just now—a paper of sorts which he has undertaken to have ready by a certain time, and it appears to his benighted intellect that a holiday is an excellent opportunity of getting it through. Mad, you see; stark, staring mad, but an excellent fellow all the same. One of the very best. I have a large experience of men, but I've never met one to compare with him for all-round goodness and simplicity of heart. We all have our failings, and there are worse things than a little shyness and reserve. If he avoids you like the plague, try to pity him for the loss it entails upon himself, and take no offence! As I said before, it's not a personal matter. He knows that you are a stranger and a woman, but I don't suppose he has the most glimmering idea of what you are really like!"

"Oh yes, he has. I was sitting in the kitchen this morning, and he came and spoke to me under the impression that I was Elspeth! The impression lasted until he got quite near. I was wearing an apron, but still,—I wasn't pleased! When he saw my face instead of hers, he fled for his life. But he *did* see it! He knows quite well what I am like."

"And in the depths of your little girl heart you think he is a strange fellow, not to want to see you again! You can't understand why he should go out of his way to be kind to Elspeth, and avoid some one infinitely more attractive. Don't be offended, but that's a wrong view to take of the case. In my brother's eyes Elspeth is more attractive than yourself, for she is poor, you see, and ugly, and leads a life of all work and no play. He might be able to do her a good turn. Besides, he has known her for several years, and has had time to become reconciled to her existence, so to speak. Custom goes a long way with shy people. George would rather beard a den of lions than face the company in the inn parlour on a wet evening, but he is a welcome guest in the kitchen, and Mrs McNab adores him to the extent of submitting to muddy boots without a murmur. He cracks jokes with her in a free-and-easy manner which strikes awe into the heart of tremblers like myself. It's my first visit to the Nag's Head, and I'm still in the stage of abject submission. She's a wonderful woman!"

Margot smiled with returning composure. She divined her companion's desire to change the subject of conversation, and was quite willing to further his efforts. What she had already heard concerning George Elgood supplied ample food for meditation.

Viewed in dispassionate light, it was not wholly disconcerting, for if the citadel could but once be stormed, there seemed a certainty of gaining sympathy and consideration. She must be content to wait in patience, until the hermit had become reconciled to her existence; but Ron, as a fellow-man, could venture on advances on his own account.

She must talk to Ron in private, and try to instil into him some of her own energy and enterprise. He was a dear, wonderful fellow, but absolutely wanting in initiative. Poets, she supposed, were always dreamy, impracticable creatures, unfitted to attend to practical interests, and dependent upon the good offices of some adoring woman working meekly in the background.

Her eyes brightened eloquently as she watched her brother's approach along the winding path. What a handsome young figure of manhood he made in his Norfolk jacket and knickerbockers, the close-fitting deerstalker cap showing the light chestnut hair, from which no barber's shears could succeed in banishing the natural kink and curl. No one would suspect, to look at him, that he cherished poetical ambitions! Margot was English enough to be thankful for this fact, illogical as it may appear. She was proud to realise that he looked a thorough sportsman, and in absolute harmony with his surroundings, and instinctively her pride and affection voiced themselves in words. The Chieftain might not be the rose, but he was at least near the rose, and it would be well to enlist his interest as well as that of his brother.

"Doesn't he look splendid?"

Mr Elgood started, and for a moment his round face expressed the blankest bewilderment, then his eyes lit upon Ron, and comprehension dawned.

"Ah, yes," he returned indifferently, "nice-looking lad! Pity he hasn't more to say for himself. What's he supposed to do? Business or profession?"

"It's not decided. He has not long come down from Cambridge. He is quiet, but he is very clever, all the same. Much cleverer than most boys of his age."

"Humph!" The Chieftain's tone was distinctly sceptical. "Yes! Good degree?"

Margot's colour heightened in embarrassment.

"Nothing special. Only a pass. It isn't in *that* way that his cleverness shows."

"Just so! Just so! I've met men like that before. Well, don't spoil him, that's all. Worship him in your heart, but not to his face. Looks to me as if he needed hardening up. A bit moony and sentimental. What? Don't mind my saying so, do you?"

"Not a bit!" returned Margot proudly; but she cared horribly, all the same, and for the moment her liking for her companion suffered a distinct eclipse. "I know him, you see, and understand him as no stranger can do. He needs appreciation, for he is too apt to lose faith in himself, and he is not sentimental at all. He has plenty of sentiment, but that's a different thing!"

"Yes—Um!" responded the Chieftain mischievously, his little eyes twinkling with amusement as they scanned the girl's flushed, injured face. "Quite so! Sorry I spoke. He is, without doubt, an unusually gifted young man." He bowed towards Margot, with an inference too transparent to be mistaken, and at which she was obliged to laugh, despite herself.

Ronald joined them at this moment, and looked from one to the other with his big, dreamy eyes. Margot was irritated to see that he looked even more absent-minded than usual, just when she was anxious that he should show to most advantage. He asked no questions in words, however, but Mr Elgood hastened to reply to the unspoken query in his eyes.

"Your sister and I have been having an argument. I don't know how it came about. Hate arguments myself, especially on a holiday. Besides, it's a waste of time. Whoever knew any one converted by an argument? Each one goes away more satisfied than ever that he is in the right, and that his opponent is talking rubbish; present company excluded, of course. So far as I can remember, we were discussing cleverness. If you were asked for a definition of a clever man, what would you say? How would you describe him?"

Ronald stood in the centre of the road, his hands clasped behind his back, his brows knitted in thought. Ninety-nine people out of a hundred would have answered such a question off-hand with a few light words; Ron bent the weight of his mind to it, with whole-hearted earnestness.

"Cleverness!" he repeated slowly. "It's a poor word! There's no depth in it. When a man is called clever, it means, I think, more an ability to display a superficial knowledge than any real, stored-up wisdom. It may even be a double-edged compliment!"

"Scored!" cried the Chieftain gaily, as he waved his stick in the air, and led the way forward with a jaunty tread. "Proposed, seconded, and carried that cleverness is a delusion to be sedulously avoided! Just what I always said. I've known clever people in my day—squillions of them, and, my hat! how stupid they were! That little lass dabbling in the lake is wiser than the whole crowd." He pointed to a fair-haired child wading by the side of the tarn. "The spirit of childhood—that's what we want! the spirit of joy in present blessings, and untroubled trust for the future. That little lass has a life of hardship and toil ahead—but what does she care? The sun shines to-day, and the funny wee mannie fra the inn is going to gie her a bawbee for goodies. It's a bad habit which he has fallen into; a shocking bad habit, but he canna cure himself of it." He threw a penny to the smiling, expectant child, then turning sharply to the left, led the way across the low-lying ground towards the base of the nearest hill.

Margot noticed that, as he went, he turned from time to time quick, scrutinising glances at Ron's face, as though trying to satisfy a doubt, and classify him in his own mind. Evidently the lad's serious, somewhat pedantic manner of replying had invested him with a new interest, but when he spoke again it was only in reference to the afternoon's expedition itself.

"I am not going to take you far," he announced. "I object to walking, on principle. What I maintain is, that we were never intended to walk! If we had been, we should have had four legs, instead of two. I never walk if I can possibly induce something else to carry me. And climbing is another mistake. What is it that one admires about mountains? Their height and grandeur! Very well, then, where is the point of vantage from which to view them? The base, of course. Climb up to the top, and you lose the whole effect, to say nothing of chucking away your valuable breath. See that little path winding up the slope? That leads to the moors, and when you are once on the moors you can walk about on the level all day long, if you are so disposed, and the air goes to the head of even a lazy old fellow like myself, and makes me quite gay and frisky. You two youngsters can go on ahead and engage in light conversation, while I puff along in the rear. At my age and bulk even the most witty conversation palls when climbing a hillside. When you get to the end of the footpath sit down and wait till I arrive, and take no notice of me till I get my wind. Then we'll start fair. Off with you!"

Margot ran forward, laughing, and she and Ron were soon scrambling up the hillside, side by side.

"That's a good fellow. I like him! He will be very interesting when one gets beneath the surface," pronounced the boy thoughtfully.

Margot nodded emphatically.

"I'm going to love him! I feel it in my bones, and he is going to love me too, but unfortunately he's the wrong man. He says that his brother hates women, and will do all he can to avoid me, so you must take things into your own hands, Ron! I can't help you, so you must help yourself. You will have to cultivate his acquaintance, and get him to take you about, and talk to him, and try to get intimate. You will, won't you? Promise me that you will!"

She looked with anxiety into the lad's face as she spoke, for previous experience had proved that Ron possessed the full share of those failings which are most characteristic of his temperament: a sudden cooling of interest at critical moments; a shirking of responsibility, an inclination to drift. It was a part of the artistic nature, which had an irritating effect on more practical mortals. Now, as she feared, he remained as placidly unmoved by the intelligence as if it had no bearing whatever on his own prospects.

"Oh, all right. I'll see! You can't rush things, if a fellow keeps out of your way. Our opening will come in time, if we leave it to chance and don't worry. I believe I am going to do really good work here, Margot! I had an idea last night, after you had gone to bed, and I was watching the stars through the pines. I won't read it to you yet, for it wants working up, but it's good—I am sure it is good! And that little stream along from the house; I found a song motif in that,—'*Clear babbling over amber bed*!' How's that for a word-picture? Shows the whole thing, doesn't it? The crystal clearness of the water; the music of its flow, the curious golden colour of the rocks. I'm always pleased when I can hit off a description in a line. I'm glad we came, Margot! There's inspiration in this place."

But for once Margot refused to be sympathetic.

"You did not come for inspiration, you came for a definite, practical purpose; and if you write a hundred poems, it won't make up for neglecting it. Now, Ron, wake up! I shall be angry with you if you don't do all you can for yourself. Promise me that you will try!"

"All right! All right! Do let us be happy while we have the chance, Margot. We had enough worry at home, and this place is perfect. Let us be wise children, and take no thought for the morrow. What would Elgood think of you, beginning to worry about the future, the moment his back was turned? She was a pretty illustration, wasn't she?—that little bare-headed child. Did you notice her hair? Almost white against the russet of her skin."

Margot grunted unsympathetically. She was out of breath with scrambling up the hillside, a trifle out of temper also, and consequently not in the mood to enthuse over artistic contrasts. She did not speak again until the summit was reached, and she threw herself on the ground to rest, and wait the arrival of the Chieftain. His gasps and grunts could already be heard in the distance, for, notwithstanding his various handicaps, he was surprisingly nimble, and in a few moments a round scarlet face hove into sight, and a round grey body rolled over on the ground by her side.

"Piff! piff! whew–w! Don't look at me, please—I don't like—being stared at by ladies—when my—complexion is flushed!" he gasped brokenly, mopping his face with a large silk handkerchief. "Every time—I—come up here—I vow I'll—never come again; but when *I'm* once up, I—never want to go down!"

He flourished his handkerchief to the left, pointing out the wide moorland, beautiful in colouring with its bright rank greens, and the bloomy purple of heather undulating gently up and down like the waves of an inland sea.

The pure rarefied air fanned the heated faces of the climbers, and with every moment seemed to instil fresh life and vigour. It was easy to believe that, once started, one would wander on and on over this wonderful moorland, feeling no fatigue, possessed with the desire to go farther and farther, to see what surprise lay beyond the next hillock.

After all, it was Mr Elgood who made the first start. One moment he lay still, puffing and blowing, bemoaning past youth, and bewailing loss of strength; the next, like an indiarubber ball, he had bounced to his feet, and was strutting forward, waving his short arms in the air, the white silk handkerchief streaming behind him like a flag.

"*Allons, mes enfants*! No lolling allowed on the moors. Keep your eye on that green peak to the right, and make for it as straight as a die. A few hundred yards away is a cottage where, if we are very polite and ask prettily, the guid-wife will give us a cup of buttermilk, the Gaelic substitute for afternoon tea. In a certain spot, which shall be nameless, I should as soon think of drinking poison in glassfuls, but after a stretch on the moors it tastes like nectar! Take my word for it, and try!"

That was the first walk which Ron and Margot had ever taken over a Scotch moor, and to the last day of their lives they remembered it with joy. The air went to their heads so that they grew "fey," and sang, and laughed, and teased each other like a couple of merry-hearted children, while the Chieftain was the biggest child of the three.

At times he declared that he was tired out and must turn back, but hardly were the words out of his mouth, than, lo, he was dancing an impromptu hornpipe with astonishing nimbleness and dexterity! He took a lively interest in all that his companions did and said, and did not hesitate to put question after question in order to arrive at a fuller understanding of any case in point; but London, and all that took place in London, remained a forbidden topic. He was the Elgood of Elgood, and they were "his bonnie men," and life outside the Highlands had ceased to exist.

Margot was delighted that the little man should have a chance of seeing Ronald in one of his lightest, most boyish moods, for from the expression of his face she feared that he had not so far previously been favourably impressed by the lad's personality. Now it was impossible not to admire and laugh as Ron played imaginary bagpipes on the end of his walking-stick, or droned out lugubrious ballads in imitation of a strolling minstrel who had visited the inn the night before. The ballad dramatised the circumstances of the moment: the perilous ascent, the wandering of three strangers across the moor, the flowing bowl which was to refresh and strengthen them for the return journey. Ron's knowledge of the native dialect was so slight that he fell back upon the more stately phraseology of the early English poets, introducing a strange Scotch term now and again with irresistibly comic effect.

The two listeners cheered him on with bursts of delighted laughter, while at an unexpected clever turn, or apt stringing together of words, the Chieftain would clap his hands and caper with delight.

"Good! good!" he would cry. "Neat! neat!" while his twinkling eyes surveyed the boy with increasing respect. "Do you often improvise?" he asked, when the ballad came to an end, and when Ron replied truthfully enough in the negative, "Well, I have heard many fellows do it worse!" was his flattering comment.

Margot had expected more, and felt that more was deserved, for the ballad had been quite a brilliant effort to be rattled off on the spur of the moment, but she could only hope that, in conclave with his brother, the Chieftain might be more enthusiastic, and manage to impress upon that absent-minded genius that the boy was worthy of his notice and study.

In due time—a very short time, as it appeared—the cottage was reached owned by the "guid-wife," who was ready to give—not sell—draughts of buttermilk to the passers-by. Margot was a little chary of the first taste, but the keen moorland air had done its work, and she too found it as nectar to the palate. The guid-wife "had no English," but the two women conversed eloquently with the language of the eyes, concerning the sleeping baby in its cradle, and the toddling urchins around the door. Here in the solitude this brave woman of the people reared her family, made their garments, tended them when they were sick, cooked for them, baked for them, washed for them, mended for them, and kept the three-roomed cot as exquisitely clean as hands could make it. The girl who dusted the drawing-room and arranged a few vases of flowers as her duty in life, gazed at her with awe, and felt ashamed of her own idle existence!

The buttermilk quaffed, Mr Elgood led the way to a thick patch of heather some few hundred yards nearer home, came to a standstill, and, spreading his handkerchief under his head, lay down with great deliberation and crossed his arms in beatific content.

"Now, if you want to discover what comfort means, find a soft patch for yourselves, and take a nap before we start for home. No upholsterer on earth ever manufactured a mattress to equal a bed of heather. If you don't want to sleep, kindly keep your distance, and enjoy yourselves with discretion, for if I'm awakened in the middle of my siesta, nothing short of murder will appease me!"

He shut his eyes even as he spoke, and composed himself with a sigh of content. Margot, nothing loath, took off her cap, and, spreading her cape over the bushes, nestled contentedly into its folds. Ron scorned the idea of sleep, but as he was curious to test the comforts of the heather, down he lay in his turn; and so soft, so springy, so eminently luxurious did the new bed appear, that he felt no desire to rise. Presently his eyes dropped, rose heavily once or twice, and rose no more. Margot's head burrowed more deeply into her cape. Deep regular snores sounded from the bush where Mr Elgood reposed. All three were fast asleep!

The sun shone on them; the hum of a thousand insects rose from the grass; high in the air a lark trilled his triumphant song. It was rest indeed to sleep and dream in such surroundings!

Chapter Thirteen.

The True Church.

Life flowed on very quietly and uneventfully at the Nag's Head during the next few days. The clergyman and his son were determined walkers, who set out each morning on a new expedition over the countryside, and at the evening dinner boasted of the number of miles they had traversed. What they had seen appeared to be of secondary importance, and they were correspondingly depressed or elated according as they had fallen short of, or surpassed previous records of distance.

Mr Macalister sat in the garden, reading day-old editions of the "*Glasga He–rald*" from the front page to the last, while his wife made pilgrimages to the village shop to buy infinitesimal articles of drapery, and exchange details of domestic history with the good lady in charge of the emporium.

Mr George Elgood went out fishing in a river two or three miles distant, accompanied sometimes by his brother, but for the most part by himself. He also sat at his bedroom window, writing by the hour together, and always and at all times he avoided his fellow-guests with a quiet persistence which could not be gainsaid. By the time that Margot had been in the inn for four days, he had advanced to the point of bidding her good-night and good morning, staring steadily at a point about a yard above her head, while on one historic occasion he even brought himself to remark that it was a fine day. Once also, looking up suddenly at dinner, she met his eyes fixed upon her with an expression of intent scrutiny; but he turned aside in evident perturbation at being discovered, and though the little puss thereafter wore her prettiest dresses, and took special pains with the arrangement of her hair, the incident was never repeated.

Goaded thereto by his sister's entreaties, Ronald had proposed himself as the companion of a morning's fishing expedition, but he returned home bored and irritated, and could not be persuaded to repeat the experiment. As Mr Elgood had left him at one point in the stream, and himself repaired to another some two hundred yards distant, the opportunities for conversation had been limited, while not even a twitch of the line had rewarded his amateur efforts.

Margot coaxed, reasoned, and finally stormed, but to no avail. In a quiet, amiable fashion, Ronald could be as obstinate as a mule, and he was plainly determined to go his own way. The sun shone; the surroundings were magnificent; he was free from the jarring dissensions of home; in easy, light-hearted manner he was content to live for the moment, and shut his eyes to troubles ahead.

"Remember what the Chieftain said to as the first day we were here!" he protested vigorously. "We ought to cultivate the spirit of children; to rejoice in the present, and trust for the future; whereas you want me to begin worrying the very first thing. I do call it stupid of you, Margot!"

"But, my dear boy—remember September! September is coming, and if you don't bestir yourself to take advantage of this last chance, you will be bemoaning your hard fate, and calling out that your life is ruined! Do, for goodness' sake, descend from the clouds and be practical for once! I'd help you if I could, but how can I, when the man refuses even to look at me?"

Margot's voice took a plaintive tone as she uttered those last words. She was so unaccustomed to be ignored, that the editor's avoidance rankled in her mind. She found her thoughts persistently returning to him in every period of leisure; when he was near, she was acutely conscious of his presence; when he was absent, her mind followed after him, wondering where he was, what he was doing, and of what he was thinking. Having once seen a glimpse of the real man when, in the character of Elspeth, she had looked into his face, sparkling with youth, kindliness, and humour, she understood that the abstracted figure which sat at the table at meal-times was but the shell of the real George Elgood, and that, if the barriers of shyness and reserve could once be overcome, he would prove an even more fascinating companion than his brother. The desire to know him grew daily in intensity, while, unconsciously to herself, the personal element slowly predominated the thought of Ron and Ron's future.

Now, as the brother and sister argued together, they were hurrying along by the edge of the tarn on their way to service at the kirk, for this was Sunday morning, the fifth day after their arrival at the Glen.

Ron, as usual, had been late in starting, and before the village was reached his watch showed that it was already five minutes past the time when service began. They had been sternly directed by Mrs McNab to go to the kirk at the far end of the village, and inquire for the inn pew, but as it would take several minutes longer to traverse the length of the straggling street, Margot suggested that it would be wise to attend the nearer of the two churches.

"There can be no difference. They are both Presbyterian," quoth she, in her ignorance; so in they went, to be met in the doorway by an elder in his Sabbath "blacks," his solemn face surrounded by a fringe of sandy whisker. The pews were very narrow and very high, shut in a box-like seclusion by wooden doors; the minister, in his pulpit, was just giving out the number of the psalm, and the precentor, after tapping his tuning-fork and holding it to his ear, burst forth into wailing notes of surprising strength and volume. Margot rose automatically to her feet, to subside in confusion, as the seated congregation gazed at her in stolid rebuke. In this kirk it was the custom to sit while singing, and stand during prayers—a seemly and decorous habit which benighted Southerners had difficulty in understanding.

Big Game: A Story for Girls

The singing of the metrical psalm sounded strangely in unaccustomed ears. Of melody there seemed little or none. The notes ascended and fell, and quavered into odd, unexpected trills and shakes, but it was sung with an earnestness and an intensity which could not fail to be impressive. The women, clean and tidy in their Sabbath bravery, sat with eyes fixed unwaveringly on their books; the children piped lustily by their sides; at the door of the pews the heads of the different families peered over their spectacles at the printed words, their solemn, whiskered faces drawn out to abnormal length.

In a corner by himself sat a weather-beaten old shepherd, singing with closed eyes, his shaggy head waving to and fro in time with the strain. Up in this lonesome glen those words had been his stay and comfort during a life of hardship. Like David of old, he had sung them on the mountainside, and they had been as a guide unto his feet, a lamp unto his eyes. He needed no book and no spectacles to enable him to join his note to the strain. Margot looked at him with a thrill of understanding and reverence. A saint of God, a lowly dweller on earth, for whom was waiting one of the "higher" places in the kingdom of heaven.

The sermon was long and rambling, and somewhat difficult for Southern ears to follow; there was a solemn collection taken in small boxes secured to long wooden handles, thrust in turns down the various pews with somewhat comical effect; then the service was over, and Margot and Ron came out into the village street, to find themselves face to face with a stream of worshippers who were returning from the farther kirk. Foremost among the number was Mrs McNab, large and imposing to behold in her Sabbath best, with her small husband ambling meekly by her side. Margot smiled at her in friendly fashion, and was dismayed to receive in return a glare of incredulous anger. What had she done to offend? She could not imagine what was wrong, and continued to stare blankly after the unbending figure, until presently her eye encountered another well-known face bent upon her with a smile. The Chieftain and his brother were close behind; so close that even the Editor's shyness could not attempt an escape. In another moment they were walking together, Margot between the two men, Ron on the outside, a few paces apart from the rest.

Margot glanced from one to the other with puzzled eyes. The Chieftain beamed upon her frankly. The Editor looked, and looked away, knitting his brows in embarrassment.

"What have I done?" she cried eagerly. "Why is Mrs McNab so cross? All was peace and joy when we left the inn. I had done my very best to help her, and now—you saw how she scowled! How can I possibly have offended her in this short time?"

The Chieftain chuckled softly.

"A good deal, I'm afraid! I'm sorry for you, after all your efforts at conciliation. It's bad luck that you should have stumbled upon an unforgivable offence. I'm afraid that there is no doubt that you will be turned out of the inn, neck and crop. Not to-day, perhaps, as she won't send out the trap, but certainly to-morrow morning."

"I shan't go!" protested Margot defiantly. If eviction had been probable, she did not believe that the Chieftain would have taken it in so unperturbed a fashion; but it was evident that she had committed some offence, and that he was aware of its nature. "But what have I done?" she continued urgently. "That's what I want to discover. There can't be any harm in going to church!"

"Oh, can't there, just? That's the whole crux of the matter. You went to the wrong church!"

There was a pause of stunned surprise while Margot gasped, and Ron's sleepy eyes brightened with curiosity.

"The wrong church! How can that be? They are both Scotch Presbyterians? There is no difference between them?"

"Only this difference, that the members of one kirk are hardly on speaking terms with the members of the other! That their leaders are at law together in the Courts, and that feeling runs so high, even in this sleepy hollow, that Mrs McNab, being a Free, refuses to sell milk to the 'Wees,' and is shamed to the heart to think that a guest living under her house-roof should have condescended to attend their service. It will be all over the Glen this afternoon that the bonny lady fra the inn chose to give her offering of siller to the 'Wees,' and they will bear themselves haughtily in consequence. Mrs McNab feels that she has been humiliated the day in the eyes of the neighbourhood. No wonder she looks coldly upon you!"

Margot flushed with resentment and indignation, but before she could speak Ron burst into impetuous speech.

"They quarrel? Up here? A handful of men and women among the great mountains? How can they do it? How can they harbour ill-feeling?"

"And what can they quarrel about? There must be such tiny, trivial differences. I am thankful I am not a Dissenter!" cried Margot proudly. "There are so many sects that one gets muddled among them all, and even in the same one it appears that there are differences! I am thankful that I belong to the Church."

The Chieftain looked at her quietly.

"To which Church?"

"The Church of England, of course."

"Oh!" He elevated his light eyebrows expressively. "Because its members have no quarrels with one another?"

Margot frowned uneasily.

"Oh, well—I suppose they have. But at the worst there are two parties, as compared to a dozen. You cannot deny that we are more united?"

"I should not boast too much about the unity of a Church in which civil war is permanently in progress; and what about charity and humility of mind? Suppose now, suppose for a moment that a family of strangers come to live in the house next your own in town, and you discover among other things that they are Dissenters. How does it influence your attitude towards them?" He thrust his ruddy face nearer, staring fixedly into hers. "Answer me that! Feel just the same? Exactly the same? No cooling off in the intention to call? *Quite* sure you never used the expression, 'only Dissenters!' and passed by on the other side?"

Margot's cheeks blazed. Her lids dropped, and the corners of her mouth drooped in self-conscious shame. There was a moment's silence, then a low murmur sounded on her ear, and, looking up quickly, she saw the Editor's dark face turned upon his brother, with reproach written large in frowning brow and flashing eye. He was taking up the cudgels in her defence; reproaching his own brother for forcing her into an awkward position.

Margot's heart gave a leap of joy at the discovery; in the flash of an eye her mood, her outlook on life, the very scene itself, seemed transfused with new radiance and joy. The sun seemed to peep out through the grey clouds, the underlying anxiety and worry of the past days took to itself wings, and disappeared. Her brown eyes thanked him with a glance more eloquent than she was aware; she laughed softly, and her laugh was sweet as a chime of bells.

"Yes, I have! I confess it. I've been narrow-minded and uncharitable, and a snob into the bargain. I've no right to throw stones... What Church do you belong to, Mr Elgood?"

The little man stood still in the middle of the road, throwing out his arms on either side, with a gesture wonderfully eloquent. His round, chubby face shone with earnestness and exaltation.

"To the Church of Christ! The Church of loyalty, and obedience, and love towards the brethren! To the Church of Christ, wherever I find it! When will Christians learn to remember the points on which they agree, rather than those on which they differ? The questions of form and ceremony; of Church government and ritual; how small they are, how unutterably trivial, compared to the great facts of the Fatherhood of God, and the sacrifice of Christ! Did the Power who made every one of us with different faces and different forms, expect us all to think mathematically alike? I cannot believe it! It is our duty to trust in God and love our brethren; to live together in peace, seeing the best in each other, acknowledging the best, thinking no evil! To see men who make a profession of religion quarrelling and persecuting each other for trivial differences, is a ghastly spectacle—a ghastly spectacle!" He walked on, swinging his short arms to and fro, then suddenly looked up with a keen glance into Ron's eager face.

There were no traces of dreaminess in the brown eyes at this moment; the dilated pupil gave to them an appearance of extraordinary depth and intensity; it was easy to see that the lad had been swept off his feet by the rugged force of the speaker's words, and was kindled into a like enthusiasm.

Lads of nineteen and twenty make it so much a matter of principle to suppress all exhibition of feeling, that it is almost startling to come across one who is not ashamed to betray a little human emotion. Mr Elgood evidently found it so, for he continued to cast those quick peering glances until the inn was reached, and the little party separated, to prepare for the midday dinner.

Margot walked slowly up the steep staircase leading to her room, and sat herself down on the bed to think out the problem. More and more did she long to pierce through the armour by which the strange, silent man was enveloped; but how was it to be done? Opportunities were few and far between, and now, for the first time in her life, confidence in her own powers deserted her, and she was overcome by a strange new feeling of humility and doubt. Who and what was she, that such a man should stoop to accept her friendship; poor, unlettered girl that she was, while he was acknowledged as one of the leading intellects of the day? Yet deep in her heart the thought lingered that between this man and herself existed a certain affinity, which, given an opportunity, might bridge over greater gaps than that of intellect and learning. How was that opportunity to be gained? She might be willing to sacrifice much to attain it, but there was one thing that could never be thrown on one side—her natural maidenly pride and dignity! Not even for Ron's sake could she bring herself to make advances to a man who, so far from exhibiting any desire for her company, had gone markedly out of his way to avoid it.

Ron himself was useless in such circumstances, a creature of moods, living for the moment only, content to forget the future in the enjoyment of present good. To drive him into the Editor's company against his will could do no good, since he would certainly reveal himself in his worst light, and in aggravating, topsy-turvy fashion he had taken a violent fancy for the wrong brother.

The Chieftain's geniality and candour, his boy-like lightness of heart on the one hand, his passion for right on the other, were fast developing a species of hero-worship in the lad's mind. Margot foresaw that, as time passed by, the two would grow closer together, and that any chance of intimacy with the other brother would retreat helplessly into the background. Unless—! Her face flamed as a possible solution of the difficulty darted suddenly into her mind. Could she? Dared she risk it? Yes, she could. It would be difficult, but she could bring herself to face it, if after a few days' consideration it still seemed the only way out of the difficulty.

Margot rose from the bed, and began quietly to prepare for dinner. Her face looked grave and anxious, but it had lost its troubled, fretted expression. She had made up her mind what to do, and with the decision came rest and ease of mind.

Chapter Fourteen.

Music hath Charms.

For the next two days it rained incessantly, and Margot sat in the little parlour of the inn talking to Mrs Macalister, or rather listening while Mrs Macalister talked, and playing draughts with Mr Macalister, who had relapsed into hopeless gloom of mind, and was with difficulty prevented from rushing home by the first train.

"The doctor said we were to keep him from the office for a good month at least, and there's not three weeks of the time gone by. If he goes back now, what will be the use of spending all this money on travelling and keep, and what not? It will be all clean waste," sighed the poor dame sadly. "He's a bit fratchety and irritable, I'm free to admit, but you should not judge a man when his nerves are upset. There's not a better man on earth than Mr Macalister when he has his health. It's dull for a man-body to be shut up in an inn, without the comforts of home, and feeling all the time that there's money going out. It is different when he can be out and about with his fishing and what not.—If you could just manage to amuse him a bit, like a good lassie!..."

The good lassie nodded reassuringly into the troubled, kindly face.

"I'll do my best. I have an old father of my own, who has nerves too, and I am used to amusing him. I'll take Mr Macalister in hand till the weather clears."

It was not a congenial task, for, truth to tell, Mr Macalister was not a beguiling object, with his lugubrious face, lack-lustre eyes, and sandy, outstanding whiskers; nor did he in the first instance betray any gratitude for the attention bestowed upon him. A stolid glance over his spectacles was his first response to Margot's overtures; his next, a series of grunts and sniffs, and when at last he condescended to words it was invariably to deride or throw doubt on her statements.

"Tut, nonsense! Who told you that? I would think so, indeed!" followed by another and more determined retreat behind the *Glasgow Herald*.

In the corner of the room Mrs Macalister sat meekly knitting, never venturing a look upwards so long as her spouse was in view, but urging Margot onward by nods and winks and noiseless mouthings, the moment that she was safe from observation.

It had its comic side, but it was also somewhat pathetic. These two good commonplace souls had travelled through life together side by side for over thirty years, and, despite age, infirmity, and "nearves", were still lovers at heart. Before the wife's eyes the figure of "Mr Macalister" loomed so large that it blocked out the entire world; to him, even in this hour of depression, "the wife" was the one supreme authority.

Fortunately for herself and her friends, Margot was gifted with sufficient insight to grasp the poetry behind the prose, and it gave her patience to persevere. Solution came at last, in the shape of the wheezy old piano in the corner, opened in a moment of aimless wandering to and fro. Margot was no great performer, but what she could play she played by heart, and Nature had provided her with a sweet, thrush-like voice, with that true musical thrill which no teaching can impart. At the first few bars of a Chopin nocturne Mr Macalister's newspaper wavered, and fell to his knee. Margot heard the rustle of it, slid gradually into a simpler melody, and was conscious of a heavy hand waving steadily to and fro.

"Ha-ha!" murmured Mr Macalister, at the end of the strain. "Hum-hum! The piano wants tuning, I'm thinking!" It was foreign to his nature to express any gratification, but that he had deigned to speak at all was a distinct advance, and equal to a whole volume of compliments from another man.

MARGOT ESSAYED ONE SCOTCH AIR AFTER ANOTHER.

"Maybe," he added, after a pause, "if ye were to sing us a ballad it would be less obsearved!"

So Margot sang, and, finding a book of Scotch selections, could gratify the old man by selecting his favourite airs, and providing him with an excuse to hum a gentle accompaniment. Music, it appeared, was Mr Macalister's passion in life. As a young man he had been quite a celebrated performer at Penny Readings and Church Soirées, and had been told by a lady who had heard Sims Reeves that she preferred his rendering of "Tom Bowling" to that of the famous tenor. This anecdote was proudly related by his wife, and though Mr Macalister cried, "Hoots!" and rustled his paper in protest, it was easy to see that he was gratified by the remembrance.

Margot essayed one Scotch air after another, and was instructed in the proper pronunciation of the words; feigning, it is to be feared, an extra amount of incapacity to pronounce the soft "ch," for the sake of giving her patient a better opportunity of displaying his superior adroitness.

Comparatively speaking, Mr Macalister became quite genial and agreeable in the course of that musical hour, and when Margot finished her performance by singing "The Oak and the Ash," he waxed, for him, positively enthusiastic.

"It's a small organ," he pronounced judicially, "a ve–ry small organ. Ye would make a poor show on a concert platform, but for all that, I'm not saying that it might not have been worse. Ye can keep in tune, and that's a mearcy!"

"Indeed, Alexander, I call it a bonnie voice! There's no call for squallings and squakings in a bit of a room like this. I love to hear a lassie's voice sound sweet and clear, and happy like herself, and that's just the truth about Miss Vane's singing. Thank ye, my dear. It's been a treat to hear you."

The broad, beaming smile, the sly little nod behind Mr Macalister's back, proclaiming triumph and delighted gratitude—these sent Margot up to her room heartened and revived in spirits, for there is nothing on earth so invigorating as to feel that we have helped a fellow-creature. The sunshine came back to her own heart, even as it was slowly breaking its way through the clouds overhead. She thrust her head out of the window, and opening her mouth, drank in great gulps of the fresh damp air, so sweet and reviving after the mouldy atmosphere of "the parlour." Over the mountain tops in the direction from which the wind was blowing the clouds were slowly drifting aside, leaving broader and broader patches of blue. Blue! After the long grey hours of rain and mist. The rapture of it was almost beyond belief! A few minutes more, and the glen would be alight with sunshine. She would put on boots, cap, and cape, and hurry out to enjoy every moment that remained.

The strong-soled little boots were lifted from their corner behind the door, and down sat Margot on the floor, school-girl fashion, and began to thread the laces in and out, and tie them securely into place. Then the deerstalker cap was pinned on top of the chestnut locks, and the straps of the grey cape crossed over the white flannel blouse. Now she was ready, and the sunshine was already calling to her from without, dancing across the floor, and bringing a delicious warmth into the atmosphere.

Margot threw open the door and was about to descend the narrow staircase, when she stopped short, arrested by an unexpected sound. Some one was singing softly in a room near at hand, repeating the refrain of the ballad which she had taken last on her list. The deep bass tones lingered softly on the words—

"And the lad who marries me,

Must carry me hame to my North Coun–tree!"

George Elgood was echoing her song in the seclusion of his own room! He had been indoors all the time, then, listening to her while she sang! Margot's cheeks grew hot with embarrassment, yet in the repeated strain there was a suggestion of appreciation, of lingering enjoyment which did away with the idea of adverse criticism.

"Oh, the Oak and the Ash,"—the strain seemed to swell in volume, growing ever nearer and nearer. "And the lad who marries me—"

The door flew open, and they stood facing one another, each framed as in a picture in the lintel of the doorways, divided only by a few yards of boarded passage. The strain came to an abrupt conclusion, frozen upon his lips by the shock of surprise and embarrassment. For the third time in their short acquaintance Margot looked straight into his eyes; for the third time recognised in their depths something that in mysterious fashion seemed to respond to a want in her own nature; for the third time saw the lids drop, heard an unintelligible murmur of apology, and watched a hasty retreat.

For a moment Margot stood motionless, an expression of wounded pride clouding the young rounded face, then very slowly descended the staircase, traversed the length of the "lobby," and stood outside the door, looking anxiously to right and left.

There he was, a strong, well-built figure in knickerbockers and Norfolk coat striding rapidly up the hill path to the right,—trying, no doubt, to put as much distance as possible between himself and the objectionable girl who seemed ever to be appearing when she was not wanted. For a long minute Margot stood gazing miserably ahead, then turning resolutely to the left, came face to face with the Chieftain returning from the village with his pockets bulging with papers.

His sudden appearance at this moment of depression had a peculiar significance to the girl's mind. Doubt crystallised into resolution; with a rapid beating of the heart she determined to grasp her courage in both hands, and boldly make the plunge which she had been meditating for some days past.

Chapter Fifteen.

Revelations.

At sight of Margot the Chieftain first beamed delight, and then screwed his chubby face into an expression of concern.

"Halloa! What's up? You look pretty middling doleful!" cried he, casting an eloquent glance towards the inn windows, then lowering his voice to a stage whisper, "Macalisteritis, eh? Too much stuffy parlour and domestic reminiscences? Never mind! Pack clouds away, and welcome day! The sun is shining, and I have a packet of bull's eyes for you in one pocket and a budget of letters in another. No, you don't! Not one single one of them to read in the house—come and sit on a stone by the tarn, and we'll suck peppermints and read 'em together. Wonderful how much better you'll feel when you've had a good blow of fresh air. I was prancing mad when I went out this afternoon, but now—a child might play with me!"

He threw out his short arms with his favourite sweeping gesture, his coat flapped to and fro in the breeze, he stepped out with such a jaunty tread on his short broad feet, that at sight of him Margot's depression vanished like smoke, and she trotted along by his side with willing footsteps.

"That's better! That's better! Never saw you look melancholy before, and never want to again... 'Shocking disappearance of dimples! A young lady robbed of her treasures! Thief still at large! Consternation in the neighbourhood!' Eh! How's that? Young women who have been endowed with dimples should never indulge in low spirits. It's a criminal offence against their neighbours. Where's your brother?"

Margot laughed at the suddenness of the question. It was one of the Chieftain's peculiarities to leap upon one like this, taking one unawares, and surprising thereby involuntary revelations.

"I don't know," she answered truthfully. "Over the hills and far away, I suppose—studying them in a new aspect. He loved them yesterday in the rain; to-day he felt sure that it would clear, and he wanted to see the mists rise. He does so intensely love studying Nature."

"Humph?"

Margot looked at him sharply, her head involuntarily assuming a defensive tilt.

"What does 'Humph' mean, pray?"

"Just exactly and precisely what it says!"

"It doesn't sound at all flattering or nice."

"Probably not. It wasn't intended to be."

"Mr Elgood, how can you! What can you have to say about Ron that isn't to his credit? I thought you liked him! I thought you admired him! You must see—you *must*—that he is different from other boys of his age. So much more clever, and thoughtful, and appreciative!"

"That's where the pity comes in! It's pitiful to see a lad like that mooning away his time, when he ought to be busy at football or cricket, or playing tricks on his betters. What business has he to appreciate Nature? Tell me that! At twenty—is it, or only nineteen?—he ought to be too much engrossed in exercising his muscles, and letting off steam generally, to bother his head about effects of sun and mist. Sun and mist, indeed! A good wholesome ordinary English lad doesn't care a toss about sun or mist, except as they help or hinder his enjoyment of sport!"

"Ronald is not an 'ordinary English boy'!"

"Hoity-toity! Now she's offended!" The Chieftain looked at his companion's flushed cheeks with twinkling eyes, not one whit daunted by her airs of dignified displeasure. "Don't want me to say what isn't true, do you? He's a nice lad—a very nice lad, and a clever one into the bargain, though by no means the paragon you think him. That's why I'm sorry to see him frittering away his youth, instead of making hay while the sun shines. He'll be old soon enough. Wake up some fine morning to find himself with a bald head and stiff joints. Then he'll be sorry! Wouldn't bother my head about him if I didn't like the lad. Have a peppermint? It will soothe your feelings."

The parcel of round black bull's eyes was held towards Margot in ingratiating fashion. It was impossible to refuse, impossible to cherish angry feelings, impossible to do anything but laugh and be happy in the presence of this kindest and most cheery of men. Margot took the peppermint, and sucked it with frank enjoyment the while she sat by the tarn reading her letters. Having received nothing from home for several days, the same post had now brought letters from her father, Edith, and Agnes, to say nothing of illustrated missives from the two small nephews. Mr Vane's note was short, and more an echo of her own last letter than a record of his own doings.

"Glad to know that you like your surroundings—pleased to hear that the weather keeps fine—hope you will enjoy your excursion," etcetera, etcetera.

Just at the end came a few sentences which to the reader's quick wits were full of hidden meaning.

"Agnes is taking the opportunity of your absence to organise a second spring cleaning. It seems only the other day since we were upset before. I dined at the club last night. It is difficult to know what to do with oneself on these long light evenings.—I would run away over Sunday, if I could think of any place I cared to go to... Town seems very empty."

"Poor dear darling!" murmured Margot sympathetically, at which the Chieftain lifted his eyes to flash upon her a glance of twinkling amusement. He made no spoken comment, however, but returned to the perusal of his own correspondence, while Margot broke open the envelope of Agnes's letter.

Two sheets of handwriting, with immense spaces between both words and lines—"My dear Margot," as a beginning—"Your affectionate sister, Agnes Mary Vane," as a conclusion. Thrilling information to the effect that the charwoman was coming on Friday. Complaints of the late arrival of the sweep. Information requested concerning a missing mat which was required to complete a set. Mild disapproval of the Nag's Head Inn. "I cannot understand what you find to rave about in such quarters." A sigh of impatience and resignation was the tribute paid to this letter, and then Margot settled herself more comfortably on the stone, and prepared to enjoy a treat—a real heart-to-heart talk with her beloved eldest sister.

Edith had the gift of sympathy. Just as Agnes never understood, Edith always seemed able to put herself in another's place, and enter into that person's joys and griefs. She herself might be sad and downcast, but in her darkest hour she could always rejoice in another's good fortune, and forget her own woes in eager interest and sympathy. Now, sitting alone in the dreary lodging-house sitting-room in Oxford Terrace, she was able mentally to project herself into the far-off Highland glen, and to feel an ungrudging joy in the pleasure of others. Never a hint of "How I envy you! How I wish I were there!" Not a mention of "I" in obtruding, shadow-like fashion from first to last, but instead, tender little anecdotes about the boys; motherly solicitude for their benefit, and humble asking of advice from one younger and less experienced than herself; an outpouring of tenderness for her husband, and of a beautiful and unbroken trust and belief, which failure was powerless to shake.

"Jack is working like a slave trying to build up the ruins of the old business. It is difficult, discouraging work, and so far the results are practically nil, but they will come. Something will come! More and more I feel the conviction in my heart that all this trouble and upheaval have been because God has some better thing in store for us both. We have only to wait and be patient, and the way will open.—I don't want to be rich, only just to have enough money to live simply and quietly. We are so rich in each other's companionship that we can afford to do without luxuries. Last night we had a dinner of herbs—literally herbs—a vegetarian feast costing about sixpence halfpenny, but with such lots of love to sweeten it, and afterwards we went out for a stroll into the Park, and I wore the hat you trimmed, and Jack made love to me. We *were* happy! I saw people looking at us with envious eyes. They thought we were a pair of lovers building castles in the air, instead of an old married couple with two bouncing boys, having the workhouse in much nearer proximity than any castle—but they were right to envy us all the same. We have the best thing!"

The letter dropped on to Margot's knee, and she sat silent, gazing before her with shining eyes, her face softened into a beautiful tenderness of expression. For some time she was unconscious that her companion had returned his own letters to his coat pocket, and was lying along the ground, his head resting upon his hand, watching her with a very intent scrutiny; but when at last her eyes were unconsciously drawn towards him, she spoke at once, as if answering an unspoken question.

"What a wonderful thing love is!"

The Chieftain's light eyebrows were elevated in interrogation.

"In connection with the 'dear darling' previously mentioned, if one may ask?"

"That was my father. I love him dearly, but just now I was thinking of the other sort of love. This letter is from my eldest sister. She was a beautiful girl, and could have married half a dozen rich men if she had wished, but she chose the poorest of them all, a dear, good, splendid man, who has been persistently unsuccessful all the way through. Everything—financially speaking, I mean,—has been against him. They have had continual anxiety and curtailment, until at last they have had to let their pretty house and go into dingy lodgings. My father is very down on Jack. He is a successful man himself, and don't you think it needs a very fine nature to keep up faith in a person who seems persistently to fail? But my sister never doubts. She loves her husband more, and idealises him more, than on the day they were married."

"And you call that man unsuccessful?"

Margot hardly recognised the low, earnest tones: her quick glance downward surprised a spasm of pain on the chubby face, which she had always associated with unruffled complacency. It appeared that here also lay a hidden trouble, a secret grief carefully concealed from the world.

"Isn't that rather a misuse of the word? A man who has gained and kept such a love can never be called a failure by any one who understands the true proportions of life. With all his monetary losses he is rich... And she is rich also... Richer than she knows."

Margot's hand closed impulsively on Edith's letter and held it towards him.

"Yes, you are right. Read that, and you will see how right you are. There are no secrets in it—its just a word-photograph of Edith herself, and I'd like you to see her, as you understand so well. She's my dearest sister, whom I admire more than anybody in the world."

Mr Elgood took the letter without a word, and read over its contents slowly once, and then, even more slowly, a second time. When at last he had finished he still held the sheet in his hands, smoothing it out with gentle, reverent fingers.

"Yes!" he said slowly. "I can see her. She is a beautiful creature. I should like to know her in the flesh. You must introduce us to one another some day. I haven't come across too many women like that in my life. It would be an honour to know her, to help her, if that were possible." He sighed, and stretching out his hand laid the letter on Margot's knee. "You are right, Miss Bright Eyes, love is a wonderful thing!"

Margot glanced at him with involuntary, girlish curiosity, the inevitable question springing to her lips before Prudence had time to order silence.

"Do you—have you—did you ever—"

The Chieftain laughed softly.

"Have I ever been in love, you would ask! What do you take me for, pray? Am I such a blind, cold-hearted clod that I could go through the world for forty-five years and keep my heart untouched? Of course I have loved. I do love! It was once and for ever with me—"

"But you are not—"

"Married? No! She died long ago; but even if she had lived she was not for me. She would have been the wife of another man; a good fellow; I think she would have been happy. As it is, we remember her together. She was a bright, sunshiny creature who carried happiness with her wherever she went... To have known her is the comfort of our lives—not the grief. We have lived through the deep waters, and can now rejoice in her gain... Do you know there is something about yourself which has reminded me of her several times! That is one reason why I like being with you, and am interested in your life. I should like you to think of me as a friend, and come to me for help if you were ever in need of anything that I could give."

The colour rushed into Margot's cheeks, and her heart beat with suffocating quickness. Here was the opportunity for which she had longed, offered to her without any preliminary effort or contriving on her own part! The place, the time, the person were all in readiness, waiting for her convenience. If through cowardice or wavering she allowed the moment to pass, she could never again hope for another such opening. Already the Chieftain was watching her with surprise and curiosity, the softness of the last few minutes giving place to the usual alert good-humour.

"Hey? Well! What is it? What's the trouble? Out with it! Anything I can do?"

"Mr Elgood," said Margot faintly, "you are very good, very kind; I am most grateful to you. I hope you *will* help me, but first there is something I must say... I—I have been deceiving you from the beginning!"

"What's that?" The Chieftain sat up suddenly and stared at her beneath frowning brows. "Deceiving me? *You*? I don't believe a word of it! What is there to deceive me about, pray? You are not masquerading under a false name, I suppose? Not married, for instance, and passing yourself off as single for some silly school-girl freak?"

"Oh no! Oh no! Everything that I have told you about myself is true, absolutely true."

"I knew it. You are not the sort that could act a lie. What's all the fuss about, then?"

"What I have told you is true, but—but—I have not told you *all*!"

"I should think not, indeed! Who expected that you should? I am not at all sure that I care to hear it."

"Oh, but—I want to tell you!"

The Chieftain chuckled with amusement. He was evidently comfortably convinced of the non-importance of the forthcoming revelations, and Margot's courage suffered another ebb as she returned his unsuspicious glance.

"I—we—we knew that you were staying at the Nag's Head!"

The Chieftain cocked a surprised eyebrow, startled but unresentful.

"You knew that we were here, before you arrived, and met us in the flesh? Is that so? I wonder how you heard! I make it a rule to keep my holiday plans as secret as possible, for the very good reason that a holiday *is* a holiday, and one wants a change of companionship as well as scene. How in the world did you hear that we were bound for Glenaire? I'm curious!"

Margot's eyelids fell guiltily, but Nature had generously endowed these same lids with long black lashes, the points of which curled up in a manner distractingly apparent when shown in contrast with a flushed pink cheek; so it happened that instead of being hardened by the sight, the Chieftain drew a few inches nearer, and smiled with genial approval.

"Well, out with it! *How* did you hear?"

"I—asked!"

"Asked?" The brow became a network of astonished wrinkling. "You asked? Whom did you ask? And why? What did you know about us, to give you interest in our comings or goings? This grows curiouser and curiouser! I imagined that we were as absolute strangers to you as you were to us."

"It—it—there was the magazine—it was because of the magazine."

"Oh, indeed! You knew the name through the magazine! I understand!" The Chieftain straightened himself, and the laugh died out of his eyes. For the first time in the history of their short acquaintance Margot saw his face set in firm, hard lines, the business face which had been left at home, together with the black coats and silk hats of City wear, and seeing it, trembled with fear. But it was too late to retreat; for better or worse she was bound to go forward and complete her half-finished revelations.

"I wanted to get to know your brother, because he is the editor of the *Loadstar*, and I had heard people say that he was the most powerful literary man in London; that if he chose to take up any one who was beginning to write he could do more to help than any one else. We know no literary people at home, and I wanted to. Badly!"

"I see! Just so. Written a novel, and want help to get it into print," returned the Chieftain slowly. He had drawn down his lips into an expression of preternatural gravity, but the hard look had disappeared. The murder was out, and he was not angry; he might pretend to be, but Margot was too sharp-witted to be frightened by a pretence.

She drew a sigh of relief as she replied—

"No, indeed. Couldn't to save my life. It's—Ron! I was thinking of him, not of myself. He is a poet!"

The Chieftain groaned aloud, as if in pain.

"Oh, I know you won't believe it, but he is! He writes wonderful poems. Not rhymes, but poems; beautiful poems that live in your mind. He will be another Tennyson or Browning when he is a little older."

The Chieftain groaned again, a trifle more loudly than before.

"It's true! It really is true. You must have seen yourself that he is different from other boys of his age. You heard him reeling off those impromptu lines the other day, and said how clever they were! I have seen you looking at his face when he has been thinking out some idea. I knew what he was doing, and you didn't; but you guessed that he was different from ordinary people."

"I saw that he was mooning about something, and wondered if he was right in the head! If he'd been my boy, I should have taken care to keep his nose so close to the grindstone that he would have no time to moon! Poet, indeed! Didn't you tell me that your father was a successful business man? What is he about, to countenance such nonsense?"

"He doesn't!" replied Margot sadly. "No one does but me, and that's why I had to act. Father agrees with you. He doesn't care for books, and looks down upon literary men as poor, effeminate sort of creatures, who know nothing of the world. He is ashamed that his only son writes verses. Ron detests the idea of business, but he has had to promise father that he would go into his office if at the end of a year he had had no encouragement to persevere in literature. But how is a young unknown poet to make himself known? The magazines announce that they can accept no unsolicited poetical contributions; the publishers laugh at the idea of bringing out a book by a man of whom no one has heard. A boy might be a second Shakespeare, but no one would believe in him until they had first broken his heart by their ridicule and unbelief. The year is out in September, so matters were getting desperate, when at last I—thought of this plan! I felt sure that if a man who was a real judge of literary power met Ron face to face, and got to know him, he would realise his gifts, and be willing to give him a chance. It was no use trying in London in the midst of the full pressure of work, but in the country everything is different. I knew a man who knew a man in the office of the *Loadstar*, and asked him to find out your brother's plans—"

As she was speaking Margot was conscious of a succession of stifled chuckles which her companion vainly tried to suppress. The Chieftain's amusement had evidently overmastered his threatened displeasure, and when at length she paused, he burst into an irresistible guffaw of laughter, rubbed his hands together, and cried gleefully—

"Stalked him! Stalked him! Poor old George! Big game, and no mistake. Ran him to earth... Eh, what? Bravo, bravo, Miss Bright Eyes! You are a first-class conspirator."

He laughed again and again, with ever-increasing merriment, laughed till his eyes disappeared in wrinkles of fat, till the tears streamed helplessly down his cheeks. His portly form shook with the violence of his merriment; he kicked the air with his short, fat feet.

Margot stared at this strange exhibition in an amazement, which gradually changed into annoyance and outraged dignity; so that when at last the Chieftain sat up to mop his eyes with a large silk pocket-handkerchief, he beheld a very dignified young lady sitting by his side in a position of poker-like rigidity, with her head tilted to an expressive angle.

"Sorry!" he panted hastily. "Sorry I smiled. A compliment, you know, if you look at it in the right light. It's such an uncommonly good idea, and so original. 'The Stalking of the Editor'—eh? Well, now that you have made such a rattling good beginning, why don't you go on and prosper? Here you are; there he is; the field is your own. Why don't you go in and win?"

Margot's face fell, and her haughty airs vanished, as she turned towards him a pair of widely-opened eyes, eloquent with plaintive surprise.

"But I can't! How can I, when he runs away the moment I appear? I made Ron go fishing with him one day, but he went off and left him alone, and now it's no use persuading any more. Ron says it is only waste of time! As for me, I have hardly spoken a word to him all this time, though I feel that if I did really know him, I—" she hesitated, knitting her brows, and pursing her soft red lips—"I could make him understand! I decided at last to confide in you, because you have been so kind and friendly to us from the first that I felt sure you would be willing to help. You will, won't you? Even if personally you don't approve of a literary career, will you give Ron a chance of living his life in his own way? If your brother approved of his writings, and helped him to a beginning, even the very smallest beginning, father would be satisfied that he was not wasting his time."

The Chieftain clasped his hands around his knees, and sat staring at her with thoughtful gaze. His eyes rested upon the clear childlike eyes, the sweet lips, the broad, honest brow, as though studying them in a new light, and with regard to some problem suddenly presented to the mind. Whatever was the question waiting to be decided, the answer was self-evidently favourable, for his eyes lightened, he stretched out an impetuous hand, and laid it upon her arm.

"Right!" he cried heartily. "Right! I'll help you! The lad's a good lad, and a clever lad; but what I do will be for your sake, not his! You are a dear girl! The dearest girl I have ever met—save one! For the sake of the bit of her that lives again in you, I am at your service. You shall have your chance. From to-day forward I will see to it that George makes a member of our party wherever we go. He has done enough writing; it is time that he began to play. Make him play, Miss Vane! He has been old all his life; teach him to be young! He is the best fellow in the world, but he is fast asleep. Wake him up! There is just one condition, and that is, that you leave your brother and his scribblings alone for the time being! Don't mention them, or any question of the sort, but be content just to show yourself to George, your own bright, natural girl-self, as you have shown it to me. Learn to know one another, and forget all about the boy. His turn will come later on! You promise?"

"Ye–es!" faltered Margot shyly. "Yes, I do; but you must promise too—that you will, that you won't, won't let your brother think—"

The Chieftain touched her arm once more, with a gesture of kindly reassurement.

"Don't you worry, little girl! He shall have no thoughts about you that are not altogether chivalrous and true. It's not you who are going to move in this matter, remember! You've given it over into my hands; it is I who am to pull the strings. No, you needn't thank me. It strikes me that we are going to work out pretty even over this business. If you want help for your brother, I need it just as badly for mine. I have realised for a long time that he needed a medicine which no doctor could supply." He looked into her face with a sudden radiant smile. "It strikes me I might have searched a very long time before finding any one so eminently fitted to undertake his cure!"

Chapter Sixteen.

Raspberry-Picking.

Margot awoke the next morning with the pleasant feeling that something was going to happen, and as she dressed, curiosity added an additional savour to the anticipation. What would happen? How would the Chieftain set to work? Would the Editor consider himself a victim, or yield readily to the temptation? Certainly he had so far manifested no anxiety to enjoy her society, had, indeed, seemed to avoid her at all points; and yet, and yet— Margot possessed her full share of a woman's divination, and, despite appearances, the inward conviction lingered that if the first natural shyness could be overcome, he would soon become reconciled to her companionship, and might even—she blushed at her own audacity!—*enjoy* the change from his usual solitude.

Like a true daughter of Eve, Margot did her best to help on this happy *dénouement* by taking special pains with her toilette, putting on one of her prettiest washing frocks, and coiling her chestnut locks in the most becoming fashion, and the consciousness of looking her best sent her down to breakfast in the happiest of spirits.

Other countries may carry off the palm for the cooking of the more elaborate meals of the day, but surely no breakfast can touch that served in a well-ordered Scottish household. The smoothly boiled porridge, with its accompaniment of thick yellow cream; the new-laid eggs; the grilled trout, fresh from the stream; the freshly baked "baps" and "scones," the crisp rolls of oatcake; and last, but not least, the delectable, home-made marmalade, which is as much a part of the meal as the coffee itself. He must be difficult to please who does not appreciate such a meal as Mrs McNab served each morning to her guests in the dining-room of the Nag's Head!

It was when Margot had reached the marmalade stage, and George Elgood, a persistent late-comer, was setting to work on his ham and eggs, that the Chieftain fired the first gun of the assault.

"When are you going to invite us all to come up and have tea with you in your fairy dell, George?" he demanded suddenly. "What do you think of this fellow, Mrs Macalister, finding a veritable little heaven below, and keeping it to himself all this time? There's an easy ascent by the head of the glen for those who object to the steeper climb; there's shade, and water and everything that the most exacting person could want for an ideal picnic. To be in the country on a day like this, and not to go for a picnic seems to me a deliberate waste of opportunity. What about this afternoon, eh? That will suit you as well as any other time, I presume?"

To say that the Editor appeared surprised by this sudden threatening of his solitude, would be to state the case too mildly. He looked absolutely stunned with astonishment, and his predicament was all the more enhanced by the fact that already murmurs of assent and anticipation welcomed the idea from his neighbours to right and to left. He stared incredulously into his brother's face, wrinkled his brow, and stammered out a laboured excuse.

"I'm afraid I— The dell is in no sense my property—No doubt it would make a capital site for a picnic, but I—I have no right to pose as host!"

"Rubbish, my boy! You are not going to get out of it so easily as that. We expect you to act as master of the ceremonies, and show us the beauties you have kept to yourself so long. Yes, and to catch some trout for us, too! What do you say to that, Mrs Macalister? How does freshly grilled trout strike you as an accessory to a picnic? We'll have two fires, with the kettle on one, and the gridiron on the other, and Mrs McNab will send up a hamper of good things to complete the feast. We'll leave George to manage that, as he knows how to get round her; only do the thing well when you are about it; that's all I have to say! We shall bring rattling big appetites, shan't we, Miss Vane?"

Margot's glance passed by his to dwell with remorseful commiseration on the Editor's perturbed face. This was her own doing; a direct consequence of her appeal of the day before! The expression of the brown eyes was wonderfully eloquent, and meeting them the Editor bestirred himself to smile back a grateful recognition. By this time, however, the murmur had grown into definite speech; Mrs Macalister was stating at length her life's experience as to picnics, and laying down the law as to what was necessary for their success; the clergyman and his son were debating how to reach the dell from the farthest point of the day's expedition; Mr Macalister was slowly repeating—

"Trout! Grilled trout! It's a strange-like idea to have fish at a picnic!"

It was plainly too late in the day for the Editor to refuse an invitation which had already been practically accepted! With a better grace than might have been expected he resigned himself to his fate, and the smile which he sent round the table was very charming in its shy cordiality.

"I shall be delighted if you will honour me by coming so far; and no doubt with Mrs McNab's help I shall be able to provide refreshments. Shall we say half-past four?"

"Four o'clock would be better. We want plenty of time to linger over tea, and ramble about afterwards," said the Chieftain firmly; and there being no dissent from this amendment, the Editor nodded assent, and, gathering his papers in his hand, hurried out of the room.

Margot followed on the first opportunity. She felt the eyes of the Chieftain fixed on her face from across the room, and could imagine the twinkle of humorous meaning with which they would be alight but she felt too self-conscious and ill at ease to respond. Like a frightened little rabbit she scuttled upstairs to her own room and remained there, busying herself with odd pieces of work until the inmates of the inn had taken themselves off for their morning's excursions, and quiet reigned throughout the house. Then, and not till then, she opened her door and peered cautiously at that other door across the landing. It was closely shut, and taking for granted that within its portals the bewildered scholar was making the most of his free hours, Margot crept quietly down the staircase, and turned to the right towards the kitchen. It occurred to her that she might be able to help Mrs McNab in her preparations for the afternoon, and by doing so relieve the pangs of her own conscience. All this work, and worry, and bewilderment, on her account—as a response to her appeal! She blushed guiltily, hardly knowing whether to feel more gratified or annoyed with the Chieftain for so speedy a demonstration of his power; dreading the moment when they should meet again, and she must perforce brave the mischievous messages of his eyes.

The kitchen door was closely shut. Mrs McNab was too capable a housewife to allow the noise and odour of culinary preparations to invade the rest of the house; but by this time Margot was sure of her welcome, for scarcely a day had passed by that she had not offered her services, and been condescendingly permitted to shell peas, stone fruit, or whip up snowy masses of cream. Mrs McNab always accorded permission with the air of an empress conferring an order upon some humble suppliant, but none the less Margot felt assured that she appreciated the help, and would have missed it, had it not been forthcoming.

This morning she tapped on the door, opened it, and thrust her head round the corner, to behold a tableau which remained fixed irrevocably in heart and memory. In the middle of the floor stood the mistress of the inn, arms akimbo, engaged in laying down the law in characteristic, downright fashion to some one who sat perched upon the dresser with hands thrust deep into knickerbocker pockets, and feet in rough climbing boots swinging nonchalantly to and fro; some one with a bright, almost boyish face alight with fun, laughter, and defiance.

For the second time Margot beheld the real George Elgood denuded of his mask of shyness and reserve, and thrilled at the recognition. This sunny, stone-flagged kitchen seemed fated to be the scene of unexpected meetings! She would have retreated in haste, but at the sound of her entrance Mr Elgood jumped hastily to the floor, and Mrs McNab authoritatively waved her forward.

"Here she is to speak for herself! Come yer ways, Miss Vane. I was saying to Mr Elgood that maybe he'd listen to your advice, as he willna tak' mine. You're a leddy, and ken how such things should be done, and if there's any call to waste the morning, and run into daft-like expense, when everything a reasonable body need want is lying ready to hand—"

Margot looked from one to the other in bewilderment, her spirits rising with the discovery that for the first time in their short acquaintance the Editor met her glance with an expression of relief rather than of dread. He was smiling still, and the boyish look lingered on his face, making him appear an absolutely different creature from the grave, formidable hermit to whom she was accustomed.

Margot's eyes danced, and she answered as naturally as if she had been speaking to Ron himself.

"I don't know in the least what I am giving an opinion about—but I am not a 'reasonable body,' and as a rule the result of 'daft-like expense' is very nice! I'm afraid that isn't what you wanted me to say, Mrs McNab, but I must be honest. Perhaps I may feel differently when I know what I am talking about."

"Your picnic!" cried Mrs McNab.

"My picnic!" corrected the Editor. "I never gave a picnic before, and I'm weighed down by responsibility. My brother refuses to help me, and Mrs McNab is a Spartan, and nips my suggestions in the bud. She thinks we ought to be satisfied with bread and butter; I want cakes and fruit; I want her to bake, and she says she has no time to bake; I want to send over to Rew on the chance of getting strawberries; she says she has no one to send. If you agree with me, Miss Vane, perhaps she will make time; I know by experience that she is always better than her word!"

Mrs McNab sniffed ironically.

"There's scones for ye, and good fresh butter—what do ye want forbye? Ye'd get nae mair if ye were at hame, and it's not going to kill ye, walking a couple of miles. I've something else to do on a Thursday morning than waste my time messing over things that aren't needed."

Mr Elgood leant against the dresser, and surveyed her more in sorrow than in anger.

"Now what have you to do?" he demanded. "It's absurd to pretend that there is anything to clean, because you never give a thing a chance to become dirty. There is cold meat for lunch, as you yourself informed me, so there's no cooking on hand. This house goes by machinery, with Elspeth to stoke up the motive power. What can be left for you? I can't think of a single thing."

"Maybe not. A man-body never kens what goes on under his nose, though he'd be keen enough to find out if anything went wrong. It's the day I clean my candlesticks and brasses. They don't go on shining by themselves, whatever ye may think."

"Candlesticks and brasses!" George Elgood repeated the words with gloomy emphasis, fixing the speaker with reproachful eyes. "Candlesticks and brasses! And you put such things as those before *me*, and the first—one of the first, favours I have ever asked! ... A big plum cake, with almonds at the top, and a round of shortbread; it seems to me a most moderate request. There's not a soul in the inn who will notice a shade of extra polish on the candlesticks to-night, but they will all bear me a lifelong grudge if I don't give them enough to eat. Have you ever been to a picnic where you were expected to be satisfied with bread and butter, Miss Vane?"

Margot's shake of the head was tragic in its solemnity.

"Never! and I don't intend to begin. I know where we can get some fruit, at any rate, for I heard the woman at the grocer's shop saying that she had raspberries to sell. That is far easier than sending over to Rew, and I'd be delighted to take a basket and bring back all I can get. While Mrs McNab makes the cakes!"

Mrs McNab sniffed again, but vouchsafed no further answer. Mr Elgood's face brightened, and he cried eagerly—

"That is kind of you! Raspberries are very nearly as good as strawberries, and it would be splendid to get them so near at hand. I—er—" he frowned, with a momentary return to his old embarrassment—"I will come too, and carry the basket, for we must hope to have a fairly heavy load."

Margot could hardly believe in the reality of this sudden change of position, as she set out for the village ten minutes later, with George Elgood by her side. He carried the basket lent by Mrs McNab, and swung along with big easy strides, while she trotted by his side, a pretty girlish figure in her cool white frock. It was left to her to do the greatest share of the talking; but one reassuring fact was quickly discovered, namely, that her companion's shyness seemed to consist mainly in the dread of breaking strange ground, for once the first plunge over he showed none of the expected embarrassment or distress. If he could not be called talkative, he was at least an appreciative listener; not a single point of her conversation missed its due share of interest; while his deep, quiet laugh proved an incentive to fresh flights of fancy. For a whole ten days had Margot been waiting for her opportunity, and now that it had come she was keen to turn it to the best possible advantage. Had the Chieftain been at hand to watch her with his quizzical glance, she might have been tongue-tied and ill at ease; even Ronald's presence would have brought with it a feeling of self-consciousness; but in the kindly solitude of the mountain road she could be herself, without thought of any one but her companion. Remembering the warning which she had received, she kept the conversation on strictly impersonal topics, avoiding even the mention of Ron's name, but never had ordinary topics seemed so interesting, or the way to the village so extraordinarily quickly traversed!

Inside the fusty grocer's shop the good Mrs Forsyth manifested none of a Southerner's delight at the advent of a customer for her superfluous fruit; she appeared, indeed, to receive Margot's first inquiry in a somewhat flisty and off-hand manner, as though advantage were being taken of a careless word, which she had not expected to have taken in serious earnest. George Elgood, distinctly rebuffed, muttered unintelligible words of apology, but already Margot was beginning to understand the dour Northern manner, and pressed the attack with undiminished eagerness. Thus coerced, Mrs Forsyth was forced to acknowledge that she wouldna deny that she had raspberries in the garden; and that it seemed a pity they should waste, as she hadna the time to "presarve." There was no telling—maybe when the children came hame from school in the afternoon they wouldna be above picking a basketful, and taking it down to the inn.

"But we want them now! We want as many as you can possibly spare, but we must have them to take back with us now!"

"And who's to pick them for ye, I would ask?" demanded Mrs Forsyth with scathing directness. "I've the shop to mind, and the dinner to cook; it's not likely I can be out picking fruit at the same time, and there's not anither soul in the house forbye mysel! I'm thinking you'll have to wait, or do without!"

"We could pick them ourselves!" pleaded the Editor eagerly. "You would have no trouble except to measure the fruit after it is gathered, and tell us what we owe! I don't care how much I pay. I want some fruit this morning, and if I can't get it from you I shall have to drive over to Rew. That would cost five or six shillings for the trap alone, so you see I shall get off well, even if you charge me twice the usual price."

But here again the benighted Southerner found himself brought up sharply against an unexpected phase of Scottish character, for Mrs Forsyth was distinctly on her high horse at the thought of being offered more than her due. She had her price; a fair-like price, she informed him loftily, and she stuck to it. She wasna the woman to make differences between one person and anither. Justice was justice, and she would like to meet the man who could say she had ever stooped to accept a bribe.

So on and so on, while once again George Elgood hung his head abashed, and glanced in distress at his companion. In the delight afforded by that appeal Margot felt equal to dealing with ten Mrs Forsyths, each equally unreasonable and "kamstary."

"We will leave the price to you; we will leave everything to you!" she cried gaily. "I know it's asking a great deal to be allowed to come into your garden and pick for ourselves, but we are rather in a difficulty, for this gentleman is giving a picnic this afternoon, and Mrs McNab has no fruit to give us. It would be a favour not only to us, but to the whole party if you would say Yes. *Please!*"

The way in which Margot said "Please!" with head on one side, and upraised, beseeching *eyes*, was one of the most fatal of her blandishments. Even the redoubtable Mrs McNab had succumbed at the sight, and in her turn Mrs Forsyth also was overcome. She made no further objections, but led the way through the house into a long stretch of vegetable garden, the end portion of which was thickly planted with raspberry bushes.

"Help yourself!" she said briefly. "You're welcome to all that's fit to eat."

So the two who had been strangers, and had suddenly developed into a kind of partnership of aim, set to work to fill the basket, which for better convenience was slung over a branch of one of the bushes.

The sun shone down on them; the life-giving breeze blew round them; they were alone together among the flowers and the scented herbs. They worked side by side, laughing over their efforts, comparing their takings, gloating over the quickly-filling basket like a couple of children recognising each other as playmates, and disdaining the ordinary preliminaries of acquaintanceship.

"It's so kind of you to help me!" said the man.

"It's so kind of you to let me!" returned the maid.

"I—I have noticed that you seem always to be helping people."

"I didn't think you noticed anything at all!"

He had not intended to say so much. She did not stop to consider what she was implying. Both blushed, relapsed into silence, and picked fruit assiduously for several moments, before beginning again—

"I am afraid this picnic will be a great bore to you."

"Indeed, I think it is going to be a pleasure. I should have thought of it before, but that sort of thing does not come easily to me. I have lived too much alone!"

"You have your work—you have been absorbed in your work."

"Have I? I'm afraid that is not altogether true!"

Margot glanced up surprised, met the dark eyes fixed full upon her, and looked hurriedly away.

"I have been finding it increasingly difficult to be absorbed," he continued dreamily. "I have heard you all laughing and talking together downstairs, and my thoughts have wandered. Once you sang... Do you remember that wet afternoon when you sang? I did not seem able to write at all that afternoon."

The basket was full of fruit by now; Margot lifted it by one handle; George Elgood lifted it by the other. They walked down the sunlit garden into the house.

Chapter Seventeen.

The Picnic.

Every one agreed that there never had been such a picnic, that it was impossible that such a picnic would ever occur again. In those northern regions it is a rare joy to find a day that is a very incarnation of summer; hot, yet not too hot; bright, yet not glaringly oppressive; a day when even the old and ailing feel it a joy to be alive, and the young and strong unconsciously break into song, and find it impossible to curtail their footsteps to a staid walking-pace.

George Elgood's "fairy dell" stood in a gorge between two mountains; a strip of velvet green grass sheltered from the wind, such as the monks of old loved to select as the site of the monasteries whose ruins are still to be seen scattered over our land. The Editor had discovered this retreat, and mentally adopted it as his own, keenly resenting the intrusion of strangers; yet to-day he stood surrounded by hampers and impedimenta, playing host to every guest in the inn, and, wonder of wonders! conscious of an unusual sense of satisfaction in so doing.

Up the winding path they appeared, one by one, the clergyman and his son arriving first of all, hot and breathless after climbing a record distance in a record time. Next Mrs Macalister, red and shiny of face, holding up her skirts to display a pair of large, flat-heeled boots. By her side the originator of the expedition, the genial Chieftain, walking with his usual springy tread, twirling aloft an umbrella which he fondly believed to be sheltering the good dame from the rays of the sun, but which never approached much nearer to her head than a couple of yards. Next, Ronald walking alone, as his custom was; thinking his own thoughts, and gazing around with eyes quick to behold that deeper vision which is revealed only to the chosen few. The boy poet, young, strong, and ardent, with his life ahead, and following him with weary tread the tired-out man of the world, weighed down with a sense of his own infirmities, pining after the office desk and the city smoke, and finding nothing but satiety in the lonely hillside—Mr Macalister, with the furrows graven deep as stone on his brow, his lack-lustre eyes glancing wearily around. During the walk uphill Margot had been his companion, cheering him by her merry prattle, but, now that the destination was reached, she hung back, as though anxious to hide herself from view. Marvellous and unprecedented humility, for Margot Vane deliberately to choose a place in the rear!

It was impossible, however, for the only young woman of the party to remain in the background during the hour which followed, and, willy-nilly, Margot found herself forced into a foremost position; almost, it might be said, into the position of hostess to George Elgood's host. While Mrs Macalister sat on a bank and fanned herself with her pocket-handkerchief, while the Chieftain built up the fires after a patent fashion of his own, Margot unpacked the hampers and laid out the contents on a tablecloth, carefully fastening down the corners with stones from the brook.

There was a goodly supply of eatables, for, as usual, Mrs McNab had proved better than her word. White bread and brown, scones and "cookies" galore, and a flat, round cake of most appetising appearance. There were also little pots of home-made preserves; a large bottle of cream, and a wonderfully exact and thoughtful supply of those smaller necessities which are so often forgotten on such occasions.

There was a frying-pan also, to cook the trout which had been duly caught to order, and were lying in readiness in a shady corner—two big shining fellows, such as would have delighted any fisherman's eyes to behold. The second fire was built for their special benefit, and, as usual, each separate member of the party had his own suggestion to make as to its construction.

"Pile all the wood in a heap, and set fire to it! It's as easy as tumbling off a wall!" cried the Chieftain, suiting the action to the word, and puffing cheerfully at clouds of smoke.

"You've built it far too tightly. Pull the branches apart, and lay 'em criss-cross—"

"The best way is to get one or two big stones and use them as a grate. Then you can get a draught underneath—"

"Quite so! and just as the water begins to boil, the whole thing collapses, and the kettle is upset!"

"Why can ye not bring up a methylated spirit lamp, and use its own stand as ye would at home?"

This last in Mr Macalister's weary accents, and a loud groan of disapproval from the younger members of the party testified to the unpopularity of the idea.

"Oh, Mr Macalister, no! How horribly prosaic! It's just because we do use it at home that we couldn't think of it in a fairy dell. It's a thousand times more romantic to use faggots."

"Well, well! It's a matter of taste. I should say a spirit lamp was as romantic as smoked water; but don't mind me, don't mind me! I have no call to interfere—"

"Mr Macalister was always a very handy man about the house. If anything went wrong with the kitchen range, I would say to the girl, 'Wait till your master comes home!' As long as he had his health we never sent for a workman. There's very few could lay a fire better than he, if he took the trouble—"

"Tuts, tuts!" Mr Macalister frowned darkly at the faithful wife who so loyally chanted his praises, then, turning on his heel, paced solemnly down the dell. The Chieftain seized a sheet of the *Glasgow Herald* and vigorously fanned the dying flame; Margot coughed, choked, and spluttered before the clouds of smoke, and retreated in dismay to the more distant fire which George Elgood was sheltering with an open umbrella. Behind the impromptu tent he knelt, poking gingerly at the smouldering wood, but at Margot's approach he sat back on his feet, lifting to hers a laughing, boyish face.

"No go! The wretched thing won't light! How is Geoff getting on?"

"Your brother?" It was the first time that Margot had heard the Chieftain called by his Christian name, and it struck her as wonderfully appropriate for so bright and happy a personality. "He isn't getting on at all! His measures are more drastic than yours, and he is at present occupied in fanning smoke into every one's face, and knocking down sticks wholesale in the process. My hopes of tea are dwindling into the far distance—"

"What about grilled trout?" queried the Editor, pointing with a grimy finger at his own travesty of a fire. "At this rate, it seems as if we should have to come down to buns and milk; in which case I should never again be able to hold up my head before Mrs McNab. She told me that it was madness to think of cooking fish in the open."

"But it isn't, and it shan't be, and we'll make up our minds that we *will*!" cried Margot gaily. "Let us build up a little grate of stones, on which the pan can rest, and lay more faggots round the outside, to get warm and crisp before they are needed. We must keep the flame as clear as possible, so you can go on feeding it gently, while I attend to the fish. Big stones! We must pick them carefully from the side of the stream. The little ones are no use. I'll go!"

"No, no! I'll go!" He sprang to his feet as he spoke, and the umbrella, loosed from its moorings, pitched promptly forward, and alighted in the middle of the fire. There was only the tiniest of flickering flames, but, after the contrary nature of things, though it had scorned to undertake the grilling of trout, it seemed eager to seize upon twilled black silk, and to scorch it into a hole. Margot squealed; George Elgood pounced and stamped and dragged, until the ground was scattered over with smoking faggots, and the last pretence of fire had disappeared.

Just at this moment of thwarted ambition a whoop and crow of triumph sounded across the green, and behold the Chieftain capering round a dancing flame, and Mrs Macalister approaching with a brimming kettle.

"Quick! Quick!" cried Margot, flying brook-wards. "We'll have it laid again in a moment. The ground is warm, and so are the sticks, so it will light more quickly this time. I'll lay it afresh on two or three stones while you bring the rest. Big ones! Big ones!"

"But your frock, your pretty frock!" The Editor cast a commiserating glance at the dainty lawn flounces, already splattered with wet; but Margot only laughed, and ran eagerly back to her task.

The tea would be ready first, but that was only right and proper. The company would have time to be seated, and to help themselves to cream and sugar to their liking, and while they were even yet enjoying the first fragrant sips, the smoking trout would emerge from the pan, and triumphantly take its place on the festal tablecloth.

Gingerly picking up the smoking faggots, Margot piled them up in careful criss-cross fashion, sheltering them the while with the stones which the Editor carried back from the brook. Dress and hands alike suffered in the process, but she minded nothing for that. It was recompense enough to hear the crisp crackling of wood, to see the dancing gold of the flame. Almost as soon as the artificial grate was complete, the heat was strong enough to put on the frying-pan, and soon the fish was spluttering and sending forth a pleasant fragrance, at which the picnickers sniffed with anticipatory enjoyment.

A curious company they looked, seated on the ground around the well-spread table; very different from the usual party on like occasions, when a solitary adult is admitted on sufferance to play chaperon to a number of light-hearted youngsters. To-day youth was the exception rather than the rule, and a stolid reserve took the place of hilarious enjoyment. Yet even here the softening effects of tea and trout, and cakes and scones gradually made themselves felt. The clergyman waxed anecdotal, his grim face twitching with unexpected humour, as he related various sayings and doings of his brethren; the son insisted upon refilling the kettle, and superintending its second boiling. Mr Macalister assisted himself to two helpings of trout, and his wife's disapproving gaze softened into complacence at the sight of the zest which replaced his usual languid distaste.

By the time that third cups of tea had been served round, the subject of music had been introduced, and the company had been made aware of the fact that a one-time singer of note was among their number. From this point it seemed only one step until Mr and Mrs Macalister were safely launched upon the strains of "Hunting Tower."

There sat he at the one end of the low-spread cloth, eyes shut, brows elevated until they almost touched the locks of sandy hair which discreetly veiled his bald crown, his right hand sawing the air in time to the melody. There sat the guid-wife, beaming goodwill on all around, her bonnet-strings untied, her kindly face flushed to a peony red as the combined result of excitement and indigestion. There was not left much to boast of in the *timbre* of either voice; indeed, regarded as a musical effort, the duet must have been classed as a failure, had it not been for the hearty sincerity with which the words were voiced.

"Be my guidman yoursel, Jamie,

Marry me yoursel, laddie,

And tak' me ower to Germanie,

Wi' you at hame to dwell, laddie!

"I dinna ken how that wad do, Jeanie,

I dinna ken how that can be, lassie,

For I've a wife and bairnies three,

And I'm no sure how ye'd agree, lassie!

"Dry that tearful eye, Jeanie;

Grieve nae mair for me, lassie,

I've neether wife nor bairnies three,

And I'll wed nane but thee, lassie!

"Blair in Athol's mine, lassie,

Fair Dunkeld is mine, lassie,

Saint Johnstoun's Bower, and Hunting Tower,

And a' that's mine is thine, lassie!"

A burst of applause greeted the concluding words, under cover of which Margot's eyes and those of George Elgood met with instinctive sympathy.

"Aren't they dears? Don't you love to hear them?"

"Indeed I do! There's so much poetry underlying the prose. To me they are far more interesting than a pair of young callow lovers, whose affection has known no trial."

"Oh!" gasped Margot, and grimaced over her plate. She could not go so far as that, and had not bargained for such a degree of enthusiasm. As she stood side by side with the portly songstress a few minutes later, washing and drying dishes preparatory to packing them away in the hampers, she found herself still pondering over the Editor's reply, and wondering if really—literally!—he could be more interested in this plain elderly woman than in a young attractive girl, like—like—

And then Miss Margot blushed, and tucked away a fold of the lawn skirt on which the mark of smoky fingers was painfully apparent!

When the hampers were packed ready for the return to the inn, an awkward silence fell upon the little company, while each one looked at the other, mutely interrogating as to what should happen next. It seemed ill-mannered to depart directly after being fed, yet no one knew what to do, or who should take the lead, seeing that the host himself appeared serenely unconscious of his duties. Once again it was the Chieftain who came to the rescue with a brilliant suggestion.

"Now we must clear the courts for Olympian sports, suitable for the occasion! To set the ball a-rolling, I'll give you my celebrated impersonation of the reel, as performed by the prize dancer at the Athol Sports. Miss Vane! A word in your ear. Will you retire with me to the green-room behind those trees?"

Margot followed dimpling with amusement, and for the next ten minutes outbursts of laughter floated to the ears of the company, and kept them happily expectant of what was to come. Once or twice Margot darted across the green to open a hamper, and pilfer some mysterious article, which she made haste to cover beneath a cloth, and on her return would follow fresh explosions of mirth, the deep "Ha, ha!" of the Chieftain mingling with her own silvery trills of laughter.

Presently out he marched—"The Elgood of Elgood," stepping daintily across the carpet of grass, his stockinged feet criss-crossed with bindings of tape, Mrs Macalister's plaid shawl flounced round his substantial waist, and hanging therefrom to the depth of the knee. A roller towel was swathed across his body, and swung gallantly over his shoulder; sideways on his head was perched a cap of brown paper, secured across the chin with a shoelace, while held aloft in his hands was an empty milk-bottle, from the mouth of which issued the wailing notes of a bagpipe.

"Pity me, what's this?" cried Mr Macalister, in amaze.

"Did ever any one see the like?" echoed his astonished wife.

The clergyman gazed over the top of his spectacles with eyes bulging with astonishment. Ron clapped his hands, and sent up a great shout of delight, while George Elgood sat on the grass clasping his knees with his hands, and shaking with laughter.

"Good old Geoff! Go it, Geoff! Keep it up. Dance, man, dance! Leave the pipes to us—we'll pipe for you. Give your mind to your steps!"

Even as he spoke he and Ron seized bottles on their own account, and turned themselves into imaginary pipers, rivalling each other in turns and twists and long-drawn-out notes, till presently the infection spread, and every single member of the family was swelling the orchestra, Mr Macalister beating time with vigorous sawings of the arm and shakings of the head. So they piped, this motley assembly of old and young, while in the centre of the green the Chieftain twirled and leapt, and twirled again, and stamped his feet, and gave vent to loud staccato whoops—as deliciously comic a spectacle as one would meet in the course of a very long day.

Then at last, with purple face and gasping breath, he collapsed on the grass, and rolling over on his side lay panting, the while the onlookers exhausted themselves in applause.

"If they could see him now! If they could see him now!" cried George Elgood rapturously to himself; and Margot caught the words, and questioned curiously—

"Who? Whom do you mean?"

"The people at home. In town! What would they think?"

"Does he behave so differently in town?"

He cast at her a glance more eloquent than words. "Different!" he echoed beneath his breath. "Different!" But though she waited eagerly for a further explanation, it did not come. The Chieftain was already sitting up, mopping his damp face, and gesticulating energetically towards the other members of the party.

"Now then! Go ahead. I've led the way. Mr Macalister, your turn, sir! Who's afraid?"

Mr Macalister shook his head. He was not afraid of any man, but his days were past for playing the fool! Not to say there had not been a time when he could dance a reel with the best! There was young Mr Menzies now—

Young Mr Menzies, the clergyman's apathetic son, blushed crimson at the suggestion, and shook his head until it seemed in danger of falling off altogether. George Elgood stoutly denied his ability to "play tricks," and tiresome, aggravating Ron flatly refused to improvise a poem on the day's doings, throwing away a valuable opportunity with a recklessness which made his sister long to shake him.

Nobody would do anything! The Chieftain sat on the grass, divesting himself of his make-up, the while he roundly denounced his companions as the laziest, slackest, most unsportsmanlike crew whom it had ever been his misfortune to meet.

"But if you won't play singly, you must play in bulk, for play you shall! We are out for a picnic, and must behave as sich. Up with you now, every man-jack of you!" he cried, suiting the action to the word, and springing to his own feet with the surprising ease and elasticity which characterised all his gestures. "We'll start hide-and-seek along the Glen. We'll hide, and,"—he glanced round, with an air of innocent inquiry—almost too innocent, it appeared in the eyes of one watcher at least!—and pointed a fat forefinger at his brother and Margot as they sat side by side—"you two will seek! Miss Vane and George... Give us ten minutes to hide ourselves discreetly, and then start out on your search. Between the two fireplaces shall be 'Den!' Are you ready?"

Apparently they were all ready. Mrs Macalister creaked and gasped, and finally rose to her feet; the men travelled after her in a long, straggling row. Margot and the Editor were left to themselves.

Chapter Eighteen.

Trout Fishing.

There was a short, somewhat embarrassed silence while Margot kept her eyes fixed on the scene of the late meal, the two smouldering fires, the piled-up hampers and baskets, and the Editor drummed with his fingers, and chewed his moustache.

"Er—" he began haltingly at last. "How do you think it has gone?"

"You mean the—"

"Picnic! Yes. My first entertainment. I feel responsible. Think they enjoyed it at all?"

"I'm sure of it. Immensely! They thawed wonderfully. Think of the duet! To hear Mr Macalister singing was a revelation. It has been a delightful change from the ordinary routine. And the trout! The trout was a huge success. How amiable of it to let itself be caught so conveniently!"

The Editor smiled, with the conscious pride of the experienced fisherman.

"There was not much 'let' about it. He led me a pretty dance before he gave up the struggle, but I was on my mettle, and bound to win. Do you know anything about fishing, Miss Vane?"

"I?" Margot laughed happily. "Just as much as I have gleaned from watching little boys fish for minnows in Regent's Park! I don't think I have ever particularly wanted to know more. It seems so dull to stand waiting for hours for what may never come, not daring to speak, in case you may scare it away! What do you think about all the time?"

He turned and looked at her at that, his lips twitching with amusement. Seated on the ground as they were, the two faces were very near together, and each regarded the other with the feeling of advancing a step further in the history of their acquaintance.

"He really *is* young!" decided Margot, with a sigh of relief. "It's only the frown and the stoop and the eyeglasses which make him look as if he were old."

George Elgood looked into the pink and white face, and his thoughts turned instinctively to a bush of briar roses which he had seen and admired earlier in the day. So fresh, and fair, and innocent! Were all young girls so fragrant and flower-like as this? Then he thought of the little prickles which had stung his hand as he had picked a bud from the same bush for his buttonhole, and smiled with latent mischief. After all, the remembrance did not lessen the likeness. Miss Margot looked as if she might—under provocation—display a prickle or two of her own!

"What do I think about?" he repeated slowly. "That is rather a difficult question to answer; but this good little river, I am thankful to say, does not leave one much time for thought. There's a little channel just beyond the bridge that is a favourite place for sea trout. Would you like to see it?"

"Might I? Really? Oh, please!" cried Margot, all in a breath. Her very prettiest "please," accompanied by a quick rise to her feet which emphasised the eagerness of her words.

George Elgood lost no time in following her example, and together they walked briskly away towards the head of the dell; that is to say, in the opposite direction to that taken by the other members of the party. George Elgood had picked up his fishing-tackle as he went—by an almost unconscious impulse, as it seemed—and unconsciously his conversation drifted to the all-absorbing topic.

"If we take a sharp cut across this hill—I'll give you a hand down the steep bits!—we hit the river at the best spot. You have been grumbling at the wet weather, but you will see the good effects of rain, from a fisherman's point of view. The river is full from bank to bank, rushing down to the sea. It is a fine sight, a river in flood! I don't know anything in Nature which gives the same impression of power and joy. That's where Norway has the pull. Her mountains can't compare with the Swiss giants, but everywhere there is a glorious wealth of water. No calm sleeping lakes, but leaping cataracts of rivers filling whole valleys, as my little stream here fills its small banks; roaring and dashing, and sparkling in the sun. Norway is perfection, from a fisherman's point of view; but there is plenty of sport to be found nearer home. I have had no cause to complain for the last fortnight. This way—to the right! It's just a little rough going at first, but it cuts off a good mile. You are sure you don't mind?"

Margot's laugh rang out jubilantly. She scrambled up the steep mountain path with nimble feet, easily out-distancing her guide, until the hilltop was reached, and she stood silhouetted against the sky, while the wind blew out her white skirts, and loosened curling tendrils of hair.

Below could be traced the course of the river, winding in and out in deep curves, and growing ever broader and fuller with every mile it traversed. The sunlight which played on it, making it look like a silver ribbon, played also on the yellow gorse and purple heather; on the long grey stretch of country in the distance; on that softer blue plain joining the skyline, which was the sea itself. A breath of salt seemed to mingle with the aromatic odour of the heather, adding tenfold to its exhilaration.

As Margot stood holding on to her hat, and waiting for her companion's approach, she felt such a glorious sense of youth and well-being, such an assurance of happiness to come, as is seldom given to mortals to enjoy. It was written in her face, her radiant, lovely young face, and the light in the eyes which she turned upon him made the shy scholar catch his breath.

"You did that well! Magnificently well!" he cried approvingly. "But you must take the descent carefully, please. There are one or two sudden dips which might be awkward if you were not prepared. I know them all. Shall I,—would you,—will you take my hand?"

"Thank you!" said Margot, and laid her hand in his with an acceptance as simple as if he had been her own brother. It was a very pretty little hand, in which its owner felt a justifiable pride, and it lay like a white snowflake in the strong brown palm stretched out to meet it.

For just a moment George Elgood kept his fingers straight and unclasped, while he gazed downward at it with kindling eyes, then they closed in a tight, protecting clasp, and together they began the descent.

For the most part it was easy enough, but the awkward places came so often and unexpectedly that it did not seem worth while to unloose that grasp until the bottom was safely reached. Margot had a dream-like sensation of having wandered along for hours, but in reality it was a bare ten minutes before she and her guide were standing on level ground by the side of the rushing river.

"Thank you! That was a great help," she said quietly. George Elgood, with a sudden access of shyness, made no reply, but busied himself with preparation.

"I'll just make another cast, to show you how one sets to work. I take a pretty big fly—the trout like that. These are the flies—all sizes, as you see. I am rather proud of them, for I make them myself in the winter months, when one can enjoy only the pleasures of anticipation. It's a good occupation for a leisure hour."

"You make them yourself!" Margot repeated incredulously, stretching out her hand to receive one of the hairy morsels on her palm, and bending over it in unaffected admiration. "But how clever of you! How can you have the patience? It must be dreadfully finicky work!"

"It is a trifle 'finicky,' no doubt!" He laughed over the repetition of the word. "But it's a refreshing change to work with one's hands sometimes, instead of one's brain. Now shall I give you your first lesson in the art? Don't imagine for a moment that fishing means standing still for the hour together, with nothing more exciting than the pulling-in of your fish the moment he bites. That's the idea of the outsider who does not know what adventure he is losing, what hope and suspense, what glorious triumph! Like most things, it's the struggle that's the glory of the thing, not the prize. Shall I soak this cast for you, and give you your first lesson?"

"Oh, please! I'd love it! It would be too kind of you!" cried Margot eagerly. She had not the faintest idea what "soaking a cast" might mean, and listened in bewilderment to a score of unfamiliar expressions; but it is safe to affirm that she would have assented with equal fervour to almost any proposition which her companion made.

There and then followed the first lesson on the seemingly easy, but in reality difficult, task of "casting," the Editor illustrating his lesson by easy, graceful throws, which Margot tried in vain to imitate. She grew impatient, stamping her feet, and frowning fiercely with her dark eyebrows, while he looked on with the amused indulgence which one accords to a child.

"Are you always in such a hurry to accomplish a thing at once?"

"Yes, always! It's only when you don't care that you can afford to wait."

"It sometimes saves time in the end to make haste slowly!"

"Oh, don't confound me with proverbs!" cried Margot, turning a flushed, petulant face at him over her shoulder. "I know I am impetuous and imprudent, but—the horrid thing *will* twist up! Don't you think I might have a demonstration this time? Let me watch, and pick up hints. I'm sure I should learn more quickly that way, and it would be less boring for you. Please!"

At that he took the rod, nothing loth, and Margot seated herself on the ground, a trifle short of breath after her exertions, and not at all sorry to have the chance of looking on while some one else did the work. She was intently conscious of her companion's presence, but he seemed to forget all about her, as wading slightly forward into the stream he cast his fly in slow, unerring circuit. How big he looked, how strong and masterful; how graceful were the lines of his tall lean figure! From where she sat Margot could see the dark profile beneath the deerstalker cap, the long straight nose, the firmly-closed lips, the steady eyes. It was the face of a man whom above all things one could trust. "A poor dumb body," Mrs Macalister had dubbed him, scornfully; but Margot had discovered that he was by no means dumb, and that once the first barriers were broken, he could talk with the best, and bring into his conversation the added eloquence of expression. She recalled the lighting of his absorbed eyes as he had looked down at her own white hand, and flushed at the remembrance.

Margot had often pitied the wives and sisters of enthusiastic fishermen who had perforce to sit mum-chance in the background, but to-day she was conscious of no dissatisfaction with her own position. She possessed her full share of the girl's gift of building castles, and it would not be safe to say how high the airy structure had risen before suddenly the rod bent, and the Editor's intent face lit up with elation. The fish was hooked; it now remained to "play" with him, in professional parlance, till he could be landed with credit to himself and his captor.

For the next half-hour Margot was keenly, vividly interested in studying the tactics of the game. The reel screamed out, as the captive made a gallant dash for liberty; the Editor splashed after him, running hastily by the side of the river, now reeling in his line, now allowing it full play; and at the distance of a few yards she ran with him, now holding her breath with suspense, now clasping her hands in triumph, until at last, his struggles over, the captive floated heavily upon the stream.

It was the end for which she had longed throughout thirty of the most exciting moments that she had ever known; but now that victory was secured, woman—like she began to feel remorse.

"Oh, is it dead? Have you killed it? But it's horrid, you know—quite horrible! A big strong man like you, and that poor little fish—"

"Not little at all! It's a good six-pounder," protested the fisherman, quick to defend his sport against depreciation. "No—he's not dead yet, but he soon will be. I will just—"

"Wait! Wait! Let me get out of the way." Margot flew with her fingers in her ears, then pulled them out to cry—"Is it done? Is it over? Can I come back?"

"Yes; it is all right. I've put him in my bag. You will appreciate him better in his table guise. I'll take him back as a peace-offering to Mrs McNab, for her own evening meal. We have already had our share at the pic—"

Suddenly his hands fell to his sides, he straightened himself, and turned his eyes upon her, filled with puzzle and dismay.

"The pic—"

"—Nic!" concluded Margot faintly. Rosy red were her cheeks; a weight as of lead pressed on her eyelids, dragging them down, down, beneath his gaze. "I—I—*forgot*! We were to have gone to find them! Do you suppose they are—hiding still?"

He laughed at that, though in somewhat discomfited fashion.

"Rather not! Given us up long ago. It must be getting on for an hour. I can't think how I came to forget—"

Margot glanced at him shyly beneath her curling lashes.

"It was the fish! A fisherman can't be expected to remember anything when he is landing a trout!" she suggested soothingly. Nevertheless she remembered with a thrill of joy that his forgetfulness had dated back to a time when there had been no fish in prospect. "Do you suppose they have gone home?"

"We will go and see. From that mound over there we can overlook the path to the inn. Perhaps we had better keep a little in the background! It would be as well that they should not see us, if they happened to look up—"

If it were possible to feel a degree hotter, Margot felt it at that moment, as she followed George Elgood up the little hillock to the right, and, pausing just short of the top, peered stealthily around. A simultaneous exclamation broke from both lips; simultaneously they drew back, and crouched on their knees to peer over the heather.

There they went!—straggling in a row in the direction of the inn, the party of revellers who had been so basely deserted.

First, the clergyman, with his hands clasped behind his back, his head bent in thought; a pensive reveller, this, already beginning to repent a heavy, indigestible meal; next, Mrs Macalister, holding her skirts in characteristic fashion well up in front and sweeping the ground behind; a pace or two in the rear, her spouse, showing depression and weariness in every line of his body. Yet farther along the two young men carrying the empty hampers; last of all, at quite a little distance from the rest, the figure of the Chieftain stepping out with a tread even more conspicuously jaunty than usual, his hands thrust deep into his pockets, his head turned from side to side, as if curiously scanning the hillsides.

At one and the same moment Margot and the Editor ducked their heads, and scrambled backwards for a distance of two or three yards. There was a moment's silence, then instinctively their eyes met. Margot pressed her lips tightly together, George Elgood frowned, but it was all in vain; no power on earth could prevent the mischievous dimples from dipping in her cheeks; no effort could hide the twinkle in his eyes—they buried their heads in their hands, and shook with laughter!

When at last composure was regained, George Elgood pulled his watch from his pocket, glanced at the time, and cried eagerly—

"There is still an hour before we need be back for dinner. As well be hanged for a sheep as a lamb. Let us go back to the river, and try our luck once more!"

Chapter Nineteen.

A Telegram.

It was a very shamefaced Margot who made her appearance at the dinner-table that evening; but, to her unspeakable relief, she found that there was no cause for embarrassment. Instead of the meaning glances and joking remarks which she had dreaded, she was greeted with the ordinary kindly prosaic welcome, and not even Mrs Macalister herself ventured an innuendo. The Chieftain was the only one who alluded to the non-appearance of the searchers, and the manner in which he did so was a triumph of the commonplace.

"Muddled up that hide-and-seek finely, didn't we?" he cried cheerily. "Afraid you had all your trouble for nothing. I happened to catch a glimpse of you heading off in the wrong direction, so turned into 'It' myself, and rooted them all out of their lairs. Then we played some sensible, middle-aged, sitting-down games, and strolled home in time for a siesta before dinner. Very good picnic, I call it. Great success! We'll have another, one of these fine days."

"'Deed yes, and we will!" assented Mrs Macalister genially. "It stirs a body up to have an outing now and then. I was thinking, why shouldn't we drive over to B— and see the old castle and all the sights? I've been hankering to go ever since we arrived; but it mounts up when you drive about by yourselves. If we shared two carriages between us, it would make all the difference, and it seems foolish-like to be in a neighbourhood and not see what there is to be seen. You can get carriages from Rew, they tell me, if you order them a day or two before."

To the amazement of the company, it was George Elgood of all others who hastened to second the proposal.

"A capital idea!" he cried. "B— is one of the finest old ruins in Scotland. Of course we must go; it would be worse than foolish to go home without seeing it. I have been before, so I could act as guide, and those who possess cameras had better take them also, as the place is rich in subjects."

The clergyman and his son pricked up their ears at this, photography being with them only a degree less absorbing a pastime than that of walking; Ron awoke suddenly to the remembrance that his half-plate camera had never been unpacked since his arrival; and the three vied with each other in asking questions about the proposed excursion, and in urging that a date should be fixed. Before the meal had come to a conclusion, plans were mapped out, and a division of labour made, by which one person was held responsible for the hiring of carriages, another for the promised food, while George Elgood was left to arrange the plan of campaign.

"We are a happy family, we are, we are, we are!" hummed the Chieftain, under his breath, as he cast a twinkling glance across the table to where Margot sat, as demure to outward seeming as she was excited at heart.

"Why do you avoid me?" he demanded of her plumply, the next morning, when, after several unsuccessful attempts, he ran her to earth by the side of the tarn. "Scurry out of my way like a frightened bunny whenever I come along. Won't do, you know! Not going to trouble myself to do you good turns, if you round on me afterwards, and avoid me as if I were the plague. What's it all about?"

"Nothing," stammered Margot confusedly. "I only felt rather— You *do* tease, you know, and your eyes twinkle so mischievously that I felt that discretion was the better part of valour."

"Well, don't do it again then, that's all, or I may turn rusty and upset the apple-cart. No reason that I know of why I should be ostracised, because I try to help my fellow-creatures. What are you doing over here? Reading? What a waste of time! Much better come and chuck stones into the lake with me."

Margot's brown eyes widened in reproof.

"Don't you like books?"

"Hate the sight of 'em! Especially on a holiday. Never want to see as much as a line of print from the time I leave home to the time I return. Especially,"—his eyes twinkled in the mischievous manner to which exception had just been taken—"especially poetry! Don't mind my saying so, do you?"

"Not a bit," returned Margot promptly, tossing her first stone into the lake with a vehemence which held more than a suspicion of temper. "Of course I never—one would never—*expect* you to like it. It would be the last thing one would expect—"

"Too fat?"

She blushed at that, and had the grace to look a trifle distressed.

"Oh, not that altogether. It's a '*Je ne sais quoi*,' don't you know. One could tell at a glance that you were not a literary man."

The Chieftain chuckled, bent down to gather a handful of stones, and raised a red smiling face to hers.

"Well, well, we can't all be geniuses, you know! One in a glen is about as much as you can expect to meet in these hard times. But I can chuck stones with the best of 'em. That one was a good dozen yards beyond your last throw. Put your back into it, and see what you can do. It's a capital way of letting off steam."

Margot was tempted to protest against the accusation, but reflection prompted silence, since after all she *was* cross, and there was no denying it.

She took the little man's advice, and "let off steam" by the vigour and determination with which she hurled pebbles into the lake, making them skim along the surface in professional manner for an ever longer and longer space before finally disappearing from sight.

The Chieftain cheered her on with example and precept, and, as usual, irritation died a speedy death in the presence of his bright, cheery personality. While they were still laughing and cheering each other on to fresh exploits, a lad from the post office passed along the road, and the Chieftain wheeled round to call out the usual question—

"Anything for me? Is the post in already?"

The lad shook his head. He was a red-headed sociable-looking creature who seemed only too glad to enliven his walk by a chat *en route*. His teeth showed in a cheerful smile as he replied—

"The post willna be here for an hour or mair. It's just a telegram!"

'THE POST WILLNA BE HERE FOR AN HOUR OR MAIR; IT'S JUST A TELEGRAM!'

A telegram! It said much for the peaceful seclusion of the Glen that the very sound of the word brought a chill of apprehension to the listening ears. No one received telegrams at the Nag's Head. One and all the visitors had sojourned thither with the aim of getting away as far as possible from the world of telegrams, and electric trams, and tube railways, and all the nerve-shattering inventions of modern life. Their ambition was to outlive the sense of hurry; to forget that such a thing as hurry existed, and browse along in peaceful uninterrupted ease.

To-day, however, in that far-away world beyond the heather-clad mountains something must have happened of such importance to some member of the little party that it could not wait for the leisurely medium of the post, but for good or ill had demanded instant attention.

Margot and the Chieftain stood in silence for a moment before he asked the second question.

"Who is it for?—What's the name?"

"Macalister!"

The name was pronounced with the lengthy drawl to which the hearers were growing familiar. They looked at each other with sighs of relief, followed swiftly by contrition.

"I hope nothing is wrong! I hope it's not bad news. Poor Mr Macalister's 'nearves'!"

"No, no! Nothing of the sort. Why imagine evil? Always look at the bright side as long as you can. Take for granted that it is good news, splendid news—the news he would like most to hear. Cut along, laddie! People pay for telegrams with the intention of getting them to their destination as quickly as possible. We'll defer the pleasure of a conversation to our next merry meeting."

The red-headed one grinned complacently and continued on his way, whistling as he went. There was about him no suggestion of a harbinger of bad tidings; the sun shone from a cloudless sky, and awoke sparkling reflections in the water; the scene was one of unbroken peace and happiness, and yet, and yet,—some shadow seemed to have fallen on Margot's soul, so that she could no longer take any interest in the mere throwing of stones. Her heart followed the footsteps of the messenger down the winding path, and stood still as he entered the inn.

"What is it, little girl? You look as if you had seen a ghost!"

The Chieftain stood observing her with an expression of kindly concern, for the pretty face had turned white beneath its tan, and the brown eyes were wide and tense, as if beholding something hidden from ordinary gaze. She gazed fixedly, not back in his face, but past him down the lane towards the inn.

"I'm—afraid! I *feel* it is not good news. It means trouble—big trouble! It is hanging over me like a cloud!"

He looked at her swiftly, and his face changed.

"Come then," he said quietly, "we will go back. If it is trouble, we may be able to help. I never ignore presentiments; they are sent to us all from time to time, and if we are faithful we obey them, like a summons. One came to me years ago. It was late at night, and I was just off to bed, when suddenly it came—the remembrance of a friend far off; the insistent remembrance; the certainty that he needed me, and that I must hasten to help. By all the laws of common sense I should have shrugged my shoulders and gone to sleep; but what are we, to judge by our own poor knowledge the great unknown forces of God? I went out there and then, caught a midnight train, and was at his house by seven in the morning. His wife met me on the stair and said, 'How did you know?' ... He lay dying in his bed, and all that night he had been calling for me. There was something I could do for him, better than any one else. He wished to place it in my hands before he went, and God had mercifully provided the opportunity. Never say that anything is impossible in this world, little girl! According to your faith so shall it be unto you."

Margot did not answer except by a faint, strained smile. Her eyes were fixed upon the doorway of the inn, waiting for the reappearance of the messenger, but he did not come, and the delay lent weight to her apprehension.

They spoke no more, but walked silently side by side, until they drew near to the inn, when suddenly the silence of the Glen was broken by a strange, unaccustomed sound.

What was it? Whence did it come? From some animal surely; some animal in pain or fear, piteously making known its needs! It could not be the moan of human woe! Yet even as she passionately denied the thought, Margot recognised in her heart that it was true, and darting quickly forward made her way into the inn parlour. The messenger still stood outside the door, waiting in stolid patience for instructions, and by his side was Mrs McNab, wiping floury hands in her apron, in evident perturbation of spirit.

On the plush-bedecked sofa in the corner of the parlour the half-inanimate form of Mrs Macalister swayed helplessly to and fro, while on either side stood two men—her husband and George Elgood—looking on in helpless, masculine fashion. Her cap had fallen back from her head, her ruddy face was bleached to a livid grey, from her lips came from time to time that pitiful, hopeless wail. At first it seemed to have no definite sound, but as one listened it took to itself words,—always the same words, repeated again and again—

"My lassie! My Lizzie! Oh, my lassie!"

"Nay, dearie, nay! You mustna give way. She's better off. You must be strong. We'll bear it together."

It was Mr Macalister who spoke; but Margot hardly recognised the voice, hardly recognised the face, which, for all its pallor and quiver of pain, was yet strong and calm. All trace of the peevish discontent that had hung like a cloud over the man had vanished like a mist; his bowed back seemed to have straightened itself and grown erect; the whining voice was composed and full of courage. He had forgotten his nerves in the presence of a great calamity; nay, more than that—he had forgotten himself; his one care and anxiety was for his wife!

The tears smarted in Margot's eyes; she ran forward, dropped on her knees before the chair, and clasped her strong young arms round the swaying figure, steadying it with loving, gentle pressure. The wan eyes stared at her unrecognisingly for a moment, then, at the sight of her girlish beauty, old memories returned, and the tears began to rain.

"Lizzie's gone! Lizzie's gone! I'll never see her again. All in a moment, and me so far away. My little Lizzie!... I canna bear it!..."

"She never suffered, mother. She knew nothing about it. It's better for her than a long, painful illness. You must be thankful for her sake." Mr Macalister looked down at Margot, and bravely essayed an explanation. "It was an accident. We've just heard. Instantaneous, they say. The mother's sore upset, but she's a brave woman. She'll bear it bravely for all our sakes. We'll need to get back to Glasgow."

"Yes. I'll help! I'll pack for her. Don't trouble about anything. I'll see that it is all right. You'll let me help you, dear, won't you?" Margot put up a tender hand, to straighten the cap on the poor, dishevelled head; and something in the simple, daughterly action seemed to reach the poor woman's heart, and bring with it the first touch of calmness. She sat up and looked blankly from side to side.

"I—I'm sorry! I shouldna give way. I never lost a child before, you see, and Lizzie was such a one for her mother. I wrote to her only last night. She leaves two bairnies of her own, but they are so young. They'll never remember her!" The pitiful trembling began again, whereupon George Elgood's hand held out a glass of water, and Margot took it from him to lift it to the quivering lips.

"They will need you all the more, and you must be strong for their sakes. That's what she would wish, isn't it?"

"Yes, yes. I must take care of the children. And Fred—poor Fred! but he hasn't loved her as I have done for nearly thirty years. Father, when can we get back?"

"I'll see, my dearie. I'll see! Leave all to me. I'll settle it all, and this good lassie will pack your things. Ye need trouble for nothing, my lass,—ye need trouble for nothing."

He laid his broad hand on his wife's shoulder with a gesture infinitely tender, then turned and went stumbling out of the room, while Margot's eyes met the tear-drenched ones above her with a flash of enthusiasm.

"He is—*splendid*!"

Even at that moment Mrs Macalister showed a faint kindling of response.

"Didn't I tell ye? When a man's out of health ye canna judge. When he's in his usual, there's no one to touch Mr Macalister."

With an instinctive movement Margot turned her head upward till her eyes met those of George Elgood, and exchanged a flash of mutual understanding. It heartened her like a drink of water in a thirsty land, for underlying the pity and the kindliness she recognised something else; something that existed for herself alone, and which seemed to bring with it an electric thrill of happiness.

Outside in the "lobby" the Chieftain was looking up trains in his own *Bradshaw*, and arranging with Mrs McNab for the long drive to the station, while Mr Macalister was writing out a return message with trembling fingers.

"Come upstairs with me, dear!" said Margot gently. "You shall lie on the bed while I do the packing. It's a long journey, and you must be as fresh as possible when you arrive. They will be waiting for you, you know, and expecting you to comfort them. You have told me how they all rely upon you. You wouldn't like to fail just when they need you most!"

Mrs Macalister raised herself feebly from her chair, but her poor face quivered helplessly.

"I'm a broken reed for any one to lean on. I can only remember that Lizzie's gone. There's no strength left in me. She was the flower of the flock. And me so far away!"

For the next hour the poor woman lay on the bed in her room, now sobbing in helpless paroxysms of grief, now relating pitiful, commonplace anecdotes of the dead daughter so dearly beloved, a dazed helpless creature, unable to do a hand's turn for herself, while her husband crept in and out, quiet, resourceful, comforting, full of unselfish compassion. Margot had hard work to keep back her own tears, as he clumsily pressed his own services upon her, picking up odd garments, folding them carefully in the wrong way, and rummaging awkwardly through the drawers.

The trap was to be ready to start by twelve o'clock, and ten minutes before the time Margot carried a sponge and basin of water to the bedside, bathed the poor, tear-stained face, brushed the straggling locks of grey hair, and helped to fasten bonnet and cloak. It was pathetic to see the helplessness into which grief had stricken this capable, bustling woman. She lifted her chin, to allow the strings of her bonnet to be tied by Margot's hands, and sat meekly while the "dolman" was hooked. It was like dressing a big docile baby; like a child, too, the manner in which she clung to her husband's arm down the narrow stair.

Mrs McNab was standing below in the lobby, her hard face flushed to an unnatural red. She held a basket in her hand filled with dainty paper packages containing fruit, sandwiches, and cakes. Unable to voice her sympathy, she had put it into deeds, striving to ensure some comfort for the long journey ahead.

Mrs Macalister smiled a pitiful travesty of a smile in acknowledgment, and her friends pressed her hand, mercifully refraining from speech. When it came to parting from Margot, however, that was a different matter. Mrs Macalister stooped from the seat of the trap to kiss the girl's cheek once and again.

"You're a guid lassie," she said, trembling. "I would have been lost without you! The Lord bless you, my dear!"

"Ay! and she *shall* be blessed!" added Mr Macalister's voice, deeply.

Margot thrilled at the sound of those words, and stood back on the path watching the departing wheels through a mist of tears. They had gone, those two good, loving, simple creatures, and in all likelihood she would never see them again; for a moment their lives had touched, but the currents had swept them apart; they were as ships that had passed in the night. To the end of time, however, she must be the better for the meeting, for in their need they had leant upon her, and she had been able to help. They had blessed her in patriarchal fashion, and the sound of their words still rang in her ears—

"The Lord bless you!"

"Ay! and she *shall* be blessed?"

Chapter Twenty.

Criticism.

Out of sympathy and respect for Mr and Mrs Macalister, nothing more was said about the next picnic party for several days after their tragic departure from the Glen, but the intervening time was, to Margot at least, full of interest and excitement. One morning, for instance, as she strolled from the breakfast-room to the road, as was the easy custom of the hour, a hurried step followed in the same direction, and George Elgood, staring hard in an opposite direction, advanced an opinion that one lesson in fishing was mere waste of time, whereas two, or perhaps three, might possibly convey some real knowledge of the art. Er—did Miss Vane feel inclined to pay another visit to the river?

Miss Vane, poking the gravel with the points of her shoes, was—er—yes! quite inclined, if Mr Elgood was sure she would not interrupt his sport Mr Elgood, with equal eagerness and incoherence, assured Miss Vane that she would do nothing of the kind, and hurried back to the inn, murmuring vaguely concerning eleven o'clock.

In the quiet of the riverside, however, he regained his self-possession, and once more proved himself to be the most interesting of companions, the most patient of instructors. Margot thought fishing a delightful and absorbing pursuit, which was the more remarkable as she was rather stupid than otherwise in mastering the initial movements. Mr Elgood encouraged her, however, by saying that some of the cleverest "rods" of his acquaintance had been the slowest in picking up the knack. The great thing was to have plenty of practice! She ought to come up every morning for as much time as she could spare; meantime, as she had been standing so long, would she not like to sit down, and rest awhile before walking home?

Then they sat down side by side on the grassy bank, and talked together as a man and a maid love to talk in the summer of their youth, exchanging innocent confidences, comparing thoughts and opinions, marvelling that they are so much alike.

Margot faithfully observed her promise to make no references to her ambitions on her brother's behalf, and, truth to tell, her silence involved little effort, for she was guiltily conscious of being so much engrossed in her own affairs that even Ron's ambitions had faded into the background. As for the lad himself, he was happy enough, wandering about by himself studying "effects" to transcribe to paper, or scouring the countryside with the Chieftain, whom he frankly adored, despite the many exceedingly plain-spoken criticisms and exhortations received from his lips.

"Your sister has been telling me about that rhyming craze of yours," the little man said suddenly one day. "Likewise about her own very pretty little scheme for the subjugation of my brother. Told you that she'd told me, eh? Expect she did! She is pleased to believe she is a designing little adventuress, whereas as a matter of fact she's as clear as crystal, and any one with half an eye could see through her schemes. Well! I laid down the law that neither she nor you are to worry my brother about business matters during his holiday, for, to tell you the truth, he has had his full share of worry of late. But what about me? I'm a plain, common-sense, steady-going old fellow, who might perhaps be able to give you a word or two of advice! What's all this nonsense about throwing aside a post that's waiting for you, and which means an income for life, in order to live in an attic, and scribble verses for magazines? If you knew the world, young man, you would understand that you are blessedly well off, to have your way made smooth, and would not be in such a hurry to meet disappointments half way. They will come soon enough! At the best of it, you will have a hard row to hoe. Why make it worse?"

Ronald flushed in sensitive fashion, but there was no hint of offence in his manner, as he replied—

"It is hardly a question of an attic, sir. My father would not disinherit me because I preferred literature to business. I might have a pittance instead of a fortune, but I should not have to fear want. And why should I not live my own life? If I am bound to meet troubles, surely it is only right to provide what compensations I can, and my best compensation would be congenial work! I don't want to be rich. Let some other fellow take the post, and get his happiness out of it; it would be slavery to me."

"Humph! No boy likes the idea of putting his nose to the grindstone. They all kick a bit at the thought of an office desk, but nine out of ten enjoy the life when they get into the swing. It's a great secret of happiness in this world, to be kept so busy that we have not time to think of ourselves. We need work for its own sake, even more than for what it brings; but our work must be worthy. There's no real success away from that... About those verses now! It's a pleasant occupation for you to sling them together—I haven't a word to say against it as a recreation—but that's a different thing from serious work. There's only one thing which justifies a man in cutting himself adrift from the world, in opposition to the wishes of those who have his interests most at heart, and that is, a strong and solemn conviction of a special mission in life. Very well then! If you agree so far, let us proceed to consider the mission of a poet. There's only one justification for his existence—only one thing that distinguishes him from the professional rhymester whom nobody wants, and who is the bane and terror of society, and that is—*that he has something to say*! Now take your own case—a lad without as much as a moustache on his face; the son of a rich father, who has lain soft all his life, and had the bumps rolled flat before him. What do you imagine that you are going to teach the world? Do you fondly believe that you have anything to say that has not been said before, and a thousand times better into the bargain?"

Ronald looked up and gazed dreamily ahead. He had taken off his cap, as his custom was in these moorland tramps, which were becoming of daily occurrence, and his hair was ruffled on his forehead, giving an air of even more than ordinary youth to his face. The hazel eyes were dark, and the curved lips trembled with emotion; he was searching his soul for the reply to a question on which more than life seemed to depend, and while he gazed at the purple mountains with unseeing eyes the Chieftain gazed at his illumined face, and felt that he had received his answer.

The words of Wordsworth's immortal ode rushed into his brain, and he recognised that this ignorant lad possessed a knowledge which was hidden from the world. Heaven, with its clouds of glory, lay close around him, ignorant of worldly wisdom though he might be. God forbid that the one should ever be exchanged for the other!

The Chieftain was answered, but like Ron he remained silent. They walked on over the short, springy grass, breathed the clear, fresh breeze, and thought their own thoughts. It was not until nearly a mile had been traversed that Ron turned his head and said simply, as if answering a question put but a moment before—

"I sing, because I must! It is my life. I have not thought of other people, except in so far as their approval would justify me in my father's eyes. You could no doubt judge better than I if what I have to say has value or not. Will you read some of my lines?"

A curious sound broke from the Chieftain's lips, a sound something between a groan and a laugh. He frowned, pursed his lips, swung his short arms vigorously to and fro, shook his head with an air of determined opposition, then suddenly softened into a smile.

"It's a strange world, my masters! A strange world! You never know your luck! In the middle of my holiday, and a Scotch moor into the bargain! I'll try Timbuctoo another year! Nothing else for it. Where does my brain-rest come in, I want to know! You and your verses—be plagued to the pair of you! Got some about you now, I suppose? Hand them over, then,—the first that come to the surface—and let me get through with it as soon as possible!"

He plumped down on the grass as he spoke, took out a large bandana handkerchief and mopped his brow with an air of resignation, while Ronald fumbled awkwardly in his pocket.

"I have several pencil copies. I think you can make them out. This is the latest. A Madrigal—'To my Lady.'"

"Love-song?"

"Yes."

"Ever been in love?"

"No."

"What a pity when charming—poets—sing of things they don't understand! Well, well, hand it over! I'll bear it as bravely as I may—"

Ron winced, and bit his lower lip. It was agony to sit by and watch the cool, supercilious expression on the critic's face, the indifferent flick of the fingers with which the sheet was closed and returned.

"Anything more?"

"You don't care for that one?"

"Pretty platitudes! Read them before a score of times—and somewhat more happily expressed. If I were a poet—which I'm not, thank goodness!—I could turn 'em out by the score. Ten shillings each, reduction upon taking a dozen. Suitable for amateur tenors, or the fashion-magazines. Alterations made if required... Anything else in the lucky bag?"

"There's my note-book. They are all in there—the new ones, I mean, written since I came up here. You can read which you please."

Ron took the precious leather book from his pocket, and handed it over with an effort as painful as that of submitting a live nerve to the dentist's tool. As he sat on the ground beside his critic he dug his heels into the grass, and the knuckles of his clenched hands showed white through the tan. The beginning had not been propitious, and he knew well that no consideration for his feelings would seal the lips of this most honest of critics. For a few moments he had not courage to look at his companion's face, but even without that eloquent guide it was easy to follow his impressions.

A grunt, a groan, a long incredulous whistle, a sharp intake of breath—these were but too readily translated as adverse criticisms, but between these explosions came intervals of silence less easy to explain. Ron deliberately rolled over on his side, turning his back on his companion, thereby making it impossible to see his face. Those who have never trusted their inmost thoughts to paper can hardly imagine the acute suffering of the moment when they are submitted to the cold criticism of an outsider. Life and death themselves seemed to hang in the balance for the young poet during the half-hour when he lay on the heather listening to each sound and movement of his critic. At the end of half an hour the interruption came. A yawn, a groan, the pressure of a heavy hand on his shoulder.

"Now then, wake up, over there! Time to move on!"

Awake! As if it were possible that he could be asleep! Never in his life had he been more acutely, painfully conscious of his surroundings. Ron rose to his feet, casting the while a tense glance at his companion's face. What verdict would he see written on eye and mouth as the result of that half-hour's study? He met a smile of bland good-humour; the cheery, carelessly complacent smile of the breakfast-table, the smoke-room, the after-dinner game; with not one trace of emotion, of kindled feeling, or even ordinary appreciation! The black note-book was tossed into his hands, as carelessly as if it had been a ball; even a commonplace word of comment was denied.

It was a bitter moment, but, to the lad's credit be it said, he met it bravely. A gulp to a tiresome lump in the throat, a slight quivering of the sensitive lips, and he was master of himself again, hastily stuffing the precious note-book out of sight, and striving to display the right amount of interest in his companion's conversation. It was not until the inn was within sight that Mr Elgood made the slightest allusion to the verses which he had read.

"Ah—about those rhymes!" he began casually. "Don't take yourself too seriously, you know. It's a strange thing that young people constitute themselves the pessimists of the world, while the old ones, who know what real trouble is, are left to do the optimism by themselves. If you are bound to sing, sing cheerfully! Try to forget that 'sad' rhymes with 'glad,' and don't feel it necessary to end in the minor key. That rhyming business has a lot to answer for. I like you best when you are content to be your natural, cheerful self!"

"You think, then—you do think—some of them a little good?"

Ron's wistful voice would have melted a heart of stone. The Chieftain laid a hand on his arm with a very kindly pressure.

"There are some of 'em," he said cheerfully, "which are a lot better than others. I'm not partial to amateur verses myself, but I don't mind telling you for your comfort that I've seen worse, before now—considerably worse!"

Poor Ron! It was bitter comfort. In the blessed privacy of his own room he sat himself down to read over the pages of the little black book with painful criticism, asking himself miserably if it were really true that they were feeble amateur efforts, tinged with pretence and unreality. Here and there a flush and a wince proved that the accusation had gone home, when a vigorous pencil mark on the side of the page marked the necessity for correction, but on the whole he could honestly refute the charge; could declare, with the bold yet humble conviction of the true craftsman, that it was good work; work well done; work worth doing!

The dreamy brown eyes sent out a flash of determination.

"I *can*!" said Ron to himself. "And I *will*!"

Chapter Twenty One.

A Mountain Mist.

Three days later a wagonette was chartered from Rew, to drive the diminished party to the scene of the haunted castle. Margot felt rather shy in the position of the only lady, but a mild proposition that she should stay at home had been so vigorously vetoed that she had nothing more to say.

"If one clergyman, plus one brother, plus one bald-headed veteran, aren't sufficient chaperons for one small girl, things are coming to a pretty pass indeed!" protested the Chieftain vigorously. "If you stay at home, we *all* stay, so that's settled, and the disappointment and upset will be on your head. Why all this fuss, I should like to know? One might think you were shy."

Margot pouted, and wriggled her shoulders inside her white blouse.

"I *am* shy!"

"You are, are you? Hadn't noticed it before. Of whom, if one may ask?"

She turned at that, and walked back to the inn, nose in air, but thereafter there were no more demurs.

It was indeed a very decorous little party which sat in two rows of three, facing each other in the wagonette during the eight-mile drive. The clergyman and the Chieftain, with Margot between them; and opposite, the three dreamers: the Editor, Ron, and young Mr Menzies,—each apparently too much immersed in his own thoughts to care for conversation. Margot was quite thankful when the drive came to an end, outside castle walls, grim and grey, but imposing as ever, though they were in reality but a shell, surrounding a plot of innocent green grass. There were isolated towers still standing, however, approached by winding stone stairways, and short lengths of walks along the ramparts, and quaint little barred windows through which one could view the surrounding country. When Margot thrust her pretty laughing face through one of these latter to greet her friends below, every photographer among them insisted upon snap-shotting her then and there, and for a good half-hour she was kept busy, posing in various attitudes, to give the desired touch of life to the pictures.

Photography over, the next duties were to partake of lunch and to wander round the small, and it must be confessed somewhat uninteresting little village; then,—since the return home counted as one of the chief attractions in the programme—the little party broke up into two, the clergyman and his son preferring the longer route, round by the roads, the other four to take the short—cut across the moors.

A five-mile walk across the moors! Given health, settled skies, and congenial society, it would be difficult to name a more exhilarating occupation for a summer afternoon; but, truth to tell, the weather had taken a decided turn for the worse since midday, and it needed some optimism to set forth on a long exposed walk.

The subject had been discussed at lunch with special reference to Margot, as the only lady of the party; but, as she aptly observed, she was bound to get back somehow, and, as a choice of evils, preferred to walk through rain, rather than sit still to be soaked through and through on the seat of the wagonette. It was therefore decided to make an early start, and allow no loitering by the way; but when the village had been left about a mile behind an unexpected delay occurred. The Chieftain thrust his hands into his pockets, and stopped short in the middle of the road, with an expression of dismay.

"Eh, what! Here's a fine kettle of fish! Where's my bunch of keys? They were here as safe as houses, a few minutes back. I was jingling tunes on them as we passed the school. You heard me jingling 'em! Dropped them on the road, I suppose, and walked on like a blind bat. Serves me right to have to turn back to find 'em. Can't lose my keys, you know. Got to find them somehow, or there'll be the mischief to pay. You'll have to go on, George, and take Miss Vane with you. There's no time for conundrums, if you want to get home dry." He looked towards Ron with questioning eyebrows. "Feel inclined to keep me company? I don't fancy that walk by my lonesome."

"Of course I do. I should not think of leaving you behind by yourself, sir," returned Ron eagerly. "We can't have far to go, and we can soon catch up the others, if we make a sprint for it. Go on, Margot. We'll be after you in no time."

In the circumstances there was nothing else to be done, nor indeed, after a long morning spent in wandering about as a party, was Margot inclined to quarrel with the fate which provided an interesting *tête-à-tête* for the walk home. She contented herself with expressing profuse sympathy for the Chieftain's loss, and with prophesying cheerfully that the keys were certain to be found, then promptly dismissed the subject from her mind, and gave herself up to the enjoyment of the moment.

"I really think we are wise not to wait about," George Elgood said, in accents of self-vindication, as they moved on together. "The glass is high, but I don't like the look of things, all the same, and for your sake shall be glad when we are nearer home. Are you pretty warmly dressed, if the rain should come on?"

"Don't I look it? I couldn't possibly have anything more suitable than this tweed coat and skirt. It doesn't matter how wet it gets. It won't spoil."

"I was thinking about your own comfort, not of the clothes. You never carry an umbrella with you, I notice!"

"I can't be bothered! Showers are such an everyday occurrence up here, that one would be doing nothing else. I rather like the feel of the rain on my face, and besides,"—she laughed mischievously, "it's good for the complexion!"

"Is that so?" he asked gravely, his dark eyes dwelling on the soft, rounded cheeks, which grew a shade more pink beneath his gaze. Suddenly his lips twitched, with the one-sided, humorous smile which brought the youth into his face. "I don't think the need in that direction is so pressing that it could not be postponed with advantage, for to-day at least. Do you mind walking fairly quickly? I shall feel more comfortable when we are nearer home."

Margot was serenely indifferent whether it rained or not, but none the less she appreciated the Editor's care for her welfare, which showed itself in a dozen little graceful acts during the first part of their walk. For one unaccustomed to women's society he was marvellously observant, and Margot felt a sweeter satisfaction in being so protected than in all her former independence. They climbed the hillside which led to the moor and set out radiantly to traverse the grey expanse; grey and cheerless to-day in very deed, with a thick, blanket-like dampness in the atmosphere of which dwellers in southern climes are happily ignorant.

George Elgood turned up the collar of his coat, and Margot thrust her hands into her pockets, shivering slightly the while, but neither made any complaint in words. As usual, it was left to Margot to do most of the talking; but though her companion's responses were short, they were yet so sympathetic and appreciative, that there was never any difficulty in finding a fresh subject. Like most couples with whom friendship is fast making way for a warmer emotion, personal topics were the most appreciated, and what was happening in the world—the discoveries of science, the works of the great writers—palled in interest before sentences beginning with, "I think," and, "Do you think?"

"I wish—"

"Have you ever wished—?"

They looked at each other as they spoke, with bright, questioning glances, which seemed ever to hail some precious new discovery of mind, drawing them closer and closer together. The hour of

THEN THEY AWOKE TO THE CONSCIOUSNESS OF DANGER.
[See page 262.

enchantment had come, when they moved in a world of their own, unconscious of external accidents. The moisture hung in dewdrops on the Editor's cap, Margot's hair curled damply on her forehead; but they felt neither cold nor discomfort. It was unusually dark for the time of day, and had grown mysteriously darker during the last half-hour; but visitors to the Highlands become philosophically resigned to sudden and unpleasant atmospheric changes, and fall into the way of ignoring them as far as possible.

It was only when they reached a point in the moor from whence the ground sloped sharply downward towards the Glen that they awoke to the consciousness of danger, for instead of a rolling stretch of green surrounded by purple hills, they seemed to be looking down into a cauldron of floating mist and steam, blocking out the view, confusing the eyes, and slowly but surely concealing the familiar landmarks.

Margot and the Editor stopped short with simultaneous exclamations of dismay, then wheeled quickly round, to see what lay behind. Here indeed the fog was much less dense, but the distance was already obliterated, while long, smoke-like tendrils of mist were closing in on every hand. The signs which they had noted had portended something worse than rain; something which the dwellers in moorland regions learn to fear and dread above all other phenomena,—a mountain mist!

George Elgood's face was eloquent with self-reproach.

"This is my fault! Where were my eyes, that I did not see what was happening? The darkness should have warned me long ago. I am horribly ashamed of myself, Miss Vane!"

"You needn't be. It's as much my fault as yours. I did notice the damp on my face, but I thought it was rain. What are we to do?"

It was a simple question, but terribly difficult to answer. With every moment those rolling masses of mist settled down more densely over the hillsides. To walk forward was to walk blindfold over a treacherous country; to return seemed hardly more propitious, though as a choice of evils it was the one to be preferred.

"We must go back. We can't have come more than two or three miles. We must get back, and drive round by the road. Probably we shall meet Geoffrey and your brother *en route*!"

Even as he spoke the Editor turned and led the way towards the little village which had been left behind less than an hour before. There was no time to waste, for the darkness was increasing, and the clammy dankness of the air struck to the very marrow.

"I shall never forgive myself if you suffer through this. It was my business to look after you. There's only this slight excuse—that we were mounting towards the highest part of the moor, which was naturally the clearest. The mist seems to have gathered from all around."

Margaret looked and shivered, but hastened to appease his anxiety.

"I think we *did* notice, but as we were expecting rain, a little mistiness was natural. We could not tell that it was going to spread like this. Never mind! It will be quite an adventure to brag about when we are back in town. 'Lost on the Scotch moors! Tourists disappear in a mist!' It would make a thrilling headline, wouldn't it?"

She laughed as she spoke, but the laugh had rather a forced tone. Suddenly she became conscious that she was tired and chilled, that her coat was soaked, and her boots heavy with damp. Though only a few paces away, the figure of her companion was wreathed with tendrils of mist; they were floating round her also; blinding her eyes, catching her breath, sending fresh shivers down her back. A pang of fear shot through her at the thought of what might lie ahead.

Like two grey ghosts they struggled onward through the gloom.

Chapter Twenty Two.

Lost on the Moor.

George Elgood's haste to reach the end of the moor gave wings to his feet, so that Margot had much ado to keep pace. Contrary to expectation, the fog did not lessen as they advanced, but closed in upon them thicker and thicker, so that the ground beneath their feet became invisible, and progress was broken by sundry trips and stumbles over projecting mounds of heather. The air seemed to reek with moisture, and a deadly feeling of oppression, almost of suffocation, affected the lungs, as the curling wreath of mist closed overhead.

Half an hour earlier Margot had felt that any sort of adventure (if experienced in George Elgood's company) must of necessity be enjoyable, but during that swift silent retreat she was conscious of a dawning of something perilously like fear. Her breath came in quickened pants, she kept her eyes fixed in a straining eagerness on the tall figure looming darkly ahead. If she once lost sight of him, what would become of her? It made her shudder to think of being left alone upon that shrouded moor!

Every now and then as he walked, the Editor gave voice to a loud "coo-ee," in hope that the echoes might reach the ears of his brother and Ronald, who should by now be approaching in the same direction; but no reply floated back to his anxious ears.

"Perhaps they have gone round by the road," he suggested tentatively. "If they were some time in following, they may have seen the fog, and come to the conclusion that discretion was the better part of valour."

"Ron wouldn't go another way if he thought I was in danger! He promised father to take care of me. I know he will come."

"Then we are bound to meet; unless—" George Elgood stopped short hurriedly. It was not for him to open his companion's eyes to the fact that the direction which they were taking had become a matter of speculation, as one after another the familiar landmarks faded from view.

The two brothers might pass by within a few yards, or their paths might diverge by miles, but in either case they would be equally invisible. The only hope was to go on sending out the familiar cry, which would at once prove their identity. "Not that we should be any better off with them than without!" he told himself dolefully.

Margot did not ask for a completion of the unfinished sentence, perhaps because she guessed only too truly its import. A few steps farther on her foot came in contact with a stone hidden beneath a clump of furze; she stumbled, tried in vain to recover herself, and fell forward on her knees. The shock and the severe pricking which ensued forced a cry of dismay, and the Editor turned back hurriedly, and uttered a startled inquiry.

"Miss Vane, where are you?"

"I'm here!" replied a doleful voice, and a dark form stirred at his feet. "I—*fell*! On a horrid bush! My hands are full of prickles."

"I'll light a match while you get them out. It's my fault. I might have guessed what would happen. I'd like to kick myself for being so thoughtless."

"Please don't! We don't want any more tribulations. I—I'm quite all right!" cried Margot, with tremulous bravery. The flicker of a match showed a pale face, and two little hands grimed with dust and earth. She brushed them hastily together, and peered up into his face. "It's pretty thick, isn't it?"

"Abominably thick! I have heard of the sudden way in which these mountain mists come on, but I've never been in one before. I could kick myself once more for not having noticed it sooner. I suppose I was too much absorbed in our conversation."

The match died out, and there was a moment's silence, in which Margot seemed to hear the beating of her own heart. Then in the darkness a hand lifted hers, and placed it against an arm which felt reassuringly solid.

"You must let me help you along. A moor is not the easiest place in the world to cross in the dark. You won't mind my shouts? I want to let the other fellows know where we are, if they are within hearing."

"Oh, I don't mind. I'll shout, too! They must be near. It seems ridiculous that we can't see each other."

But still no answering cry came back, and Margot's sense of comfort in the supporting arm gradually gave place to a revival of her first dread. She shivered, and swallowed a lump in her throat before daring a fateful question.

"Mr Elgood, do you know—have you the faintest idea where we are going?"

His arm tightened over her hand, but he made no attempt at prevarication.

"No, I haven't! For the last five or ten minutes it has been purely guess-work."

"We may be going in the wrong direction, or round and round in a circle!"

"We may—I am afraid it is more than probable. I have been thinking that it might be better to stay where we are. We can't have strayed very far out of the course as yet, but—" Again he stopped, and this time Margot completed the sentence.

"I know! It's not safe to wander about when we can't see what is ahead. I've been thinking the same thing. We had better sit down and wait. They will come to look for us. I'm sure they will come, and there's a cottage somewhere near, where we have been for milk. That's another chance. If we keep calling the people, they may hear us."

"Oh yes, yes! Some one will hear, or the mist will rise as suddenly as it fell. It will be only for a short time," returned the Editor sturdily. "Now look here—the ground is soaking—you can't possibly sit on it without something underneath. If you could spare your cape it would serve us both as a rug, and I'm going to wrap you up in my coat."

He loosened his arm, as if to take off the said coat forthwith, but Margot's fingers tightened their grasp in very determined fashion.

"You are not! I won't wear it. I absolutely refuse to do any such thing. How can you suggest such a horridly selfish arrangement—I to wear your coat, while you sit shivering in shirt-sleeves? Never! I'd rather freeze!"

"Put it the other way. Am I, a man, to hug my coat, and let a girl sit on the soaking grass? How do you suppose I should feel? I'd rather freeze, too!"

Margot gave a quavering little laugh.

"It seems to me we have a pretty good chance of doing it—coat or no coat. If I am a girl, I'm a healthy one, and I must take my chance. Did you happen to put your newspaper in your pocket this morning? That would be better than nothing."

"Of course I did! That will do capitally. What a blessing you thought of it! There! Sit down quickly, and I'll pull a bit down under your feet. Can't I wrap that cape more tightly round you? And the hood? Hadn't you better have the hood up?"

"Yes, please! I had forgotten the hood. That will be cosy!"

Margot's cold cheeks flamed with sudden colour as she felt the touch of careful fingers settling the hood round head and face, and fumbling for the hook under the chin. At that moment at least cold was not the predominant sensation! There was a short silence while the Editor seated himself by her side, and felt in his pockets.

"You won't mind if I smoke?"

"I shall like it, especially if you have fusees. I love the smell of fusees! You don't ask me to have a cigarette, I notice, and yet it is fashionable for girls to smoke nowadays. How did you know that I didn't?"

"I *did* know! I can hardly tell why, but I am thankful for it, all the same. I am too old-fashioned to care for smoking women. A girl loses her charm when she apes a man's habits."

"Yes. I agree. I am sorry I am not a man, but as I'm a girl I prefer to be a real one, and have my clothes smelling sweet and violety, instead of like a fusty railway carriage. But men seem to find smoke soothing at times. I wish I had a feminine equivalent of it just now. It's a little bit frightening to sit still and stare into this blank white wall. Couldn't you tell me something interesting to pass the time?"

"It's a little difficult to be 'interesting' to order. What particular kind of narrative would distract you best?"

"Oh—something about yourself. Something you have done, or felt, or planned for another day. I'm so interested in people!" returned Margot, wrapping the folds of her cloak more closely round her, and slipping her hands deep down into the inside pockets. "Have you had any thrilling experiences or adventures that you don't mind speaking about? The more thrilling the better, please, for my feet *are* so cold!"

She shivered, in involuntary childish fashion, and George Elgood sighed profoundly.

"This is about the biggest adventure I've had. I was once snowed up for a night in a rest-house on one of the Swiss mountains, but we had every ordinary comfort, and knew exactly where we were, so that it didn't amount to much, after all. I was going up with my guide, and met another party of two brothers and a sister coming down, and we all took shelter together, while one of the guides returned to the village, to let the people in the hotel know of our safety. When the door was open the prospect was sufficiently eerie, but we made a fire and brewed tea, and passed the time pleasantly enough. The worst part of it was that I had to give up the ascent next day, as there was too much snow to make it prudent to go on."

"Oh! Yes! Was she pretty?"

She felt, rather than saw, his start of surprise.

"Who?"

"The sister. You said there was a girl in the other party."

"I'm *sure* I don't know! I didn't notice."

"Don't you care how people look?"

"It doesn't interest me, unless I am already attracted in other ways. At least—" he hesitated conscientiously. "I *used* not to be. I think I am growing more noticing. Geoff always said I needed to be awakened to the claims of beauty. I understand now that it may be a great additional charm."

How did he understand? Who or what had increased his power of observation? Margot hoped that she knew; longed to be certain, yet dreaded the definite information. In a little flurry of nervousness she began to talk volubly on her own account, hoping thereby to ward off embarrassing explanations.

"I seem fated to come in for adventures. I went over to Norway one summer, and the engines broke down half-way across the North Sea, and at the same time all the electric lights went out. It was terribly rough, and we rolled for a couple of hours—the longest hours I have ever known! The partitions of the cabins did not quite reach to the roof, and you could hear the different conversations going on all round. In a dreary kind of way I realised that they were very funny, and that I should laugh over them another day. Quite near us were two jolly English schoolboys, who kept ordering meals all the next day, and shouting out details to a poor sister who was lying terribly ill in the next cabin 'Monica, we are having bacon! Have a bit of bread soaked in fat?' Then Monica would groan—a heartrending groan, and they would start afresh. 'Buck up, Monica—try a muffin!' At lunch-time they pressed roast beef and Yorkshire pudding upon her, and she groaned louder than ever. She *was* ill, poor girl. In Norway there was an alarm of fire in one of those terrible wooden hotels, and we all jumped on each other's balconies to get to the outside staircases. It was soon extinguished, but it was a very bad scare. And now this is the third. Mr Elgood, do coo-ee again! Ron must be looking for me, unless he is lost himself."

The Editor put his hands to his mouth and sent forth a succession of long-drawn-out calls, which seemed as though they must surely be heard for miles around, but in the silence which followed no note of reply could be heard. In the face of such continued disappointment, Margot had not the courage to go on making conversation, but relapsed into a dreary silence, which was broken only by the gentle puff-puff of the Editor's pipe. In the darkness and silence neither took note of time, or realised how it sped along. Only by physical sensations could it be checked, but gradually these became disagreeably pressing.

Margot's feet were like ice, her fingers so cold as to be almost powerless; but as the minutes passed slowly by the active discomfort was replaced by a feeling of drowsy indifference. She seemed to have been sitting for years staring into a blank white wall, and had no longer any desire to move from her position. It was easier to sit still, and wait upon Fate.

Beneath the veil of darkness her head drooped forward, and she swayed gently from side to side. For some time these movements were so slight as to pass unnoticed by her companion, but as the drowsiness increased the muscles seemed to lose control, the swayings became momentarily more pronounced, until she tilted violently over, to recover herself with a jerk and a groan. Then indeed George Elgood was startled into anxious attention.

"What is it? What is the matter? Are you in pain?"

The inarticulate murmur which did duty for reply seemed only to whet anxiety still further.

"Miss Vane, are you ill? For pity's sake tell me what is wrong!"

Another murmur sounded faintly in his ear, followed by an incoherent—"I'm only—asleep! So—very—tired!"

With a sharp exclamation the Editor leapt upwards, and the drowsy Margot felt herself suddenly hoisted to her feet by a pair of strong arms. The arms retained their hold of her even after she was erect, shaking her to and fro with almost painful energy.

"But you *must* not sleep! Margot, Margot, awake! I can't let you sleep. It is the worst thing you could do. Speak to me, Margot. Tell me you understand. Margot! Darling! Oh, do rouse yourself, and try to understand!"

Margot never forgot that moment, or the wonder of it. She seemed to herself to be wandering in a strange country, far, far away from the solid tangible earth—a land of darkness and dreams, of strange, numbing unreality. Her eyes were open, yet saw nothing: impalpable chains fettered her limbs, so that they grew stiff and refused to move; an icy coldness crept around her heart. Hearing, like the other senses, was dulled, yet through the throbbing silence a sound had penetrated, bringing with it a thrill of returning life. Some one had called "*Margot*" in a tone she had never heard before. Some one had said, "*Darling*!"

Back through the fast-closing mists of unconsciousness Margot's soul struggled to meet her mate. Her fingers tightened feebly on his, and her cold lips breathed a reply.

"Yes—I am here! Do you want me?"

Something like a sob sounded in the Editor's throat.

"Do I want you? My little Margot! Did I ever want anything before? Come, I will warm your little cold hands. I will lead you every step of the way. You can't sit here any longer to perish of cold. We will walk on, and ask God to guide our feet. Lean on me. Don't be afraid!"

Then the dream became a moving one, in which she was borne forward encircled by protecting arms; on and on; unceasingly onward, with ever-increasing difficulty and pain.

George Elgood never knew whether he hit, as he supposed, a straight road forward, or wandered aimlessly over the same ground. His one care was to support his companion, and to test each footstep before he took it; for the rest, he had put himself in God's hands, with a simple faith which expected a reply; and when at last the light of the cottage windows shone feebly through the mist his thankfulness was as great as his relief.

As for Margot, she was too completely exhausted to realise relief; she knew only a shrinking from the light, from the strange watching face; a deathly sensation as of falling from a towering height, before darkness and oblivion overpowered her, and she lay stretched unconscious upon the bed.

Chapter Twenty Three.

Partings.

It was six days later when Margot opened her eyes, and found herself lying on the little white bed in the bedroom of the Nag's Head, with some one by the window whose profile as outlined against the light seemed strangely and sweetly familiar. She stared dumbly, with a confused wonder in her brain. *Edith*? It could not possibly be Edith! What should bring Edith up to Glenaire in this sudden and unexpected fashion? And why was she herself so weak and languid that to speak and ask the question seemed an almost impossible exertion?

What had happened? Was she only dreaming that her head ached, and her hands seemed too heavy to move, and that Edith sat by the window near a table covered with medicine bottles and glasses? Margot blinked her eyes, and stared curiously around. No! it was no dream; she was certainly awake, and through the dull torpor of her brain a remembrance began slowly to work. Something had happened! She had been tired and cold; oh, cold, cold, cold; so cold that it had seemed impossible to live. She had wandered on and on, through an eternity of darkness, which had ended in the blackness of night. Her head throbbed with the effort of thinking; she shut her eyes and lay quietly, waiting upon remembrance.

Suddenly it came. A faint flush of colour showed itself in the white cheek, and a tingle of warmth ran through the veins. She remembered now upon whose arm she had hung, whose voice it was which had cheered her onward; in trembling, incredulous fashion she remembered what that voice had said!

A faint exclamation sounded through the stillness, whereupon Edith looked round quickly, and hurried to the bedside.

"Margot! My darling! Do you know me at last?"

Margot smiled wanly. The smooth rounded face had fallen away sadly in that week of fever and unconsciousness, and a little hand was pushed feebly forward.

"Of course. I'm so glad! Edie, have I been ill?"

"Yes, darling; but you are better now. After a few days' rest you will be well again. You must not be nervous about your dear self."

"And you came?"

"Yes, darling; Ron telegraphed, and father and I came up at once. Agnes is taking care of the boys."

"So kind! I remember—it was the mist. Was—Ron—safe?"

"Yes, darling, quite safe. He and Mr Elgood arrived at the cottage very soon after you, and were so thankful to find you there."

"Is—is *everybody* well?"

Again that faint flush showed on the cheeks; but Edie was mercifully blind, and answered with direct simplicity—

"Every one, dear, and you are going to be quite well, too. You must not talk any more just now, for you are rather a weak little girl still. Drink this cup of milk, and roll over, and have another nap. It is good to see you sleeping quietly and peacefully again. There! Shut your eyes, like a good girl!"

Then once more Margot floated off into unconsciousness; but this time it was the blessed, health-restoring unconsciousness of sleep, such sleep as she had not known for days past, and from which she awoke with rested body and clearer brain.

When the dear father came in to kiss and greet her, a thin white hand crept up to stroke his hair, and pull his ear in the way he loved, whereupon he blinked away tears of thankfulness, and essayed to be fierce and reproachful.

"So you couldn't be satisfied until you had dragged the whole family after you, to the ends of the earth! There's no pleasing some people. This is my reward for being such a fool as to think you could take care of yourself!"

"Ducky Doodles!" murmured Margot fondly. As of yore, she manifested not the faintest alarm at his pretence of severity, but twitched his ear with complacent composure, and once more Mr Vane blinked and swallowed a lump in his throat. There had been hours during those last days when he had feared that he might never again hear himself called "Ducky Doodles," and what a sad grey world that would have meant!

Then came Ron, a little embarrassed, as was natural in a lad of his years, but truly loving and tender all the same, and Margot's brown *eyes* searched his face with wistful questioning.

There was so much that she wanted to ask and to hear, and concerning which no one had as yet vouchsafed information. Ron could tell her all that was to be told, which it was impossible to pass another night without knowing, yet there he sat, sublimely unconscious that she wanted to be assured of anything but his own safety. With the energy of despair, Margot forced herself to put a question.

"How are all—the others?"

"The Elgoods? They are all right. Awfully worried about you, you know, and that sort of thing. Afraid the governor might think they were to blame. The idea of your going down with pneumonia, and frightening us all into fits! I thought you were too healthy to be bowled over so soon, but a London life doesn't fit one for exposure. The governor was furious with me for bringing you to the North."

But for once Margot was not interested in her father's feelings. She turned her head on the pillow and put yet another question.

"They did not catch colds, too?"

"Oh, colds!" Ron laughed lightly. "Of course, we all had colds; what else could you expect? We were lucky to get off so easily. The Elgoods put off leaving until you were safely round the corner, but they are off first thing to-morrow."

At this there was a quick rustle of the bedclothes.

"Going? *Where*?" asked a startled voice, in which sounded an uncontrollable quiver of apprehension. "Not away for altogether?"

"Yes! Their time was up three days ago. It is awfully decent of them to have stayed on for so long. We shall meet in town, I suppose; but your Editor man is no use to me, Margot. That little scheme has fallen flat. From first to last he has never troubled to show the faintest interest in my existence, and has avoided the governor all he knew. The Chieftain is worth a dozen of him. He has kept the whole thing going this last week, amused the governor, looked after Edith, been a perfect brick to me. I'm glad we came, if it were only for the sake of making his acquaintance, for he is the grandest man I've ever known; but your scheme has failed, old girl."

From Margot's expression it would appear that everything on earth had failed. Her face looked as white as the pillow against which she rested, and her eyes were tragic in her despairing sadness. Ron bestirred himself to comfort her, full of gratitude for so heartfelt an interest.

"Never mind! You did your best, and it's nobody's fault that he turned out such a Diogenes. The governor has been awfully decent since he came up, and I don't despair of getting the time extended. He is much more amenable, apart from Agnes, and I fancy the Chieftain puts in a good word for me now and then—not on the score of literature, of course—but after they have been talking together, the governor always seems to look upon me with more—more *respect*, don't you know, and less as if I were a hopeless failure, of whom he was more or less ashamed. That's a gain in itself, isn't it?"

"'Um!" assented Margot vaguely. "I suppose they drive over to catch the evening express? Did he—they—say anything about me?"

Ron started in surprise.

"My dear girl, we have talked of nothing else *but* you, for the last week! Pulse, temperature, sleep; sleep, temperature, pulse; every hour the same old tale. You have given us all a rare old fright; but thank goodness you are on the mend at last. The doctor says it is only a matter of time."

"Did—they—send any message?"

"No! Edie said you were not to be excited. Awfully sorry to miss saying good-bye, and that sort of thing, but hope to meet you another day in town."

Margot shut her eyes, and the line of curling lashes looked astonishingly black against her cheek.

"I see. Very kind! I'm—tired, Ron. I can't talk any more."

Ron rose from his seat with, it must be confessed, a sigh of relief. He was ill at ease in the atmosphere of the sick-room, and hardly recognised his jaunty, self-confident companion in this wan and languid invalid. He dropped a light kiss on Margot's forehead, and hurried downstairs, to be encountered on the threshold of the inn by George Elgood, who for once seemed anxious to enter into conversation.

"You have been to see your sister. Did she—er—was she well enough to send any message before we go?"

"Oh, she's all right—quite quiet and sensible again, but doesn't bother herself much about what is going on. I told her you were off, but she didn't seem to take much notice. Expect she's so jolly thankful to feel comfortable again that she doesn't care for anything else."

"Er—quite so, quite so!" repeated the Editor hastily; and Ron passed on his way, satisfied that he had been all that was tactful and considerate, and serenely unconscious that he had eclipsed the sun of that summer's day for two anxious hearts!

There was little sleep for poor Margot that night, and in the morning Edith noticed with alarm the flushed cheeks and shining eyes which seemed to predict a return of the feverish symptoms. She drew down the blind and seated herself by the bedside, determined to guard the door and allow no visitors. The child had evidently had too much excitement the day before, and must now be kept absolutely quiet. But Margot tossed and fidgeted, and threw the clothes restlessly about, refusing to shut her eyes, and allow herself to be tucked up, as the elder sister lovingly advised. Her eyes were strained, and every now and then she lifted her head from the pillow with an anxious, listening movement. At last it came, the sound for which she had been waiting—the rumble of wheels, the clatter of horses' hoofs, the grunts and groans of the ostler as he lifted the heavy bags to their place. Margot's brown eyes looked up with a piteous entreaty.

"They are going! You must be quick, Edie. Run down quickly and say good-bye!"

"It isn't necessary, dear. I saw them before coming upstairs. Ron is there, and father."

"But you must! I want you to go. Quickly, before it is too late. Edie, you *must*!"

There was no denying so vehement a command. Edith turned silently away, confirmed in a growing suspicion, and yearning tenderly over the little sister's suffering. It was the younger brother, of course!—the tall, silent man, whose lips had been so dumb, whose eyes so eloquent, during the critical days of Margot's illness, and who had been the girl's companion on the misty moor. What had happened during those hours of suspense and danger? What barriers had been swept aside; what new vistas opened? Edith's own love was too sweet and sacred a thing to allow her to pry and question into the heart-secrets of another, as is the objectionable fashion of many so-called friends, but with her keen woman-senses she took in George Elgood's every word, look, and movement during the brief parting scene.

He stood aside, leaving his brother to utter the conventional farewells; his lips were set, and his brows drawn together; but ever and anon, as if against his will, his eyes shot anxious glances towards the window of the room where Margot lay. Edith moved a few steps nearer, to give the chance of a few quiet words, if it was in his heart to speak, but none came. A moment later he had swung himself up beside his brother on the high seat of the cart, and the wheels were beginning to move.

Edith went slowly back to her post, dreading to meet the gaze of those dear brown eyes, which had lost their sparkle, and become so pathetic in their dumb questioning. She had no reassuring message to give, and could only affect a confidence which she was far from feeling.

"Well, dear, they are off, but it is not good-bye—only *au revoir*, as you are sure to meet again in town before long. Mr Elgood asked permission to call upon me in town. Nice little man! He has been so wonderfully kind and considerate. I can't think why he should trouble himself so much for a complete stranger. The tall one looked sorry to go! He kept looking up at your window. He has a fine face—strong and clever. He must be an interesting companion."

Margot did not answer; but five minutes later she asked to have the curtain drawn, as the light hurt her eyes. They had a somewhat red and inflamed appearance for the rest of the day; but when Mr Vane commented on the fact, the dear, wise Edie assured him that it was a common phenomenon after illness, and laid a supply of fresh handkerchiefs on the bed—table in such a quiet and unobtrusive fashion, that they might have grown there of their own accord.

"Some day," thought Margot dismally to herself, "some day I shall laugh over this!" For the present, however, her sense of humour was strangely blunted, and the handkerchiefs were needed for a very different purpose.

Chapter Twenty Four.

A Proud Moment.

Margot's recovery was somewhat tedious, so that it was quite three weeks after the departure of the brothers Elgood before she was strong enough to face the journey home. In the meantime Edith remained in charge as nurse, while Mr Vane and Ron varied the monotony of life in the Glen by making short excursions of two or three days' duration to places of interest in the neighbourhood.

Notwithstanding the unchanged position of affairs, they appeared to be on unusually good terms, a fact which would have delighted Margot if she had been in her usual health and spirits; but she had become of late so languid and preoccupied as to appear almost unconscious of her surroundings. Once a day she did, indeed, rouse herself sufficiently to show some interest in passing events, that is to say, when the post arrived in the morning; but the revival was but momentary, and on each occasion was followed by a still deeper depression.

The elder sister was very tender during those days of waiting; very tactful and patient with little outbursts of temper and unreasonable changes of mind. She knew that it was not so much physical as mental suffering which was retarding the girl's progress, and yearned over her with a sympathy that was almost maternal in its depth.

The little sister had proved herself such a true friend during the trials of the last few years, that she would have gone through fire and water to save her from pain; but there are some things which even the most devoted relative cannot do.

Edith could not, for instance, write to George Elgood and question him concerning his silence: could not ask how it came to pass that while his brother had written to Margot, to Ronald, even to herself, he remained silent, content to send commonplace messages through a third person. As for Margot herself, she never mentioned the younger of the two brothers, but was always ready to talk about the elder, and seemed unaffectedly pleased at her sister's appreciation of the kindly, genial little man.

"But why was he so sweet to me?" Edith would ask, with puzzled wonderment. "From the moment I arrived he seemed to be on the outlook to see how he could help. And he took an interest in Jack, and asked all about him and his affairs. The astonishing thing is that I told him, too! Though he was a stranger, his interest was so *real* and deep that I could confide in him more easily than in many old friends. Had you been talking about us to him, by any chance?"

Margot turned her head on the pillow, and stared out of the window to the ridge of hills against the skyline. Her cheeks had sunk, making the brown eyes appear pathetically large and worn. There was a listlessness in her expression which was strangely different from the vivacious, self-confident Margot of a few weeks ago.

"Yes, I spoke about you one day. He liked you, because you were so fond of Jack. He was in love himself, and the girl died, but he loves her still, just the same. He tries to help other girls for her sake. He said he wanted to know you. If it were ever in his power to help you and Jack, he would do it; but sometimes no one can help. It makes things worse when they try. You might just as well give up at once."

"Margot! What heresy, dear! From you, too, who are always preaching courage and perseverance! That's pneumonia croaking, not the gallant little champion of the family! What would Ron and I have done without you this last year, I should like to know? Isn't it nice to see father and the boy on such good terms? I believe that also is in a great degree due to Mr Elgood's influence. The pater told me that he congratulated him on having such a son, and seemed to think Ron quite unusually gifted. It is wonderful how much one man thinks of another man's judgment! We have said the same thing for years past, and it has had no effect; but when a calm, level-headed man of business drops a word, it is accepted as gospel. You will be happy, won't you, darling, if Ron's future is harmoniously arranged?"

"Ron will be happy!" said Margot shortly. At the moment it seemed to her as if such good fortune could never again be her own. She must always be miserable, since George Elgood cared so little for her that he could disappear into space and leave her without a word. Formal messages sent through another person did not count, when one recalled the tone of the voice which had said, "*Margot!*" and blushed at the remembrance of that other word which had followed.

Sometimes, during those long days of convalescence, Margot almost came to the conclusion that what she had heard had been the effect of imagination only; as unreal and dream-like as the other events of that fateful afternoon. At other times, as if in contradiction of these theories, every intonation of the Editor's voice would ring in her ears, and once again she would flush and tremble with happiness.

At last the day arrived when the return to town need no longer be delayed. Mr Vane was anxious to return to his work, Edith to her husband and children; and the doctor pronounced Margot strong enough to bear the journey in the comfortable invalid carriage which had been provided.

Preparations were therefore made for an early start, and poor Elspeth made happy by such a wholesale legacy of garments as composed a very trousseau in the estimation of the Glen.

No one was bold enough to offer a gift to Mrs McNab, but when the last moment arrived Margot lifted her white face with lips slightly pursed, like a child asking for a kiss. As on the occasion of her first appearance, a contortion of suppressed emotion passed over the dour Scotch face, and something suspiciously like moisture trembled in the cold eyes.

"When ye come back again, come back twa!" was the enigmatical sentence with which the landlady made her adieu, and a faint colour flickered in Margot's cheek as she pondered over its significance.

The journey home was broken by a night spent in Perth, and London was reached on the afternoon of a warm July day. The trees in the Park looked grey with dust, the air felt close and heavy after the exhilaration of the mountain breezes to which the travellers had become accustomed; even the house itself had a heavy, stuffy smell, despite the immaculate cleanliness of its *régime*.

Jack Martin was waiting to take his wife back to Oxford Terrace, the children having already preceded her, and Margot felt a sinking of loneliness at being left to Agnes's tender mercies.

"Dear me, child, what a wreck you look! Your Highland holiday has been a fine upset for us all. What did I tell you before you started? Perhaps another time you may condescend to listen to what I say!" Such was the ingratiating welcome bestowed upon the weary girl on her arrival; yet when Margot turned aside in silence, and made no response to the accompanying kiss of welcome, Agnes felt hurt and aggrieved. From morning to night she had bustled about the house, assuring herself that everything was in apple-pie order; arranging flowers, putting out treasures of fancy-work, providing comforts for the invalid. "And she never notices, nor says one word of thanks. I can't understand Margot!" said poor Agnes to herself for the hundredth time, as she seated herself at the head of the table for dinner.

"Are there any letters for me, Agnes?" queried Margot anxiously.

"One or two, I believe, and a paper or something of the sort. You can see them after dinner."

"I want them now!" said Margot obstinately. She pushed back her chair from the table, and walked across the room to the desk where newly-arrived letters were laid out to await the coming of their owners. Three white envelopes lay there, and a rolled-up magazine, all addressed to herself. She flushed expectantly as she bent to examine the different handwritings. Two were uninterestingly familiar, belonging to faithful girl friends who had hastened to welcome her home; the third was unmistakably a man's hand,—small and compact, the letters fine, and accurately formed.

A blessed intuition told Margot that her waiting was at an end, and that this was the message for which she had longed ever since her return to consciousness. With a swift movement she slipped the envelope into her pocket, to be opened later on in the privacy of her room, and returned to the table, bearing the other communications in her hand.

"I should have thought that after six weeks' absence from home you might have been willing to talk to *me*, instead of wanting to read letters at your very first meal!" said Agnes severely; and Margot laughed in good-natured assent.

"I won't open them! It was only curiosity to see what they were. I'll talk as much as you like, Aggie dear."

It was, all of a sudden, so easy to be amiable and unselfish! The nervous irritation which had made it difficult to be patient, even with dear, tactful Edie during the last weeks, had taken wing and departed with the first sight of that square white envelope. The light came back to Margot's eyes; she held her head erect, the very hollows in her cheeks seemed miraculously to disappear, and to be replaced by the old dimpling smile. Mr Vane and Ron exchanged glances of delight at the marvellous manner in which their invalid had stood the journey home.

The letters and parcel lay unnoticed on the table until the conclusion of the meal, but as Margot picked them up preparatory to carrying them upstairs to her own room, she gave a sudden start of astonishment.

"Ron, it's the *Loadstar*! Some one has sent me a copy of the *Loadstar*. From the office, I think, for the name is printed on the cover. Who could it be?"

"The Editor, of course—as a mark of attention on your return home. Lazy beggar! It was easier than writing a letter," laughed Ron easily, stretching out his hand as he spoke to take forcible possession, for the magazine was of more interest to himself than to Margot, and he felt that a new copy was just what was needed to occupy the hours before bedtime.

Margot made no demur, but stood watching quietly while Ron tore off the wrapper, and flattened the curled paper. She was not in a reading mood, but the suggestion that George Elgood might have sent the magazine made it precious in her sight, and she waited anxiously for its return.

"It's mine, Ron. It was sent to me! I want to take it upstairs."

"Let me look at the index first, to see who is writing this month! You don't generally care for such stiff reading; I say, there's a fine collection of names! It's stronger than ever this month. I don't believe there is another paper in the world which has such splendid fellows for contribu—"

Ron stopped short, his voice failing suddenly in the middle of the word. His jaw dropped, and a wave of colour surged in his cheeks.

"It—it can't be!" he gasped incredulously. "It *can't*! There must be another man of the same name. It can't possibly be meant for *me*!..."

"What? What? Let me see? What are you talking about?" cried Margot, peering eagerly over his shoulder, while Ron pointed with a trembling finger to the end of the table of contents. Somehow the words seemed to be printed in a larger type than the rest. They grew larger and larger until they seemed to fill the whole page—"*Solitude. A Fragment. By Ronald Vane*!"

"Oh, Ron, it *is*!" shrieked Margot, in happy excitement. "It *is* you, and no one else! I *told* you it was beautiful when you read it to me that day in the Glen! Oh, when did you send it to him?"

"Never! I never so much as mentioned my verses in his hearing. That was part of the bargain—that we should not worry him on his holiday. Margot, it was you! You are only pretending that you know nothing about it. It must be your doing."

"Indeed it isn't! I never even spoke of you to him." Margot had the grace to blush at the confession; but by this time Ron had turned over the pages until he had come to the one on which his own words faced him in the beautiful distinct typing of the magazine, and the rapture of the moment precluded every other sentiment. He did not hear what Margot said, so absorbed was he in re-reading the lines in their delightful new setting.

"It *is* good; but it is only a fragment. It isn't finished. Why was this chosen, instead of one of the others?"

"I told you you would ruin it if you made it longer. It is perfect as it is, and anything more would be padding. It is a little gem, worthy even of a place in the *Loadstar*. Father, do you hear? Do you understand? Look at your son's name among all those great men! Aren't you glad? Aren't you *proud*! Aren't you going to congratulate us *both*?"

Mr Vane growled a little, for the sake of appearances; but though his eyebrows frowned, the corners of his lips relaxed in a manner distinctly complacent. Even recognising as he did the herald of defeat, it was impossible to resist a thrill of pride as his eye glanced down the imposing list of names held open for his inspection. A great scientist; a great statesman; a leading author; an astronomer known throughout the world; a soldier veteran, and near the end that other name, so dearly familiar—the name of his own son! The voice in which he spoke was gruff with emotion. "Humph! You are in good company, at least. Let me see the verses themselves. There must be something in them, I suppose, but I am no judge of these things."

Chapter Twenty Five.

"In Corn."

Meantime Margot had returned to the far end of the room, and adroitly slipped the third letter out of her pocket, feeling that it would be selfish to delay reading the contents, as they must certainly cast some light upon the present situation. Her heart sank a little as she recognised that the attention was less personal than she had imagined, but even so, it was to herself that the magazine had been directed, and that was an evidence of the fact that in publishing the poem her pleasure had been considered even more than Ronald's advancement.

She tore open the stiff white envelope and read as follows:—

"Dear Miss Vane,—

"I hear that you are to arrive home this afternoon, and intend to take the liberty of calling upon you after dinner, in the hope that you may be able to give me a few minutes of uninterrupted conversation on a subject of great importance. If you are too much fatigued after your journey, pray have no scruples in refusing me admission, in which case I shall take an early opportunity of calling again; but after the strain of the past few weeks I do not find myself able to wait longer than is absolutely necessary for an interview.

"Yours faithfully,—

"George Elgood."

"Is that from Elgood? What does he say? What does he say? Let us see what he says!" petitioned Ron eagerly; but Margot returned the letter to her pocket, resolutely ignoring his outstretched hand.

"He gives no explanation, but he is coming to-night. Coming to call after dinner, and he asks me to see him alone, so I'll find out all about it, and tell you afterwards."

"Alone!" Ron's face was eloquent with surprise, disappointment, and a dawning suspicion. "Why alone? It's more my affair than yours. I *must* thank him before he goes."

"I'll send for you, then. I suppose he wants to explain to me first. I'll be sure to send for you!" reiterated Margot hurriedly, as she disappeared through the doorway. Her first impulse was, girl-like, to make for her own room, to give those final touches to hair and dress, which are so all-important in effect, and that done, to sit alone, listening for the expected knock at the door, the sound of footsteps ascending to the drawing-room. To meet George Elgood here! To see his tall dark figure outlined against the familiar background of home,—Margot gasped at the thought, and felt her heart leap painfully at every fresh sound.

The postman, the parcels delivery, a van from the Stores, had all claimed the tribute of a blush, a gasp, and a fresh rush to the glass, before at last slow footsteps were heard mounting the stairs, and Mary's voice at the door announced, "A gentleman to see you, Miss Margot!" and in another minute, as it seemed, she was facing George Elgood across the length of the drawing-room.

The rôles of invalid and anxious inquirer seemed for the moment to be reversed, for while she was pink and smiling, he was grave and of a ghastly pallor. Nervous also; for the first words of greeting were an unintelligible murmur, and they seated themselves in an embarrassed silence.

"You—er—you received my letter?"

"Yes!" Margot gazed at the tips of her dainty slippers, and smiled softly to herself. In the interval which had passed since they last met, the Editor had evidently suffered a relapse into his old shyness and reserve. She had guessed as much from the somewhat stilted phraseology of his letter, and was prepared to reassure him by her own outspoken gratitude.

"Yes; I was so pleased!"

He gave a little start of astonishment, and stared at her with bright, incredulous eyes.

"Pleased? You mean it? You did not think it a liberty—"

"Indeed I did not. I guessed what you had to tell me, and it made me so happy."

He leaned forward impetuously, the blood flushing his cheeks.

"You had guessed before? You knew it was coming?"

"Not exactly, but I hoped—"

"*Hoped*!—Margot, is it possible that you have cared, too? It seems too wonderful to be true.—I never dreamt of such amazing happiness. At the best it seemed possible that you would be willing to give me a hearing. I did not dare to write, but this time of waiting has seemed as if it would never end..."

As he began to speak Margot faced him with candid eyes, but at the sound of his voice, and at sight of the answering flash of his eyes, her lids quivered and fell, and she shrank back against the cushions of her chair. Astonishment overwhelmed her; but the relief, the thankfulness, the rapture of the moment obliterated everything else. She gave a strangled sob of emotion and said faintly—

"It—it has seemed long to me, too!"

At that he was on his knees before her, clasping her hands and gazing at her with an expression of rapturous relief. "Oh, Margot, my darling, was it because I was not there? Have you missed me? Not as I have missed you—that is not possible, but enough to remember me sometimes, and to be glad to meet again. Have you thought of me at all, Margot?"

"I—I have thought of nothing else!" sighed Margot. She was generous with her assurance, knowing the nature of the man with whom she had to deal, and her reward was the sight of the illumined face turned upon her.

There, in a corner of a modern drawing-room, with a glimpse of a London street between the curtain folds, Margot and George Elgood found the Eden which is discovered afresh by all true lovers. Such moments are too sacred for intrusion; they live enshrined in memory until the end of life.

It was not until a considerable time had flown by that Margot recalled the events of the earlier evening, and with them still another claim held by her lover upon her gratitude and devotion. Drawing back, so as to lift her charming face to his—a rosy, sparkling face, unrecognisable as the same white and weary visage of a few hours back, she laid her hand on his, and said sweetly—

"We went off at a tangent, didn't we? I don't know how we went off, and forgot the real business of the evening; but I never finished thanking you! You must think me terribly ungrateful!"

George Elgood regarded her with puzzled, adoring eyes.

"I haven't the least idea what you are talking about, but what does it matter? What does anything matter, except that we love each other, and are the happiest creatures on earth? Business, indeed! Why need we trouble ourselves to talk about business? Margot, do you know that you have a dimple in the middle of your cheek? The most beautiful dimple in the world!"

Margot shook her head at him with a pretence of disapproval, smiling the while, so as to show off the dimple to the best advantage.

"You mustn't make me conceited. I am vain enough already to know that you love me, and have taken so much trouble to please me. It *was* kind of you!"

"What was kind, sweetheart? There is no kindness in loving you. I had no choice in the matter, for I simply could not help myself!"

"Ah, but you know what I mean! You have given me my two greatest desires! I can't tell you how happy I was when I saw it."

He stared at her for a moment, then smiled complacently.

"You mean—my note?"

"No, I didn't mean your note. Not this time. I meant the magazine!"

"Magazine!"

The accent of bewilderment was unmistakably genuine, and Margot hastened to explain still further.

"The new number of the *Loadstar* with Ron's poem in it!"

"Ron's poem!" The note of bewilderment was accentuated to one of positive incredulity. "A poem by your brother in the *Loadstar*! I did not know that he wrote at all."

Now it was Margot's turn to stare and frown.

"You didn't know! But you *must* have known. How else could it get in? You must have given permission."

"My sweetheart, what have I to do with the *Loadstar*, or any other magazine? What has my permission to do with it?"

"Everything in the world! Oh, I know exactly what has happened. Your brother has told you about Ron, and showed you his verses, and you put them in for his sake—*and mine*! Because you knew I should be pleased, and because they are good too, and you were glad to help him. He is longing to come in to thank you himself. We shall both thank you all our lives!"

George Elgood's face of stupefaction was a sight to behold. His forehead was corrugated with lines of bewilderment; he stared at her in blankest dismay.

"What *are* you talking about, sweetheart? What does it all mean? Your brother has no need to thank me for any success which he has gained. I should have been only too delighted to help him in any way that was in my power, but I have no influence with the *Loadstar Magazine*."

"No influence! How can that be when you are the Editor?"

"I am the *What*?"

"Editor! You have every influence. You *are* the magazine!"

George Elgood rose to his feet with a gesture of strongest astonishment.

"I the Editor of a magazine! My dearest little girl, what are you dreaming about? There never was a man less suited to the position. I know nothing whatever of magazines—of any sort of literature. I am in corn!"

A corn merchant! Margot's brain reeled. She lay back in her chair, staring at him with wide, stunned eyes, too utterly prostrated by surprise to be capable of speech!

Chapter Twenty Six.

An Interview with the Editor.

Could it be believed that it was the *Chieftain* who was the Editor, after all! That short, fat, undignified, commonplace little man! "Not in the least the type,"—so Ron had pronounced, in his youthful arrogance, "No one would ever suspect *you* of being literary!" so saucy Margot had declared to his face. She blushed at the remembrance of the words, blushed afresh, as, one after another, a dozen memories rushed through her brain. That afternoon by the tarn, for example, when she had summoned courage to confess her scheme, and he had lain prone on the grass, helpless and shaken with laughter!

No wonder that he had laughed! but oh, the wickedness, the duplicity of the wretch, to breathe no word of her mistake, but promptly set to work to weave a fresh plot on his own account! This was the reason why he had extracted a promise that George was not to be told of Ron's ambition during his holiday, feigning an anxiety for his brother's peace of mind, which he was in reality doing his best to destroy! This was the explanation of everything that had seemed mysterious and contradictory. He had been laughing in his sleeve all the time he had pretended to help!

George Elgood listened with a mingling of amaze, amusement, and tenderness to the hidden history of the weeks at Glenaire. Being in the frame of mind when everything that Margot did seemed perfect in his eyes, he felt nothing but admiration for her efforts on her brother's behalf.

It was an ingenious, unselfish little scheme, and the manner in which she had laid it bare to the person most concerned was delightfully unsophisticated. He laughed at her tenderly, stroking her soft, pretty hair with his big man's hand, the while he explained that he was a business man pure and simple, and had made no excursions whatever into literature; that the "writing" with which he had been occupied was connected with proposed changes in his firm, and a report of a technical character.

Margot flamed with indignation, but before the angry words had time to form themselves on her lips, the thought occurred that after all the help vouchsafed to her had been no pretence, but a very substantial reality. Ron's foot *had* been placed on the first rung of the ladder, while as for herself, what greater good could she have found to desire than that which, through the Chieftain's machinations, had already come to pass? She lifted her face to meet the anxious, adoring gaze bent upon her, and cried hurriedly—

"He—he meant it all the time! He *meant* it to happen!"

"Meant what, darling?"

"*This*!"

Margot waved her hand with a gesture sufficiently expressive, whereat her lover laughed happily.

"Bless him! of course he did. He has been badgering me for years past to look out for a wife; and when we met you he was clever enough to realise that you were the one woman to fill the post. If he had said as much to me at that stage of affairs, I should have packed up and made off within the hour; if he had said it to you, you would have felt it incumbent upon you to do the same. Instead, he let you go on in your illusion, while he designed the means of throwing us into each other's society. Good old Geoff! I'm not at all angry with him. Are you?"

Margot considered the point, her head tilted to a thoughtful angle.

"I'm—not—sure! I think I am, just a little bit, for I hate to be taken in. He was laughing at me all the time."

"But after all, he has done what you wished! I envy him for being able to give you such pleasure; but perhaps I may be able to do as much in another way. Geoff tells me that Mr Martin has had financial troubles, and there is nothing I would not do to help any one who belongs to you. I'm out of my depths in poetry, but in business matters I can count, and in this case I shall not be satisfied until I *do*."

Margot drew a long breath of contentment. "Oh, if Jack is happy, and Ron is successful, and I have—*You*!—there will be nothing left to wish for in all the world. Poor Ron! he is waiting eagerly to come in to thank you for publishing his verse, and wondering why in the world you wanted to see me alone. Don't you think you ought just to read it, to be able to say it is nice?"

"No, I don't! You are all the poetry I can attend to to-night, and for goodness' sake keep him away; I shall have to interview your father later on, but after waiting all these weeks I must have you to myself a little longer."

"Oh, I won't send for him. I don't want him a bit," cried Margot naïvely, "but he will come!"

And he did!

Waiting downstairs in the study, an hour seemed an absurd length of time, and when no summons came Ron determined to take the law in his own hands and join the conference. The tableau which was revealed to him on opening the drawing-room door struck him dumb with amazement, and the explanations which ensued appeared still more extraordinary.

George Elgood speedily beat a retreat to the study, where Mr Vane listened to his request with quiet resignation. Elderly, grey-haired fathers have a way of seeing more than their children suspect, and Margot's father had recognised certain well-known signs in the manner in which he had been questioned concerning his daughter's progress during those anxious days at Glenaire. His heart sank as he listened to the lover's protestations, but he told himself that he ought to be thankful to know that his little Margot had chosen a man of unblemished character, who was of an age to appreciate his responsibility, possessed an income sufficient to keep her in comfort, and, last but not least, a home within easy distance of his own.

Late that evening, when her lover had taken his departure, Margot stole down to the study and sat silently for a time on her old perch on the arm of her father's chair, with her head resting lovingly against his own. He was thankful to feel her dear presence, and to know that she wished to be near him on this night of all others, but his heart was too full to speak, and it was she who at last spoke the first words.

"I never knew," she said softly, "I never knew that it was possible to be as happy as this. It's so wonderful! One can't realise it all. Father dear, I've been thinking of you! ... I never realised before what it meant to you when mother died—all that you lost! You have been good, and brave, and unselfish, dear, and we must have tried you sorely many times. We didn't understand, but I understand a little bit now, daddy, and it makes me love you more. You'll remember, won't you, that this is going to draw us closer together, not separate us one little bit? You'll be *sure* to remember?"

"Bless you, dear!" he said, and stroked her hand with tender fingers. "It is sweet to hear you say so, at least. I'm glad you are going to be happy, and if I am to give you away at all, I am glad it is to a strong, sensible man whom I can trust and respect; but it will be a sad day for me when you leave the old home, Margot."

Margot purred over him with tenderest affection.

"How I wish Agnes would marry!"

"What has that to do with it, pray?"

"Then you could live with me, of course! I should love it," said Margot warmly; and though her father had no intention of accepting such an invitation, it remained through life a solace to him to remember that it had been in the girl's heart to wish it.

Next morning at twelve o'clock a daintily attired damsel ascended a dusty staircase in Fleet Street and desired to see the Editor in his den. The dragon who guarded the fastness inquired of her if

'YOU HAVE BEEN LAUGHING AT ME ALL THE TIME!'
[See page 114.

she had an appointment, and, unsoftened by the charm of her appearance, volunteered the information that Mr Elgood would see no stray callers.

"He will see *me*!" returned Margot arrogantly; and she was right, for, to the surprise of the messenger, the sight of the little printed card was followed by an order to "Show the lady in at once."

A moment later Margot made her first entrance into an Editor's den, and round the corner of a big desk caught a glimpse of a decorous, black-coated figure whom at first sight it was difficult to associate with the light-hearted Chieftain of Glenaire. As they confronted each other, however, the round face twinkled into a smile, which served as fuel to the girl's indignation. She stopped short, ostentatiously disregarding the outstretched hand, drew her brows together, and proclaimed haughtily—

"I have come to let you know that you are found out. I know all about it now. You have been laughing at me all the time?"

"Well,—very nearly!" he assented smilingly. "You are such a nice little girl to laugh at, you see, and it was an uncommonly good joke! Do you remember the day when you confided to me solemnly that you had journeyed to Scotland on purpose to stalk me, and run me to earth? You'd have been a bit embarrassed if I'd told you the truth then and there, wouldn't you now? And besides—I see quite enough of literary aspirants all the year round. It was a bit hard to be hunted down on one's holidays. I felt bound to prevaricate, for the sake of my own peace. Then again there was George! Where would George have come in? If I had confessed my identity, should I have been kept awake, as I was last night, listening to his rhapsodies by the hour together? By the way, we are going to be near relatives. Don't you want to shake hands?"

"I'm very angry indeed!" maintained Margot stubbornly—nevertheless her hand was in his, and her fingers involuntarily returned his pressure. "Are you—*glad*! Do you think I shall—do? Does he seem *really* happy?"

"Ah, my dear!" he sighed, and over the plump features there passed once more the expression of infinite longing which Margot had seen once before, when, in a moment of confidence, he had spoken of his dead love. "Ah, my dear, how happy he is! There is no word to express such happiness! George has not frittered away his affections on a number of silly flirtations—his heart is whole, and it is wholly yours. Do you owe me no thanks for bringing you together? You wanted to help your brother; I wanted to help mine; so we are equally guilty or praiseworthy, as the case may be. For myself I am very well satisfied with the result?"

Margot blushed, and cast down her eyes.

"I'm satisfied, too!" she said shyly. "Much more than satisfied—and Ron is enraptured. Have you seen him? He said he was coming to see you first thing this morning!"

"Have I seen him, indeed? I should think I had! I thought I should never get rid of the boy. I told him straight that the magazine comes first to me, and that not even a prospective sister-in-law—with dimples!—could induce me to accept a line for publication otherwise than on its own merits. But the boy has power. I can't tell yet how far it may go, but it's worth encouraging. When he gave me his manuscript book to read I was struck by one fragment, and wrote it out in shorthand, to publish as a surprise to you both. I like the lad, and will be glad to help him so far as it is in my power. I can give him a small post in this office, where at least he will be in the atmosphere; but after that his future rests with himself. What he writes that is worth publishing, I will publish, but it will be judged on its merits alone, and without any remembrance of his private associations. He will have his chance!"

He put out his hands and held her gently by the elbows, smiling at her the while with the kindliest of smiles.

"Now are you satisfied, little girl? From the moment that you looked at me with *her* eyes, and asked my help, I have had no better wish than to give it. I did not set about it quite in your own way, perhaps, but the end is the same. Don't trouble any more about the lad, but let me smooth the way with your father, while you devote yourself to George. His happiness is in your hands. Be good to him! He looks upon you as an angel from heaven! Be an angel for his sake! He sees in you everything that is good, and pure, and womanly. Be what he believes! Humanly speaking, his life is yours, and these little hands will draw him more strongly than any power in the world. It's a big responsibility, little girl, but I am not afraid! I know a good woman when I see one, and can trust George to your care. You will be very happy. I wonder if in the midst of your happiness you will sometimes remember—a lonely man?"

Margot twisted herself quickly from his grasp, and her arms stretched out and encircled his neck. She did not speak, but her lips, pressed against his cheek, gave an assurance more eloquent than words.

The End.